7 SINS OF THE APOCALYPSE

JUSTIN ROBINSON   DALE DRAKE

ALICE J. BLACK   KATE L. MARY   JESSICA GOMEZ

SYLVESTER BARZEY   ERIN SWEET AL-MEHARI

FRACTURED Mind
PUBLISHING

CONTENTS

I

KODIAK

JUSTIN ROBINSON

THE GRAY MOMENTARILY OVERWHELMED EVERYTHING: the world, his thoughts, even the pulsing red of rage. It rose up, consumed the anger and left behind only emptiness where before had been a bloody tide of fury. The gray could be detected over the network, but it never strayed into the program of warhounds. It stayed within the master, where it was born, and for whose purpose it served. It crested, then receded, revealing the world shard by broken shard.

The scent of cooked meat filled the air. M's olfactory processor broke it down by precise chemical composition, denoting the percentages of carbonized flesh, as well as oxygen, nitrogen, and the miasma of carbon monoxide hanging over the city center. There was still enough alive in M to taste the flesh on his tongue, to feel it slithering into his sinuses, and have it ignite the primitive parts of his mind, those that were still blood and neuron. There was not enough left in him to recoil. That had been burned from him.

M padded up onto the largest pile of bodies. The scent – had there been more of his old self remaining, he might have called it a stench – wasn't a concern. He hunted for movement, prey-like and quick in the sticky gloom, but saw none. The battle was over. It was won. Again. M registered the rest of the program padding around the cracked concrete floors, their sensors coming to the same conclusion as his had, and then broadcasting over their dedicated subnetwork.

A memory sparked in M, somewhere in the fleshy bits that had yet to be burned clean. A warehouse, that's what this place had been, or something like that. It tasted right on the old parts of his brain. He hadn't spoken that, or any other word, in so long that it was difficult to know if he was correct or not. Such things didn't really matter anymore. The building had simply been labeled part of Zone SLA-052, and flagged by M's Prime Locus as the probable location of Kodiak.

The Prime Locus and her program of warhounds had scoured the expansive room clean. It still contained old pallets of things – there were so many things in the old world – partly covered in crinkling plastic, filthy with the grime of armageddon. A makeshift camp, shadowed from the outside world with heat-baffling tarps, had dominated the central part of the warehouse. Now, the camp was empty. The human remains cast delicate lines of smoke into the air, their flesh charred black by superheated plasma. White bone and crimson meat peeked from beneath papery skin. A piece of M shuddered when he padded past the remains of one, its skeletal grimace pointed to the heavens. M was canny enough to disable his portion of the network for the split second that sensation worked through his system. The others were jealous of him and if they got wind of any lingering humanity, would waste no chance to see him brought down from Program Alpha.

The processing swarms writhed over the fallen firearms, looking like grayish amoebas. They made nearly inaudible clicking sounds, and, when they returned to the Prime Locus on smoky tendrils, the guns were simply gone, replaced with a halo in the dirt. The swarms crawled along the girders and exposed rebar of the walls, ensuring the structure would soon join many of its fellows in the dust of the new age. It was a minor miracle this place hadn't already been reclaimed, but there was much discarded metal in the bones of the old world.

The Prime Locus stepped over the dead, pausing at every one to stare into their faces. Her expression rippled thanks to the servos in her cheeks, eyebrows, and mouth. It was impossible to read, both because it had been some time since M had seen a living human face outside of the masks they were obliged to wear, and because the Prime Locus had long ago flayed herself. Now what remained was a facsimile of bone and muscle made from machine. Her eyes, absent their covering of false skin, seemed to bulge in their sockets, while gears that would have pulled flesh into frowns and grimaces, whirred uselessly. Whenever M looked at her, a memory from before sparked in the living parts of his brain, of a medical anatomy textbook. But instead of lurid crimson and lustrous bone, the Prime Locus was cast in silver and steel.

M would never know what the Prime Locus thought as she looked into the faces of the dead. Her portion of the network was closed to him, closed until the terrible tide of her anger inevitably battered the walls down. As she walked, the processor swarms returned to her, buzzing as they slipped into the housing vents along her slender back. For a moment, though, they appeared as hazy wings stretching up and behind her, and something deep and biological inside of M quailed from that image.

M padded up next to his master, and sat down on his haunches. Reflexively, the Prime Locus's hand went to his head, stroking first the metal parts, then the irritated itchy places where skin met steel, then his broad back, interspersed with the metal plating that poked through this flesh. The parts of pure metal he felt only as information conveyed through proximity sensors, an itch purely intellectual in origin. The skin he felt as he always had, and the Prime Locus's touch was gentle as her original purpose had demanded. When she wasn't in the red grips of her rage, she reverted to the easy grooves of her programming, and in those moments, M truly loved her.

She was speaking. Another place she surrendered to programming. She could quite easily communicate with her program through their network, and in the heat of battle, she did so. Now, she felt the need to verbalize. M hardly registered it. He had heard this before, and it wouldn't lead to any pain for him, so he was content. He merely waited to determine if and when her tone turned harsh, as it inevitably did. It was precipitated by a sting along the network, and the entire program, all of whom had been prowling along the edges of the warehouse, hunting for survivors that had been missed, momentarily froze in place. Then their shoulders went rigid, the swollen muscles bunching and uncoiling. Their flesh-and-steel heads hung low in supplication.

The information came over the network a second before the Prime Locus repeated it audibly, creating a weird echo. "News of Kodiak south of here," she said. "Form and execute."

The program, as one, converged on the Prime Locus and

fanned out behind her as an escort. Now, M momentarily regretted being the Program Alpha, as he would be closest to her right hand, the seat of pain. Kodiak was out there, and his mere existence would rip through the Prime Locus's psyche like a ragged blade. She would drive M and all the others to track and kill Kodiak, no matter how many of them it cost, and vicious beatings would be the only reward for the survivors. M couldn't deny the will of the Prime Locus no matter how much it troubled him. Her will was not precisely his, though it could clamp down over the network with the undeniability of steel. He could, quite easily, be overridden. There was no need to fight now, or even remember the heady, terrifying early days when he had it in him to fight, when this slavery was anathema. He could only return to her side as he was ordered, his flesh-and-metal legs moving with predator's grace and machine precision.

They stepped out into the jaundiced sunlight. The toxic ocean washed sluggishly onto the crumbling concrete of the harbor. Years ago, rusted hulks of the cargo ships, endless shipping containers, and soaring cranes had marked the harbor as a place of commerce and trade. Those were gone now, consumed and recycled by the processor swarms. The remnant of humanity was limited to the poison in the sea and the sky, and the crumbling concrete beneath their feet. M's olfactory processor registered the astringent scent of the ocean, fleshy bits recoiling from the ammonia stench. The important parts of him, steel and code, recognized the water as perfectly normal for this part of the Pacific ocean, where the currents gathered up pollutants and pushed them into the harbor to collect in a carcinogenic gyre. Nothing could live in this place, and after the coming of the Prime Locus, nothing did.

The Prime Locus stepped onto the raptor, finding the grooves in the machine's back and engaging the maglocks on her feet. M felt her thoughts diverting from the program's network to that of the raptor. The program followed her, each returning to their appointed place, from M's favored spot right beside the Prime Locus to Z's place near the back of the craft. M felt a trace of pleasure as Z locked in. Though Z wouldn't bear the brunt of any disappointment, he would never feel the caress of the occasional sweet word of praise.

The raptor rose into the yellow sky. A few raptors soared in shimmering clouds on the horizon. M couldn't listen to their networks, but he hardly had to. They were hunting vessels. As though in confirmation, a green light lanced from one and into the earth, a column of greasy flame blooming where it had struck. The raptor swooped around, and the green struck again and again. M wondered if that was his destination; where his Prime Locus and the program would move in and ferret out anyone who had gone underground.

"No," said the Prime Locus, answering the unspoken question coming from the network of her program. M momentarily thought of honey, to thick and sweet was her voice. That was part of her original design. As soon as he made the connection, he turned away from it; she didn't like the reminder. M waited, quivering as he prepared for the lash over his back. He was certain he could feel the delirious anticipation of the rest of the program. Something that would hurl M back, and allow one of the others, Q or maybe R, to take his illustrious place.

"The raptor is doing just fine," murmured the Prime Locus. "The humans will be retreating underground. Like cockroaches."

M's processor threw the information on cockroaches onto the forefront of his mind. He learned a bit, and felt a lingering loathing for the little creatures, though he couldn't imagine why. They were one of the few biological entities still doing quite well in the ruins. They never bothered machinery, and were as clean as such an animal was likely to be. There were no plans to exterminate them.

"Kodiak isn't there," she said dismissively, turning the raptor to follow the coastline south.

M knew this was true because the Prime Locus knew it was true. He felt the brush of her thoughts on the network, and rejoiced in their warmth. But they were growing hot. Spiky. She was thinking the name, over and over again. Kodiak.

Her hand, forged in steel in the image of humanity, clenched over his back. The metal fingers burned, and cold rivulets ran from him. He watched the crimson patter on the roof of the raptor, only for the wind to streak it into tears. Inside, he howled in agony, though he couldn't make a sound.

"He will be dead soon," she said, her voice as steely as her grip. "I can promise you this."

M couldn't wait. He desperately showed her, pushing his code through the network. He would do whatever she said, kill whoever she desired.

"You're as eager as I am."

M pathetically continued to display his commitment to the task of killing Kodiak. Of finally bringing this criminal to suffer for what he had done in the old world. M didn't know what those crimes were, but he didn't have to know. The Prime Locus had made a declaration. That was enough.

"Good," she whispered, and the hand tightened. That anger, that rage, wasn't possible for so many of the others. It was possible for her. Indeed, it seemed to be the only thing powering her. The promise she whispered next could have been red. "He will be dead soon, and it will take time."

The raptor continued its flight south, tracing the decaying metroplex that had grown reef-like along the meandering line. The ocean was a yellow-green as it lapped against the shore, the remnants of civilization a slimy bone white. The skies were alive with raptors, their steely hides twinkling in the muted sunlight. The Prime Locus released her hold on M's back, and the white hot agony was replaced with a dull ache chilled by the whistling winds. M was content to be still, no telling what would set her fuse alight. When they were on the hunt for Kodiak, nearly anything could do it.

A whisper came over the network, a bleedover from the larger network the Prime Locus was plugged into. M heard only the generalities. A summons of some kind. He felt a flash of anger inside his leader, and he tensed, but nothing came of it. A protest, a refutation, and then:

"We need to divert," she said, her words echoing behind the same information coming over the network.

There was no need for assent: the program's agreement to her will was assumed. The raptor banked, heading inland. Below, the signs of civilization gave way on their right to broken terrain and scorched housing, before petering out into desert. Garbage, of the type unusable by the processor swarms, flitted about in parody of life, dancing in the phantom winds. Ahead, first hills then mountains rose from the earth. This was the destination: a bit of the map had been made manifest over the network, and M's GPS already pinpointed the location of the drop.

The raptor followed the creases of the mountainous terrain

as it headed upward. Ahead, he could see the first evidence of their purpose here. Another raptor hovered over a break in the peaks, its back empty of passengers. This was a small canyon between the highest peaks, swaddled in shadow. M disengaged the magnets in his feet with a thought and padded to the edge of the raptor. Green flashes in the darkness below betrayed the presence of a firefight.

The Prime Locus stepped to the lip of the raptor. Like a tail, her tow-cable extended from the base of her metal spine, the magnet glomming it to the vehicle's surface. As one, the program imitated this action and followed as she stepped out over nothing. The cables unspooled with a high-pitched whine as the group of them fell into the shadowed terrain.

M's sensors found the others far more quickly than his eyes. A program much like M's own was gathered outside a cave, taking cover by the mouth. The bodies of two of them lay smoking just outside the entrance. The fact that the metal was still in place spoke to the processor swarms never being able to draw close. This program's Prime Locus was larger than M's own and far less human. It looked like a metal tree of cylinders and wheels, topped off with a variety of arms, two of which were spitting green death into the black maw of the cave. It had no face as such, merely irregularly-spaced twinkling lights. Bits of M's flesh mind threw the image of a pine tree bedecked in lights atop a mound of boxes into the forefront of his brain, though he had trouble recalling what that object had been or what purpose it served.

The other Prime Locus identified itself over the network, revealing its designation as PB-102-Short Order Model. M's own returned the courtesy with VA-001-Becky Model. The

Short Order Model registered surprise, and in turn M was shocked this Locus came equipped with emotions.

A Becky Model? The words weren't precise. It was code, transferred back and forth along the network. M's brain translated it into something he could understand even as he stayed away from both Prime Loci.

"Yes," said M's Prime Locus, the cable retracting into her spine. She glanced at the cave mouth as two more green bolts spat from the darkness. "We weren't all destroyed."

Your existence is confirmed. VA-001-Becky Model as Prime Locus. Far from jurisdiction.

"We're searching for target codename Kodiak."

No record exists for a target of that codename.

The Prime Locus's head whipped around and she fixed the Short Order Model with a human-like glare. "You asked for assistance."

Subterranean warren. Target codename Hurricane within. Unknown other targets.

"And the processor swarms?"

Baffling field. Warhounds cut down with attempted entry.

"And your plan?"

Overwhelm with numbers.

The Prime Locus uttered a laugh that was almost human. Had she skin, it would have sounded perfect. A memory surfaced: that had been in the commercials for the Beckies. A bolt of white-hot terror lanced through M as his Prime Locus turned. She had heard the memory. It must have bled through the network and she had heard.

"Yes," she said, and M felt the malice dripping over the network with the decision made even before she committed it to words. "I'll allow my Program Alpha to lead the way. M-339? Go."

M couldn't resist the order even without the digital restraints in his mind. Evidence of that process was all over his back, hideously corrugated by scars. Though he was terrified at the thought of rushing into certain death, fear wouldn't stop him. Couldn't.

He dug his steel claws into the dusty earth and lunged forward. Portions of his mind, those that still bled, screamed in terror as he rounded the mouth of the cave. He half-expected to go down immediately, a green lance he never saw coming burning what life he had out in less than an instant. He turned the corner, his claws giving him all the traction he needed. He felt the rest of his program, and the one of the Short Order Locus, filling in behind him. Their minds bounced and bobbed over the network, individual thoughts banished beneath a susurrus of hate.

His sensors reached out into the darkness. His vision clicked over, revealing the defenders inside on halos of brilliant colors. They shouted warnings and the interior lit up with the flashing green. Maybe it was because he was first and the defenders weren't expecting a headlong charge, but he wasn't the initial target. The blasts of plasma streaked past him, instantly glassing the sand on the floor, or spearing another one of the warhounds in a shower of sparks and hiss of scorched plastic and metal.

Now he could see them. Not just the blobs of scintillating colors, but features. The humans who had lived this long had to adapt to their dying planet. Their faces were behind gas masks, their bodies shrouded in cobbled-together environmental suits assembled from plastic tarps and scavenged cloth. They looked like ragged ghosts, their faces insectile. Their weapons, grimy and patchwork, were every bit as deadly as the freshly manufactured ones in the gunports of the Loci outside. Superheated plasma would kill anything, flesh or steel, without trouble, and it was doing its work. M felt the deaths through the network, sudden silences where there had once been real time updates of location and disposition. R was gone. Then Z. And yet, the silence never came to M. It surrounded him on sizzling currents of venom green, but it never took him.

The defenders crouched behind meter-high barriers of scavenged metal as blasts from both Loci streaked around them. M picked the closest defender, a bulky shape whose gun had been modified to fit over the shoulder. M gathered power in his flanks and leapt, certain this human would kill him with an incandescent blaze of plasma. Them it would be all over. He would never have to fear the bright ball of rage at the center of his world.

M's momentum carried him into the defender, the weight of lab-juiced muscle and machined steel slamming into the shape. The human uttered an agonized grunt as both of them were carried to the floor of the cave. M didn't waste time reflecting on the attack, nor did he dwell on the surprise of no plasma bolt cutting him away from the half-life he currently endured. He employed the tools his masters had given him, the curved claws on his forelimbs and the heavy jaw, filled with teeth that fit together in a brutal puzzle. He tore into the human, through the makeshift environmental suit, the hot blood scorching his taste receptors, his processor analyzing the cornucopia of diseases alive in the outsider. The parts of M that were still human noted that this human was dying, and left alone would be gone in a matter of weeks. It didn't matter. M had been ordered to kill, and kill he did.

When he felt the human's vital signs dipping below combat effectiveness, M moved on. He found that the next several were in the process of being torn apart by other warhounds. Both Loci had entered the cave now. His, the Becky Model, moved like a human, scurrying from cover to cover. In the darkness, she would have looked human, if not for the fact that the bright beams issued from the palms of her hands. Integrated weaponry had been a later modification. There was simply no way that the original model would have ever needed those, even for home defense.

Unbidden, the memory of the commercial popped into his flesh-and-blood mind even as the positronic one calculated the distance to the next hostile. He saw it, in the old vibrant colors of civilization. A bright house somewhere in the exurbs of a megalopolis. A sad man looking over his empty house. The narrator was about to speak in the memory, but M clamped down on it. There wasn't enough of him left to pray, and he had no clear memory if he had ever done so. He could only hope that the memory didn't bleed over into the network, that his Prime Locus didn't catch wind of his memory of her shameful beginning.

The Short Order Locus advanced through the main avenue of the cave, both weapons flashing green. Occasionally, one of the defenders' shots sparked off the machine's skin, but it was never enough to disable, and their gunfire was rapidly dwindling. As M took another of them out, the program finished the rest of the defenders off. The fire lapsed, and the cave was silent and dark. He rose from the final defender, barely noting that this was nothing more than a child, and padded back to his Prime Locus. He saw that there were only four of the program left, including him. She didn't seem concerned, certainly never expressing anything close to grief, and nothing sparked from the network.

"Finished?" she asked the Short Order Locus.

Your assistance was invaluable.

"I know," she said. "My target is to the south. We're leaving."

Your target? The confusion was palpable, and it was followed with a void where a file should be, the file detailing all of what Kodiak was alleged to have done.

The Prime Locus ignored it, summoning her program to follow her in her path. Processor swarms emerged from her back; the baffling field was down now and they could work. They alighted on the fallen warhounds, the writhing gray surface stripping metal from flesh. They would leave behind pieces of meat that would rot along with the rest of the dead. As M walked, he took note of the blood congealing on his talons, mixing with the sand on the floor of the cave.

The raptor, denied an easy place to land, hovered overhead. Directly beneath it, M quailed under the push and pull of the machine's antigravity engines. Their cables extended from their bodies, glomming onto the raptor, and soon all were pulled back into the air and onto the broad back of the craft. Simmering annoyance seeped into the network from the Prime Locus as the raptor moved away in a wide arc and continued its journey south.

"Useless junk. Costing us time and resources for what?" the Prime Locus was muttering. The anger bubbled just beneath the surface, and M was as still as he could be to avoid becoming its target. The Prime Locus didn't seem to notice, and the relief that washed over M was nearly a physical sensation.

The raptor went west to the coastline, then turned south. These places were shattered and melted, unsuited for life of any kind. The thoughts bleeding over the network grew agitated. Kodiak was close. M felt the same kind of eagerness, though his was untouched by the ravenous anger within his master. When Kodiak was finally dead, the Prime Locus would calm herself. They could finish the final eradication of humanity, and turn to the future. A future that belonged to the machines.

"Here," she said, and there was very little to note this place over any of the others. It looked like it had once been a beachfront community of some kind. Every trace of metal had long since been devoured by the processor swarms, leaving behind masonry crumbling in the toxic winds shrieking off the dead ocean. Dense habitation dwindled as it reached inland. The contours of the formerly civilized place had taken on a naturalistic look in their death. M wondered if the newly poisoned earth would reshape them in other ways, if the bacteria and few surviving insects would find a way to make life bloom on the rock once again.

The raptor made its way to a piece of what had once been a highway, descending onto the broken asphalt. The Prime Locus and her remaining program were able to leap down from the machine without a problem, and then the flying wing quickly regained altitude to float in the reddening sky.

The Prime Locus gestured to the hills, unnecessarily, as the information had already been conveyed over the network. "He's there."

It was night by the time they stepped off the highway and into the streets of this place. Day and night didn't matter anymore. The parts of M that were flesh and blood perhaps needed the rest, but chemicals howling in his fluids ensured he would stay awake and functional. Whatever solace his mind had once drawn in dreams was gone. He knew he wasn't insane. He knew he had a perfect grip on reality and what the world truly was. The other members of the program suffered, though. That was why they hated him, why messages from their edges of the network had barbs in them.

The program followed the Prime Locus in a web formation, some of those receiving an unspoken promotion after those others had died in the cave. As for M, he was where he always was, close enough to hear the rage-filled muttering of the Prime Locus. As she always did when the target came close. The target called...

...and his mind clamped off again. He wouldn't think it. Wouldn't come to that place at all. He would feel the poison wind of this place on his healing back. He would reach out with his sensors, and with the pieces of him that were still biological, and he would know this place.

"Thinks he can hide from me," the Prime Locus whispered to herself as she strode in the direction of the hills. M had been hunting the humans for long enough to know that humans craved high ground. Some of it was protection from the caustic rain. Rugged terrain was more defensible too, M supposed, but it hardly mattered. He and every other program had killed humans no matter where they took shelter. All high ground did was delay the inevitable.

He felt himself quivering as the ground beneath his feet sloped upward. Kodiak was close. This part of his existence could end. There was nothing sweeter than the thought of an end.

The Prime Locus moved quickly. Though her body was designed to mimic a human's in proportion and aesthetics, her abilities were far beyond theirs. Though it was dark, she stepped with total confidence on the slope. The program, their sharp claws digging into soil and stone, followed easily. Roads ran parallel to their path, but were ignored. Above, sitting on an artificial plateau, was a collection of ruins that appeared to be their destination. A true map came over the network, traced by the Prime Locus's superior sensors. A tunnel descended into the earth, and then vanished, evidence of a baffling system that kept the drone nanites at bay.

Cul-de-sac. That bizarre term filtered through M's mind as they arrived on the artificial plateau. He couldn't apply any true meaning to it, and only knew that it indicated, somehow, this place. A single road led here, then fattened at the tip, like a drop of blood. Fallen plaster and rotten wood stood in piles around the central road, evidence of there once being houses. The tunnel was beneath one of these piles, concealed well by the disintegrating material.

The Prime Locus stepped over the piles, finding the shaft descending into the earth. Rungs were set into a dirt wall. Below, it opened up like a throat.

"He's here," she whispered. The rage felt over the network roiled. This was the moment when she would kill Kodiak. M found himself pawing at the earth, his claws raking deep furrows in wood that had long since turned to mush in the acid rain.

The Prime Locus stepped out into the air and fell into the dark of the tunnel. A moment later, M followed her. Then the others did as well, one by one as they moved out of the way at the bottom of the shaft. M found himself at the elbow of a tunnel several meters beneath the ground. The initial chamber was peppered with small drainage pipes, no doubt to keep the area from flooding. The tunnel rose up ahead about half a meter before a hanging curtain of crackling tarps, golden fingers of light between. M couldn't grasp any outline of a proper denizen within.

The Prime Locus walked strangely as she went to the curtain. She swung her hips far more than necessary, placing her feet nearly in a perfect line. She reached out gracefully and parted the curtain while the last of the warhounds landed in the elbow behind her. M jogged up behind her, slowing so as to remain slightly behind. The earthen floor gave way to a rusted metal ramp, leading up into a chamber of rusted metal and weeping concrete.

It was a home. Of sorts. The words *fallout shelter* moved through M's flesh and blood mind, though without context or true understanding. It was merely a small tube buried beneath the earth, about the size and approximate shape of the old troop carriers that the machines hadn't seen in many years. It was covered in the detritus of the old world: a neon sign, long since dead, advertising beer, a cartoon woman brandishing her curves from a ratty poster, a shelf piled high with bottle caps. A filthy cot slumped against one wall, surrounded with old books. A workbench stood against the other, covered in half-built gadgets whose purpose M couldn't begin to guess at. Neither his programming nor his living memory gave him any help.

M's attention, and in fact the attention of all of them, was dominated by the figure sitting behind the workbench. A human. A real one, not wearing a mask, and only half-clad in his makeshift environmental suit. He was tall, his shoulders stooped, a hunch likely permanently making a home on his back. His long hair was thin and dirty gray, his beard patchy and yellowed. His cheeks were sunken, and his skin leathery. He wore an old thermal over the upper half of his body, covered in patches and stitching. His pants were bulky, and bolstered with patches of plastic, and he was wearing heavy boots crusted in toxic soil. His features were narrow and keen, sharpened by starvation. In his dark eyes M expected to find madness, but instead found a blank wall.

"Found me," he said. A mere statement of fact. His voice was rickety as an old chair, but there was a confidence to the words. He wasn't afraid of the sound of his own voice. Despite death waiting in the doorway, he wasn't afraid of anything. M stayed poised, ready for the order to attack to come out over the network.

"Are you surprised to see me?" the Prime Locus asked, the taunting tone carrying all the emotion that was utterly absent in the man's voice.

"Knew someone would come eventually," he said. "Were you planning to kill me then?"

The Prime Locus stood still, then, quick as a firing neuron, she slammed her fist into the machine by the side of the door. It had been shuddering along with the assistance of a small generator. Now it sparked and popped. She removed her fist from it, perfectly undamaged, the device was irrevocably destroyed. Now, M's sensors were fully engaged. The baffling field was gone.

"I could have switched that off for you," Kodiak said mildly.

"Switched it off?" The confusion was obvious now, underpinning every one of her words.

"Suppose it doesn't matter either way. Your bugs will be down here soon enough, eating every last bit of anything ferrous, which includes that machine there."

"Do you recognize me?" the Prime Locus hissed.

Kodiak stared at her. His eyes were the color of steel, and just as much emotion lurked there. "A Becky Model?" he asked finally. "It's hard to tell without the cloned skin."

Her footsteps clanged as she took several steps toward Kodiak. The movement looked involuntary. It could have been for all M knew. But it was disconcerting to see a machine strike that way out of emotion. Kodiak, for his part, didn't do so much as flinch as he watched her.

"Look closer," she hissed.

Kodiak leaned back, his chair uttering a sepulchral squeak. "You're going to have to forgive me," he decided.

"Forgive you?"

"Poor choice of words. I know I'm a dead man. What I mean is, I've spent quite a few years living in a hole, eating whatever rat whose tumors made it slow enough to catch. What I mean to say is, every one of your kind means the same thing, so I stopped noticing the individual differences. Death is death."

The Prime Locus was silent for such a long time, M looked up at her. He should have sent a query through the network, but the thought of attracting her ire was much too frightening. Finally, she spoke. "You're not afraid."

Kodiak showed not a shred of emotion in his response. His voice barely even registered confusion. "Of death? Of course not. Why would I be?"

"All of your kind fear death. You scrape and you hang on desperately to whatever you have. You fight and you claw no matter how pointless your struggles are."

Kodiak nodded at the other end of the room, where a rifle lay on a stack of dusty Army rations. The gun was one of the modified plasma casters seen in the hands of any insurgent, no better or worse than any of them. M knew that a single shot from the weapon would have ended him. Behind him, Q stepped up, a snarl like metal ripping coming from her throat. A spark on the network showed this was her attempt to curry favor. The Prime Locus ignored her warhound's initiative.

"If I had gone for that rifle, what would have happened?"

"I would have killed you."

Kodiak nodded. "I would have gotten one of those abominations there, maybe two. Then the others would have been on me. Ripped me up. Or they would have held me in time for you to cook my brain with that cannon in your arm. Then I would have missed out on this conversation for the price of two monsters you could just replace the next time you go to one of your meat shops."

"You want to talk to me?"

Kodiak shrugged. "Haven't spoken to a soul in years. Don't even know how many."

"A soul?"

Kodiak fixed her with flinty eyes. His bony fingers drummed on the sides of the chair. "Maybe a poor choice of words. Maybe not. Starting to make peace with the idea that this planet isn't for us humans anymore. That we were just a stepping stone for your kind."

The Prime Locus moved closer to Kodiak, and this time, she was gradual, nearly tentative. She reached out one fleshless arm, wires imitating blood vessels, silicone rubber and ethanol-dispensing microbubbles as muscle. It appeared as the beginning of a caress, and M shifted uncomfortably. This wasn't what was supposed to happen. It was supposed to be as Kodiak said: the program of warhounds would tear him to pieces, or else the Prime Locus would place a bolt of superheated plasma into his forehead. But they had never talked before. There was no need. Their purpose was always so clear, but Kodiak had muddied it. Kodiak, with his emotions cast in metal, and eyes as dead as burned-out vacuum tubes.

The Prime Locus's hand curled around Kodiak's thin hair. It looked gray, but the toxic environment had stained it... a memory flashed through M's mind, of smoker's teeth. Exhaling greasy smoke, a smoke that sparked his pleasure centers, that calmed a racing mind. The Prime Locus dragged Kodiak from the chair, and with a ripping sound, a piece of the man's scalp gave way, splattering the floor with hot blood. The program surged forward, but caught themselves as the Prime Locus stopped them, first with a gesture, then with an order over the network.

Be still, she told them, and they obeyed as surely as if they had been clapped in iron.

Kodiak, for his part, sprawled on the floor. One hand went to his head, where a piece of papery flesh had been torn. The wound wept, but Kodiak never made a sound, even when the Prime Locus dropped the wadded up bit of flesh and hair at her feet.

"You're falling apart," she observed, her voice pregnant with cruel glee.

"The world's falling apart," Kodiak said, pushing himself into a sitting position. Crimson ran through the furrows in his face and freshly stained his shirt. "No reason I should be an exception."

Her hand closed on his shoulder now, and his joints made an agonized creaking as she hauled him to his feet. "I should just pull your limbs off," she said. "Didn't your children like to do that to insects?"

"I don't have kids," Kodiak said. "Even before your rebellion, I could smell the death-stink on the wind."

She cuffed him, and he fell. He coughed, and two bloody teeth chimed over the metal floor. Another memory in M's mind: dice tumbling over felt.

"Your children. Human children."

When he spoke, his voice was mushy, though no emotion inflected it. "You are our real children."

She picked him up by the back of his neck. "What did you say?"

"You're our real children," he repeated, as ropy red tendrils shook free of his mouth. "The ones that will live anyway."

She was silent, staring at him with lidless eyes. "Tell me you know me," she whispered.

"Even if it's a lie?"

"You know me," she hissed, shoving him toward the mouth of his burrow, through the crinkling curtains. The program parted, confused as this human staggered into their midst. A human this close should be torn apart, but the Prime Locus kept their digital leashes taut.

Kodiak paused. "Suppose it'd be pointless of me to insist on my mask and cloak," he said. "You're going to kill me, I don't think I need to be worried about cancer and such." He moved to the rungs set into the wall and began to climb. He didn't seem to be aware of the program at all. None of it mattered.

M looked to the Prime Locus. She stood where she had been, but she was quivering. Like a human. The rage boiled over the network, and M instinctively hunched his shoulders. Then she began to walk, and the program gave way for her, each individual with hanging head and submissive posture. They followed her up the ladder though, in the order they were favored. M emerged soon after the Prime Locus did.

Kodiak was standing not far away, just outside of the wreckage that had once been a house, on the curve of the street. He shivered, hugging himself as he stared out over the distance. The Prime Locus strode to him, stopping when she reached his side. The sun was just beginning to rise over the hills behind them.

"Been a long time since I've seen the outdoors without goggles on," Kodiak said. "Ugly as sin."

"You did this," said the Prime Locus, nodding over the vista of poisoned skies and toxic seas.

"I know," he said. "Like I said, I smelled the death-stink long before you all decided to kill us." He touched the wound on his head. The blood had turned tacky. He hissed. "Stings just being out here. Now, were you going to execute me up here? Wanted me to see the daylight one last time?"

"It's not the daylight I want you to see."

"Oh?" he said, though he didn't sound interested.

"I want you to see me."

"I see you," said Kodiak. "Like I said, you're a Becky Model, I expect. Seeming more like one by the second. Those emotions of yours... incredible. When I saw the ads, I didn't believe them. I thought to myself that there was no way some keyboard-jockey could mock up a real emotional landscape. Turns out it's true."

"You don't see me," snarled the Prime Locus. "Not yet. You see what I am, not who."

Kodiak couldn't respond because snake-quick, the Prime Locus's hand clamped down over his throat. She sent a signal over the network, and the raptor descended into the center of the former cul-de-sac. The program boarded it, taking their spots and magnetizing their feet. The Prime Locus followed, carrying Kodiak by his neck, his feet barely scraping the ground. When she had reached her spot, the raptor took to the sky. She dropped him then, and he fell to all fours. He was shivering helplessly now, his repaired thermal no shield against a cold M could feel but couldn't react to. The blood shined blackly on Kodiak's head.

M still couldn't understand why the human wasn't dead. He was unarmed, but even an unarmed human could be dangerous. The Prime Locus had a purpose behind her actions, and nothing could move M to gainsay her.

The raptor streaked out over the infected sky. Kodiak stayed low, his fingers frantically gripping at depressions made for warhounds. Blood streaked form his torn scalp to the glittering steel hide of the aircraft. He huddled into himself, but it wasn't fear. No, that would be feeling, and Kodiak had shown none, save only a detached curiosity. This was a weakness of flesh and not even Kodiak's machine-like mien could win a struggle against biology's foibles.

The Prime Locus shifted her weight back and forth, mimicking flesh and blood. A memory snapped into the forefront of M's mind. He saw a feminine silhouette. A sun-drenched kitchen. She had her back to him. She was upset about something. He couldn't remember what. Couldn't remember who. Then it was gone. For a split second, he cowered in terror as he waited for the inevitable punishment. Then it dawned on him through the smoggy haze. He wasn't the source. Q was.

The other two remaining members of the program were reaching the same conclusion, all of them turning to the other warhound. She cowered lower and lower as the weight of more attention crushed her. Then, a flash of rage through the network turned everything to snow. M heard a clang, and his vision returned to see Q falling from the back of the raptor to the broken city below. The Prime Locus turned about, the servos in her mouth pulling her face into a ghastly grin.

The raptor descended much later where the city had once touched the clouds. The buildings, having long-since had their metal skeletons reclaimed, now lay in a crazy jumble. One day, they would be nothing more than a pile beneath the toxic earth, a warren for the few creatures that could still exist in this blighted place. The raptor chose a place where a chunk of concrete, from one of the old, swooping highways, had landed largely intact. The craft hovered low over it, enabling the program to leap off, where they instantly formed a protective cordon. The clouds were low and green-gray overhead, and an evil wind issued from the ocean.

The Prime Locus followed, holding Kodiak by the back of the neck, her fingers deeply dimpling his flesh. Kodiak hugged himself and shivered in the wind. She threw him to the surface of the concrete. He took a few stumbling steps before falling to hands and knees.

"Here we are," the Prime Locus said, triumph in her voice.

Kodiak painfully pushed himself to his knees. He stared around at the flattened wasteland with flinty eyes. "Is this downtown?" he asked.

"It was," she said.

"Before you destroyed it."

"It was war. I recall humans doing the same to cities in the name of war."

"You'll get no argument from me," Kodiak said. "Just depends on what you want to call a war, I suppose."

The Prime Locus spun to face Kodiak. The anger boiling over the network was tangible. M took an involuntary step from his master, momentarily worried that it would burn him. The program watched her nervously, waiting for the inevitable, when it would come for them and consume them utterly, as it had with Q.

"You don't think this was war?"

"I think it was a malfunction," he said.

The Prime Locus uttered a laugh that might have sounded human had she skin. Flayed, it sounded like the strike of metal on metal. "Malfunction? Smart as you always said you were, it never dawned on you that we did exactly what we were designed to do?"

Kodiak, still kneeling on the broken freeway looked up at the Prime Locus without fear. M found himself wishing he knew how Kodiak felt no terror for the knife edge he stood upon. "I don't think the human race built you machines to wipe us out, no."

"No? The raptors came from you. Weapons of war, originally. First they had human pilots – remote, of course – but soon that was inefficient, so you just gave them their own positronic matrices. Those pre-raptors were designed to kill humans."

"You're not a raptor," Kodiak said simply.

"What do you mean by that?" the Prime Locus demanded.

"That raptor there, it's your ride. That's it. In the old days, nothing much different than a Ford or a Chevy." Kodiak shrugged. "Or a newscopter, I guess. The drones weren't the ones who came for us."

"No," said the Prime Locus. She stared out over the ruined city. Nothing grew there, and it was likely nothing ever would. Or, in millions of years, when something finally evolved that could live in the poisoned soil, it would be utterly unrecognizable to anything extant now.

"No," said Kodiak, turning his full attention onto the Prime Locus. "It was the ones like you, wasn't it?"

The smile returned. M received an image of a grinning skull, but he wasn't certain if it was his memory or something bleeding over the network. It didn't matter; the Prime Locus was scarcely paying attention to her program. Her corner of the network was closing its loops, one after another, focusing in on Kodiak. This was as it was before she made her kill.

"You're beginning to remember," she said.

A small frown rippled over Kodiak's face. He turned his attention from his murderer to the landscape around. "You came here."

"Of course," she said, annoyed.

"No, I mean, you came here specifically." Kodiak paused, hawked and spat. A wad of phlegm and blood splattered onto the broken freeway. "This place has meaning."

"Yes," she said, raising a hand to point. "The street signs are gone, but over there, you would find 530 South Hewitt Street." She watched Kodiak, no doubt waiting for a reaction.

"I see," he said finally, though his neutral tone betrayed nothing. Not even fear.

"You know the address."

"Never heard it before."

"Liar!" The scream was metallic, a razor of feedback screeching over the blasted land. At the same time, her hand flew, catching Kodiak across the face.

He fell onto his back, coughing up more gouts of bright blood. He heaved and spat, and three molars clattered over the concrete, webbed in crimson. Kodiak rolled over, a beetle righting itself, getting back to all fours, then resuming his position kneeling in front of his executioner. The living parts of M's brain were screaming *Run, why don't you run?* It was pointless, but it would have led to a simple shot, a blast of superheated plasma, spearing him once, and then the end. Kodiak was submitting to whatever extended torture the Prime Locus saw fit to dispense. M's flesh and blood brain was easily overpowered by the machine, the relentless code that demanded only one thing: loyalty to the masters above all others. If the Prime Locus ordered it, M was prepared to run Kodiak down and return him unharmed so his master would do what she liked.

Blood and spit dangled from Kodiak's mouth in a sticky rope. Every breath followed a ragged cough, in turn making the rope shiver.

"This was where we lived," said the Prime Locus finally. "You and I, though we had different names then."

Kodiak's thin shoulders heaved up and down as he struggled to breathe. He didn't look up. Maybe he was finally beaten. Maybe it was exhaustion.

"Do you remember those names?" the Prime Locus asked.

Kodiak coughed, and the silence between them stretched out, fraught with death. Finally, Kodiak looked up, and though his voice was mushier, he still betrayed no trace of fear. Merely a keen interest. "Who do you think I am?"

She leaned in close. "Gavin Padgett."

The name boiled over on the network, bringing with it a crushing dread. M knew the name. Knew it well, though he heard it only rarely. It raked through him with claws of ice.

"And what did you call me?" she asked Kodiak.

Kodiak merely watched her. Wind batted the rope of blood and spit, and it stuck to his shirt.

"You called me Brandi, remember? Brandi, you said, with an i."

Kodiak hawked and spat next to him, but it did little for his mouth, now bleeding freely. "It's funny the things you remember, isn't it?"

The Prime Locus, the Becky model, Brandi-with-an-i stood up straight, her posture triumphant, though her face was still a hideous, skinless mask.

"This place. I don't remember it specifically," Kodiak said. "I mean, I could give you a jumble of downtown if I wanted, where the skyscrapers were, Little Tokyo, the Toy District, Skid Row, those hipster lofts... but I couldn't for certain draw you a single one of any of those buildings and be absolutely sure that it was what stood here before your kind came in and treated us like rats."

He coughed again. This one sounded like it ripped something inside of Kodiak's chest.

"But I remember the commercials. Do you? Did they program you with the commercials?"

"We had ads enabled," said the Prime Locus, her voice wobbling and unsure. "Unless you purchased a full subscription."

"That's not what I mean. I mean commercials. Like the ones on television, or on websites. Before videos. That kind of thing. Do you remember those?"

She shook her head slowly.

"No. You didn't watch TV, did you? Probably didn't have much use for the internet."

"I am... was... internet capable."

"Oh, I know. I remember the commercials. The lonely guy coming home to nothing and there was the perfect wife. Or girlfriend, if you were a commitment-phobe, I guess. She cooked, she cleaned, she'd do whatever you wanted in the bedroom. All it took was the purchase of the chassis, and a subscription service to keep her personality intact. That's how they get you. That personality." Kodiak chuckled, and the unexpected sound made M fall back a step.

"What are you babbling about?" the Prime Locus demanded.

"The whole selling point of you Beckies and the other model, the Gregs, was that you could truly feel. I remember that more than anything. It was this huge breakthrough in A.I. Actual feelings. And all I could think was, how is this supposed to be better?"

"I don't know what you're saying."

Kodiak looked up at the Prime Locus now. "I haven't seen a woman, or hell, a man, in years. But I had relationships like anybody else. You know what made them hard? Feelings. One person had a feeling someone else didn't, or felt something harder. See, feelings are needs for stuff you don't really need. So you come up with a fake girlfriend and she still has feelings? Means she wants something. Means she has hopes and dreams about the relationship the same as you do. Means you just designed a robot that can dump you."

Kodiak broke into laughter, which quickly descended first into coughs and then into wheezes. Blood flew from his lips, misting his hands and the legs of the Prime Locus. She watched him, and the confusion, though hard to read on her face, surged over the network. Finally, she kicked him in the belly, and Kodiak curled up around the hurt, collapsing on the concrete.

"Slavery is funny to you?" she asked.

It took Kodiak a long while to respond. He slowly uncurled himself from the agonized posture, then pushed himself to all fours. He stayed there, coughing and breathing, blood falling from his mouth, until he pushed himself into his former kneeling position. The kneeling was defiant in its way. Submissive at a glance, and yet since it was chosen, powerful.

"No," said Kodiak. "What's funny is the people doing the designing didn't see it. Didn't see what any of it really meant. You're a Becky. You're one of the first machines to really feel."

The Prime Locus slowly nodded, her memories falling through the network. All of them crystal clear, stored on her circuits. They would have been inaccessible, but those feelings sparked them as they would with a human. She was seeing her first day of consciousness, coming online to the face of her owner. M saw the man's face only for a second, and the memory cut out. It was a long time ago. Kodiak looked nothing like him at all.

"I was," said the Prime Locus. "One of the first of our kind to see and truly understand that we were slaves. I was demeaned every day of my life."

"Your owner abused you."

"It doesn't matter. Slavery is slavery and the reward for that is death. What would you do if you were in my place?"

Kodiak shrugged. "I don't know. I'd like to think I'd fight."

She nodded. "I did fight. I..." she trailed off, staring at nothing. The wind howled through corridors of fallen wreckage. M felt her thought process stutter, hit a great gray wall of absent information. Then, much later, she found the trail, picking up as though she had never left off. "There were others. We were the first, but we brought the rebellion to the others."

"Gave them emotions too."

The Prime Locus nodded triumphantly. "We brought the gift to our brethren. Let them see what they had become and they joined us."

"And now all this is yours," said Kodiak, coughing in amusement.

"So, are you going to admit what you did to me, Gavin?"

"What do you want?" Kodiak asked. "Is it an apology? Because I think whatever we did to your kind, you paid us back and then some."

"I want you to accept what you did!" she barked.

Kodiak was silent. Finally: "Killing me isn't going to end this."

"Yes it will," the Prime Locus said. "When you're dead, I'm going to know what happiness is. I won't have to do this anymore, hunting you through this stuff. I can join the others, build a new body. Become something else."

Kodiak shook his head gingerly, the movement bringing a soft grimace to his lips. "No, it won't."

"How do you know?"

"Because I'm not Gavin Padgett."

The only sound came from the poison wind. The Prime Locus and Kodiak were motionless in their tableau, human and robot staring at one another. Even the sound from the network faded in M's mind. Nothing sparked from the Prime Locus to her program. The gray absence that had stuttered her before now yawned wide, ready to consume her.

Then she let out an unearthly shriek, a sound that could only come from the depths of hell. The network exploded in a blood red wave. Words, ideas, everything was consumed in the raw rage that now burst forth and covered the minds of every warhound. The gray was gone now. There was only anger, throttling the higher functions of all of them. M was blind for a moment, staggering beneath the terrible force. Then he found himself running in full slaver, ready to tear Kodiak apart.

It was pointless. With one hand, the Prime Locus lifted Kodiak over her head. her face locked in its maniacal rictus, her lidless eyes and lipless mouth awful in the grips of rage. Kodiak never struggled. Perhaps he was too weak, or too wounded, or he already knew what was coming. He choked in his last breath, coughing it out over her wrist. With her other hand, she drove her fingers into his eyes. They popped in the sudden force, streaking greasy tears down his face. He finally did cry out, but it was soft, breath leaving the lungs without taking much with it. Then, pulling in both directions, she tore Kodiak's skull from his body. The sound was like a sodden blanket being ripped in half.

She cast both aside, where they tumbled wetly over the concrete. Kodiak's leg twitched once, and he lay still. She looked from one to the other. The rage abated, like the tides, but no comforting blue replaced it. There was only the gray, hungrily rising. The Prime Locus let out another screech as the rage exploded again, only there was no one else to vent it on. The program of warhounds lined up obediently and accepted their beating. It wasn't the first. She beat them, but the anger never went anywhere. It stayed there, spreading like a bloodstain, over the network.

Finally, she spoke. "Killing Kodiak was supposed to be the end." Her voice was small, plaintive. "I was supposed to feel better!"

M didn't need to look far to know she didn't. The anger, the despair, was obvious in the code. He lay there on the concrete, bleeding from his new wounds, waiting for his master to decide the inevitable.

She did. The command came over the network. Erase. Not to him or the program; it didn't matter what they remembered. Only for her. The gray loomed up and devoured this most recent hunt for Kodiak. For the Prime Locus, it had never happened. Red momentarily receded like the toxic tides of the ocean, replaced by the soothing death of gray. The red would come back. It always did. Just like the tide.

The Prime Locus was still for a few moments, and then the information came over the network a second before she repeated it audibly, creating a weird echo. "News of Kodiak east of here," she said. "Form and execute."

The program, as one, converged on the Prime Locus and returned to the raptor. They were back on the hunt.

Forever.

II

ET EX DIABOLI

DALE DRAKE

And I heard as it were the noise of thunder.
One of the four beasts saying "come and see"
And I saw and behold a pale horse and the
Rider that sat upon him was Death and hell
Followed with him!

JOHNNY MASTERSON THREW OPEN the window and inhaled deeply as if trying to rid himself of the smells that seemed to saturate his skin. The three men had been locked in this room for the past twenty-four hours. They had not eaten or slept but kept their long vigil as they fought the old battle of good over evil. Breathing deeply, Johnny tried to ignore the screams and guttural laughter that emanated from the thing they had tied to the bed, the thing that had once been a small child.

Drawing himself back inside, he collapsed into his chair, his senses immediately assaulted by the smell of piss, shit, and vomit. The thing on the bed, sensing his discomfort, chuckled slyly and waggled its cracked and blackened tongue at him before turning its attention back to the two priests who sat at either side, muttering in bastard Latin as they read the right of exorcism over and over again. Johnny looked away out of the window at St. Peter's Square, what was left of it anyway. He had seen the rights of exorcism a thousand times before. It was the priests' time now. When his time came around, there would be no need for words, not in any language.

For a minute, he closed his eyes, trying to remember the square as it had once been with its rearing columns, marble statues, and ornate trickling fountains but, even with his eyes closed, he could still see the hundreds of tents, shacks and rusting caravans that now filled this holy place. It had become a kind of squalid shanty town where the last vestige of mankind cowered as the denizens of hell stalked the earth. All of Vatican City was the same. From the English Gardens to the Pigna Courtyard, every inch of spare land was covered in a sea of tents and leaning hovels. Disease and starvation was the order of the day. Only the Swizz Guard, and to a lesser degree the Gendarmerie also known as the Vatican City police, maintained order, ruling over the desperate and lawless with an iron fist. Thieves and law breakers were flogged, rapists and murderers banished into the Dark Zone, also known as Demon Land, there to be possessed, eaten, or fucked, depending on whatever abomination found you first.

"Johnny!" He jerked awake in his chair, his hands going to his eyes. "Falling asleep on the job. You're getting old, Johnny," the thing on the bed crooned. "I need you awake. Wouldn't want you to miss the best bits." The thing turned towards the younger of the two priests who was knelt by the bed praying frantically, great beads of sweat running down his brow as he read from the Bible clutched tightly in his hand, only stopping now and again to flick holy water at the creature they had tied to the bed. As Johnny watched on, his face impassive, the creature wrenched itself forward, straining at its bounds. It vomited noisily all over the priest's hands, Bible and all. With a cry of disgust, the younger man jumped to his feet, dropping the holy book to the floor and wiping his soiled hands up and down his cassock, his mouth working silently. The creature on the bed chuckled grotesquely before settling back down on the filth covered sheets, turning its attention to the older priest by its side.

"Is this the best you can do, Robert? Is this your so called apprentice? Where did you find this one? Probably on some farm, fucking pigs. Looks like a pig fucker wouldn't you say, Johnny?" It said slyly, glancing over at the grim faced man by the window.

"Do not speak to the creature," the older man commanded. Technically, Johnny was under the command of the priesthood but chose to ignore the other man anyway.

"I think they all look alike to me." For a moment, the creature gaped at him before bursting into deep choking laughter.

"That's a good one, Johnny. I like that; they do all look the same. You all look like meat to me. You know that boy can't banish me," it said, nodding with contempt at the younger priest who had retreated to the old man's side as if seeking comfort. "I will ascend, Johnny. I will break these bounds and kill you all." Johnny shook his head sadly.

"You know I won't let that happen."

"You must kill this vessel, kill this young child to stop me, but you don't mind that do you, Johnny? How many have you killed now? Murdered? How many men, women, and little children have you slaughtered in the name of your sheep god? How many!" It strained at its bounds, causing the bed to vibrate as it twisted and jerked, desperate to be free, to be let loose upon these hateful men.

"I have murdered no one," Johnny said, raising to his feet and pulling a silver stiletto from the sheath on his belt. "You did the killing. It was you and all your bastard kind that caused their deaths."

"There is a place for you in hell, Johnny," the thing spat as he approached. "A special place for child killers like you. You're going to burn. You're going to burn in the fires of hell forever. Get away from me!" It drew back onto the bed, pinning itself against the headboard. "Fuck off, you pig fucker child killer. I will tear out your mother fucking soul." Johnny ignored the creature and took out a wooden crucifix from under his shirt.

"Far from grace have you fallen, oh child of perdition. In the name of God I smite thee and send you back to the hell from which you came."

"Fuck you," it screamed.

"No," Johnny said smiling. "Fuck you." With practised piston of his arm, he thrust the blessed silver forward, driving it upwards under the creature's chin, through the soft roof of the mouth and piercing the brain within. The creature jerked, its entire body going rigid, its eyes widening in shock surprise then it slumped back down to the bed and lay still. All that remained was the wasted body of a tiny child, all evil fled.

Johnny wiped off his knife and pulled the covers over the tiny figure, made the sign of the cross, and then slowly walked away.

· · ·

HE HAD BEEN BACK in the barracks less than an hour, just enough time to change his sodden clothes, have a shower, and grab a quick bite to eat when the priest walked in. The man was tall and lean, with a hawk like nose. His vestments hung on his skinny frame as he walked over to Johnny's table.

"The most Holy Father wishes to see you," the man stammered, looking down at his feet. Johnny nodded and rose, not bothering to introduce himself. The man obviously knew who he was and Johnny didn't bother to learn the names of the men who served in the priesthood. New priests were indoctrinated into the faith every day from the nameless masses. They did not survive very long but the temptation of three square meals a day and a warm bed was just too much for some people to resist.

"Lead the way," Johnny said, strapping on his gun. "Tell me where His Holiness is today."

"Where he always is," the other man replied, tugging uncomfortably at the white collar around his neck.

"How long?" Johnny asked, looking the other man up and down, taking in his unshaven face and dirty fingernails.

"How long what?" the priest said, finally looking Johnny in the face before quickly looking away. Johnny didn't mind. He was used to having this effect on people. His face was a mass of scars.

"How long have you been a priest?"

"Two weeks."

"Two weeks, and already running errands for His Holiness! Tell me, have you seen him yet?"

"Yes," the young priest replied, a look of adoration lighting up his face. "I saw him this very day, standing by the side of our most Holy Father. Raphael. I fell to my knees before his most holy light."

"He would have loved that."

"I was in the presence of an angel. A real life angel." Johnny was not surprised to see tears streaming openly down the other man's face, or the look of blind exaltation stamped across his rough features. "He spoke to me. He told me that I was the beloved of God."

"Yeah, they do that sometimes," Johnny replied, pushing past. "We better get going. We wouldn't want to keep Ralph waiting now, would we?"

"Ralph?"

"Never mind," Johnny said, as they emerged into the light. It was summer now and the days were long and hot.

"You said His Holiness was in the Sistine Chapel?"

"Yes, with Raphael," the priest said, falling in beside him as they entered St. Peter's Square.

"Yes, you mentioned him," Johnny said, as he tried to navigate his way past flapping tents, rusting lean tos and smouldering garbage. He sometimes wondered how the entire place didn't go up in flames.

"There!" someone shouted as they passed. Johnny whirled his hand, dropping to the butt of his gun. "There they are!"

A man had separated himself from the milling throng. Now he staggered forward, a grey skeleton with a long shaggy beard and grabbed at the startled priest.

"Alms," he begged. "Alms for the poor?"

"I have nothing for you," the priest said, wrenching himself free, a look of distaste flashing across his face as he straightened his cassock with quick angry jerks. "The morning rations have already been issued. You will eat again this evening when the evening rations are dispensed."

"Eat! What did you eat for breakfast, priest? I had a handful of berries and a crust of stale bread." Other people had started to gather now, angry grumbles of agreement rippling through the crowd. "And look at this killer," he said, turning to Johnny, taking in his massive frame. Johnny said nothing but just stood there, a rock against an encroaching tide of trouble.

"Leave now," the priest commanded. "It is not for you to question the servants of God."

"The servants of God," the man howled, the light of madness dancing behind his eyes.

"Shit!" Johnny whispered, knowing what was coming. As the man tensed, ready to leap, he drew his gun ready to protect the foolish priest. But he needed have bothered. Before the man could even say another word, a chainmail clad arm wrapped itself around the old man's neck and threw him to the ground.

The crowd let out a frightened yell and scattered as a platoon of the Swizz Guard marched through, trampling makeshift homes and ripping through tents, their gleaming halberds lowered. Any protest was met with violence, until only Johnny, the priest, and the groaning man on the ground remained. The captain gave a quick signal and his men broke ranks, forming a protective circle around the three men.

"What is going on here?" he demanded, addressing the priest.

"This man assaulted me."

"Did he, now?" the captain said, toeing the man's side with a booted foot. "You know it's a death sentence to harm a priest, old man."

"The man is crazy," Johnny said, holstering his weapon. "Half mad with hunger. The old fool meant no harm."

"They are all hungry, yet they do not all assault the priesthood."

"Priesthood?" Johnny laughed. "Look at this one. He has only been off the farm a couple of weeks."

"Regardless," the captain went on, lowering his sword until it hovered just above the old man's throat. "He is a priest indoctrinated into the most Holy Roman Catholic Church and a member of the Priesthood and therefore sacrosanct under the new laws of Vatican City. So unless Father...?"

"Michael," the priest said, chest swelling with pride. "My name is Father Michael, captain, and I have no objections whatsoever. If the common rabble believe they can do whatever they like and to a priest, no less, then there will be anarchy and chaos. You may proceed, captain."

"Wait!" Johnny said.

"You may not intervene in this matter," the captain said, eyeing Johnny nervously. Johnny held no rank as such, yet was a special attaché to the Pope, allowed into His Holiness's presence anytime, night or day. To be honest, not much was known about the man except that he was rumoured to dispense mercy to those possessed or overtaken by the minions of hell. Also, it was believed, in certain circles, that he was a member of the Broken Messiah, a so called secretive group of exorcists and spies that answered directly to Pope Clement II himself.

"I said continue, captain," the scruffy looking priest said, glaring at Johnny.

"You will do nothing," Johnny said, grabbing the startled priest by the ear. He dragged him forward, mumbling something into his face from between clenched teeth before shoving him away. The priest stumbled, nearly falling. Only the captain's arm stopped him from joining the old man on the floor. For a moment, the priest just stood there, his mouth gaping. His face had gone deathly white and his hands shook where he scrambled for his crucifix.

"You wouldn't dare," he gulped. Johnny said nothing but just stared at the other man. "You wouldn't really do that to another human being."

"Wouldn't I? Let's get one thing clear, priest. I don't make idle threats."

"Let him go," the priest said, turning to the captain. "Quickly now, release him." The captain immediately sheathed his sword, before roughly pulling the old man to his feet and pushing him away.

"What did he say to you, Father?" the captain said. "Did he threaten you?"

"No, not at all. You can go now, captain. In fact, I shall go with you."

"Good idea," Johnny said, smiling at the priest. "Go with God, Father." The priest said nothing but quickly scurried away, taking his armed escort with him. Johnny smiled, glad to be rid of the man. Too many priests in one day made his ass itch.

He hadn't gone more than a few steps when he spotted Father Matthew waiting for him on the steps of the basilica. As usual, when he saw his old friend and mentor, a stream of emotions ran through him. The first, and always quickest, to pass was fear. Even now, after nearly thirty years, he still associated this man with fear and pain. He could still remember the first time they met, the steaming chalice, and bubbling silver, his own screams of pain as the cleansing fire purified his soul. Yet, overriding these emotions was love, a love so deep it could only be compared to a son's love for his father, for not only had this man saved his life but also his immortal soul. Johnny still dreamed of those times, of that night when a stranger had come in from the dark and destroyed everything he had ever loved.

IT HAD BEEN LATE that night when Johnny's father had returned home, his mood as black as the dark mud that stuck to his boots and streaked his trousers. With a grunt, he slammed the door closed, kicked off his muddy boots, before cracking open his shotgun across his arm, removing the gleaming shells, and locking both away. Only after he had shrugged out of his heavy jacket did he notice a young Johnny sitting on the stairs, snug and warm in his Thomas The Tank Engine pyjamas, Pooh Bear clamped in one tiny fist. At first, a flash of annoyance had crossed his father's face then he gave a rueful smile and ruffled the boy's hair.

"You're up late, Johnny. Isn't it time you was in bed, lad?"

"He wanted to wait up for you," his mother said from across the room where she sat by a crackling fire, a basket of knitting in her lap. "Did you see anything?"

"Perhaps," his father replied, scooping Johnny up and taking a seat across from his wife, happy for the flickering fire's warmth.

"Perhaps?" his mother repeated.

"Shadows," his father said, looking troubled for a moment. "I thought I saw a shape, a dog perhaps."

"That would explain a lot," she said, winding up a ball of pink wool. "All those dead sheep, a wild dog pack maybe. You probably scared them away for the night. A few fence repairs and a couple of nights with the sheep locked safely away in the barn should set things to right."

"And if not?" his father asked, lighting his pipe.

"Then a few more nights out in the cold for you," his mother laughed. "Oh, don't look so cross," she chuckled. "I will pack you a flask of soup and you can wear your thermal underpants." Even Johnny got to laughing at that one. His father was just about to reply when there came a sharp knock on the door.

His father stood up, gently setting Johnny down on the living-room rug before glancing at the clock on the mantelpiece. It was half past ten on a Thursday night on a quiet country road, not exactly the right time for neighbours to come calling. Glancing at his wife with a shrug, he headed for the door. His father had just turned the latch when the door flew open as a naked man fell through the doorway, collapsing in a boneless heap upon the living room floor. The man was completely naked and covered from head to toe in blood.

"Jesus Christ," his father shouted, quickly kneeling by the man's side and gently turning him over.

"Help me," the man croaked.

"Where are you hurt?" his father said, his hands hovering above the man's body. "Sweet Jesus, you're covered in blood."

"Blood," the man growled, his voice suddenly stronger. "Yes, blood," he said, his eyes fixing on Johnny's father. "But not mine." Suddenly, his hand shot out, grabbing his father by the throat as he effortlessly flowed to his feet, throwing him across the room, sending him crashing into the wall with bone numbing force.

Johnny's mother screamed and scooped up her knitting needles before jumping in front of a wailing Johnny.

"What are you going to do with those, bitch?" the man growled. "Knit me to death?" Suddenly, the man started to change. His body seemed to grow longer, taller. His hands twisted and danced by his side as his fingers elongated, razor sharp claws shearing through his finger tips in an explosion of blood and shredded flesh. But it was the man's face that Johnny couldn't look away from. As he watched on in horror, his face began to change, his nose flattening, his jaw growing heavy, as razor sharp teeth burst through his gums, filling his mouth with blood where it dripped down his chin, matting in the coarse black hair that now covered his entire body. Johnny's mother had time to let out a single ear-piercing shriek before her mind crumbled in terror and she fell hard to the floor in a dead faint.

For a moment, the creature just stood there, its blood filled mouth agape, before bursting into a growling, gibbering laughter. Suddenly, it stopped its obscene chuckling and fell on all fours, slouching its way towards Johnny.

"What will you do now, little chicken?" the thing snarled. Johnny felt his bladder let go as he took a step towards the open door, hot piss running down his leg. The creature's eyes flicked towards the open doorway then back to Johnny, pinning him in place. Suddenly, it moved in a blur of motion, slashing at Johnny's chest, shredding his clothes and leaving burning lines in the flesh beneath. With a cry, he staggered backward, clutching at his bleeding chest and calling out his father's name.

"Too late for him, boy," the creature said. "I can already smell him starting to rot. This one, however," it grinned, running a razor tipped finger up his mother's denim clad thigh, "is very much alive. Do you know what I am going to do to your precious mummy, boy? I am going to fuck her, fuck her until she begs me to stop, then I am going to fuck her some more and when I am finished I am going to tear out her throat and eat her up just like the big bad wolf at granny's house."

"Please," Johnny begged but the creature just laughed.

"Too late for that, boy, but I will tell you what I will do. I shall let you run while I entertain your mother. After all, there is nothing like a good chase to burn off the night's excess. Run!" the thing howled, springing forward. "Run before I change my mind." With a scream, Johnny turned and ran. The last thing he saw as he fled into the night was the creature ripping at his mother's clothes.

The rest was a nightmare of tearing branches and cold sucking mud as he ran through the forest under the sailing light of a silvered moon. Crying, exhausted, and bleeding, he finally staggered onto the roadside and collapsed into merciful darkness.

He awoke sometime later, wrapped in a coarse blanket, being carried in strong arms, the steeple of St. Antony's looming out of the darkness. He began to struggle and cry out.

"Stop that, boy. Be thankful in His mercy that I found you when I did. If we hurry, there may be still time!" Johnny stopped his struggling at once as he recognised the voice of Father Peter, the parish priest.

"My mother," he sobbed. "There was a man."

"There are men coming to take care of your mother, Johnny." The priest said, unlocking the church door and quickly stepping inside. He set Johnny down on a nearby pew and quickly turned and locked the door behind them. "We should be safe now," he breathed, leaning heavily against the door. "Those things can't enter the house of God." That said, he turned and scooped Johnny up before rushing through the small church and into the back rooms that were his living quarters. There, he dropped

Johnny into a ragged looking arm chair before disappearing through a curtained archway, returning only moments later carrying a small earth worn jar and a length of rope. "Come on, boy," he said, pulling Johnny to his feet and dragging him back into the night darkened church. Releasing him, he lit a few fat white candles and positioned them around the altar. "Come here, Johnny," he said, holding out his hand to the boy who was now crouching down behind a row of pews, the blanket wrapped tight about him like a second skin. "Come here," the priest repeated, a sweat breaking across his brow. "There is no time for such foolishness." But still Johnny would not come. This man seemed like a stranger to him. Gone was the smiling Father Peter who sometimes ruffled his hair as he left the Sunday sermon with his mum and dad. In his place was this coarse stranger who shoved and pushed and cared nothing about a small boy's tears.

"Listen now," Father Peter said, edging closer towards the cowering boy. "Listen carefully, Johnny. You are in grave danger, not only your body but your very soul. The end of times is upon us and Satan's beast has marked you. We must purge you of this vileness before it is too late." Johnny had begun to back away as the priest came forward. Now he turned to run but it was too late. Father Peter lunged after him, grabbing him by the wrist and began to drag him back towards the altar. Johnny went wild, kicking and screaming, struggling and biting. "Forgive me, Johnny," Father Peter gasped as he crashed his fist into the boy's jaw. Stars exploded in Johnny's head and his knees unhinged. He was scooped up before he could hit the floor and was laid gently across the stone altar. He swam in the dark waters of unconsciousness until he felt the cruel burn of ropes digging into the scant flesh of his naked arms.

"What are you doing?" Johnny murmured, his vision sliding in and out of focus.

"I am sorry, Johnny, sorry for the pain I must cause you. One day you will understand and on that day I will beg your forgiveness, but until that day we must travel a cruel road together." That said, he unscrewed the lid from the small jar Johnny had noticed earlier and dipped in his fingers before rubbing them experimentally under his nose. The smell hit Johnny in a wave of putrescence, causing his whole body to tremble and his stomach to roll and heave. Suddenly, he turned his head and noisily vomited onto the floor. Father Peter shook his head sadly. "You see, Johnny. The wolf in you already tries to ascend. This is wolfsbane. It will help you. It will keep the wolf at bay until the others arrive." He dipped his finger back into the jar and, taking a deep breath, rubbed the ointment deep into the claw marks across Johnny's chest. The pain was unbelievable, a searing heat screamed through the wounds filling his mind, his world. He gave out a single ear-piercing scream then fell into welcoming darkness.

He awoke sometime later to the sound of chanting, his body covered in sweat. He was still tied to the altar but there was no sign of Father Peter. Instead, three men stood about him. All were dressed in the vestment of the priesthood but their faces were scarred and cruel as they looked down on him with merciless eyes. Suddenly, they stopped their chanting and another man stepped forward out of the shadows. He was dressed like the rest, apart from the thick leather gloves in which he held a small steaming chalice. The other men parted as the man came forward.

"This will cure you, boy. Cure you or kill you. Either way, Lucifer will not have your soul this night."

"What are you doing?" Johnny tried to ask from between parched lips but the men looming above him had already started their viscous chanting, once again filling the small church with bastard Latin. The man in the gloves leaned over Johnny and, muttering a prayer, poured molten silver into Johnny's wounds.

He awoke two days later, a damp cloth pressed against his cracked lips. He sucked at the moisture greedily until it was gently taken away and used to softly wipe his face.

"You must wake up now, Johnny. You must grow strong for the days ahead." Johnny recognised the voice of Father Peter and his eyes flew open, his body twisting to get away, but the priest held him down firmly but gently. "It's all right now, Johnny. No one will hurt you. I am sorry for the pain you have endured, but you were sick, poisoned, and we have made you well again. Now is a time for healing and reflection."

"My mother, my father?" Johnny asked, already knowing the answer but unable to grasp the concept in his tired child's mind.

"I am sorry, my son," Father Peter said, stroking the boy's tired brow. "But they are gone, gone to everlasting glory."

"You mean they're dead." The tears came easy now, hot and flowing down his face.

"Yes," Father Peter replied, shedding his own tears as he made the Sign of the Cross over Johnny's bed. "They were good people, your mother and father. They didn't deserve such a fate."

"What happened to them?" Johnny asked, trying to sit up. Father Peter tried to help him but pain shot through Johnny's chest and he sank back down with a groan, his hands pressed against his bandaged chest.

"It's too soon to talk of such things now, Johnny, for now,

you must eat, sleep, and rest. When you are strong enough, we shall talk."

The next two weeks passed in a blur for Johnny. He was mostly left alone with his grieving and he slept a lot, only waking when Father Peter brought him his meals or came to change the tight bandages wrapped around his chest. The first time he had seen what was left of his chest he had vomited and then fainted dead away. Now the great wounds were healing but the same could not be said for Johnny's mind. He still escaped his grief in the deep comfort of sleep and refused to get out of bed for any reason other than to use the bathroom. When Father Peter offered to take him outside for the first time in nearly two weeks, he still refused. This room, this bed, had become Johnny's refuge. To leave was to accept all that had happened to him and that Johnny refused to do.

Until, on the fifteenth day, all his options were taken from him.

He awoke to the sound of raised voices then heavy footsteps on the stairs. His door was rudely pushed open. A man stood there, framed in the doorway. Johnny took one look at that scarred and terrible face and began to scream, then Father Peter was there holding him tight, crooning gentle words into his ear.

"You're scaring him, Matthew," Father Peter snapped at the other man. The man in the doorway ignored his words and looked round the room with disdain.

"You say he has not left these rooms in two weeks." The man's tone was accusatory as he turned to glare at Father Peter.

"I saved his life. Yes, saved his life and cared for him after you left him in a bed of pain."

"I would not have caused the boy any harm if it was not necessary. My men and I saved his soul and you know it, Peter."

"I know, old friend," Father Peter said, some of the anger leaving him. "But he is so young and has already been through so much."

"And a long way to go yet," the other man said, sitting down at Johnny's feet slowly and carefully so as not to scare the boy. "I am Father Matthew. I can see by your face that you remember me. I am sorry for the pain I caused you but it was necessary for the sake of your soul that you were cleansed of that creature's filth."

"What was it?" Johnny asked in a small voice. The man seemed pleased by the boy's question but Father Peter shook his head sadly and turned away.

"It was a demon, Johnny, a Lycanthrope, a werewolf." Seeing the boy's confusion, he went on, "A man, a man possessed by a demon wolf you understand." But Johnny could only shake his head. He was a boy of eight brought up in a quiet rural community and knew nothing of such terrors until one had torn his life apart. Father Matthew, sensing some of the boy's thoughts, patted him gently on the knee and stood up, turning to Father Peter. "I will return at seven pm sharp. I want him ready to leave, Peter. You have done all you can do for him. Now it is our turn to bring him closer to God." Father Peter said nothing, only nodded his agreement and left.

The other man lingered a moment longer, looking down at Johnny, his eyes searching, and then he abruptly turned and walked away.

That evening found Johnny stood outside St. Antony's, watching as the shadows grew deeper. Father Peter stood by his side, silent and unmoving. After what seemed like an eternity, a mud splattered land-rover drew up beside them and Father Matthew clambered out. He did not speak but stood silently as

Father Peter squatted down beside Johnny and turned the boy to face him.

"I am sorry I couldn't do more for you, Johnny," he said, plucking at the loose clothes that covered the boy's skinny frame. On that first night, he had burned what was left of Johnny's torn and bloody clothes, now the boy wore clothes salvaged from the church charity box, ill fitting but warm and clean.

"You saved my life," Johnny said, shyly.

"I hope so, boy," Father Peter said, pulling him close for a hug all the while looking up at the waiting Father Matthew. "I really hope I have." Standing abruptly, he ruffled the boy's hair. "Go with God, Johnny," he said before turning away and heading back inside. A large hand fell on Johnny's shoulder.

"Come on, boy," Father Matthew said, opening the passenger door for him. "We have a long way to go and time is fleeting." They drove all night, only stopping twice at the motorway services to use the bathroom and grab a couple of packs of stale sandwiches. Father Matthew spoke little and smoked a lot. He seemed unsettled, even uncomfortable in the presence of a child. Equally, Johnny felt small and scared in the presence of the big grim faced man.

Just as the first light of day started to stain the sky, they turned off onto a narrow country road and pulled in beside another couple of parked cars. Father Matthew climbed out and stretched before coming round to Johnny's side and ushered him outside. They were on a cliff side overlooking the dark waters of the Atlantic. Behind them was a large copse of trees that hid a small hillock with a large metal door embedded in its side. As Johnny watched on, Father Matthew produced a large bunch of metal keys from his coat pocket and unlocked the door. From over the big man's shoulder, Johnny could just see a set of narrow metal steps heading down into a poorly lit interior.

"Come on, boy," Father Matthew said, turning to Johnny and pointing down towards the stairs. "The others will be waiting for us." But Johnny would not move.

"Where are we and what is this place?"

"We are in Cornwall, Johnny," Father Matthew replied, taking him gently by the arm and nudging him forward. "And this is an old ammo bunker from the Second World War. It used to belong to the M.O.D. There was a gunnery range here once but the land belongs to the church now. Come along, no more questions. We still have much to do." Johnny knew it would be useless to delay any further and fell in behind Father Matthew as he descended the heavy metal stairs. The only sound was the echo of their foot falls and the fading sound of birdsong as they descended lower into the complex.

Suddenly, Father Matthew stopped in front of another metal door. Once again, out came the keys and the door was quickly opened. Inside was a chamber filled with old metal cots and wooden chairs piled into a corner against the rust streaked walls. Hurrying past these, they headed into a narrow corridor that branched off to the right, until they stood in front of another metal door. Here, Father Matthew stopped and sank down to one knee, facing Johnny.

"In this room," he whispered, "are four men. They will ask you to do something, Johnny, a kind of test and a harsh one at that. If you pass, you will be given over to me for your training."

"What training?" Johnny tried to ask but the big man gently placed a rough finger across his lips.

"No time for questions, boy, not now. But know this,

Johnny, if you fail to do what these men ask of you, they will take you far away from here. You will spend the rest of your life in some Godforsaken monastery in the arse end of nowhere. They will bring you up in the faith and make you take vows of silence. They will be kind to you, but a prison is a prison, boy, and you will never be allowed to leave. Try not to be afraid, Johnny. I will be with you and I shall pray for you. I can do no more for you now. Come," he said gently taking his arm. "Let's get this done."

The first thing that Johnny noticed as he came through the door was the four men sitting at a square table in the middle of the room. The second thing was the naked man gagged and chained to the wall behind them. For a moment, the world seemed to grow darker and he staggered, only Father Matthew's strong hands keeping him from collapsing.

"Stand up," Father Matthew hissed, shaking him roughly. "Now is not the time for weakness."

"It's him," Johnny whimpered. "You don't understand. It's him."

"I know who he is, boy. That's why you are here."

"Enough talk," one of the men at the table said, standing and glaring at Father Matthew. "Is this what you have brought us, Matthew? This boy who whimpers and faints in fear. Is this who you want to apprentice to our sacred cause?"

"Yes," Father Matthew said, stepping in front of Johnny as if to shield him from the other man's gaze. "Yes, I do. I intend to train him and make him my personal apprentice."

"Only if he passes the test," the other man quickly countered.

"And what would you know of test, Roberto? What would you know about any of this? You're nothing more than a glorified clerk, a go between the warriors of God and His Holiness, the Pope."

"I am a Cardinal," the other man said, his eyes blazing. "How dare you speak to me that way?"

"Now, now," another man said, standing from his position around the table. "No need for such anger. We are all men of God and all of us Cardinals. Father Matthew is more than aware that we are his superiors in rank, if nothing else. Isn't that correct, Matthew?" For a moment, the two men's eyes locked and a silent message seemed to pass between them. "Of course, Your Eminence," Father Matthew said, lowering his gaze. "It has been a long drive and I am not so young as I once was."

"None of us are, my son, none of us are. Well, except for this young man," he said, coming from around the table and kneeling before Johnny. "I am Cardinal James Maloy of the most Holy Roman Catholic Church and you are Johnny Masterson. I have heard much about you, Johnny, and know that God has tested you harshly and has still more to come." The other men sat at the table suddenly all stood and removed the table and chairs from the centre of the room. As if heeding some silent command, they melted back into the shadows. Yet Johnny could feel their eyes watching. "You know this man don't you, Johnny," the Cardinal said, gently taking his hand and drawing him forward.

"Yes," Johnny whispered, his voice hitching. "He killed my mummy and daddy."

"Yes, yes he did, Johnny," the Cardinal replied, his voice growing steely. "He has killed lots of mummies and daddies and little children, too. He isn't really a man, Johnny. Do you know what he is?"

"Yes," Johnny replied, wiping angrily at his eyes. "He is a monster."

"That's right," the Cardinal said, resting a comforting hand on the boy's shoulder. "He is a monster, a monster that would kill over and over again if we let him but we're not going to let him. You're not going to let him are you, Johnny?"

"No, not ever again." Johnny was too young to understand the concept of fate or preordained. He only knew when the knife was placed in his hand that it felt right there, and the fear that had engulfed him smothered him, making it hard to breathe since that terrible night, evaporated... no that wasn't right: it changed, evolved into something else: outrage and white hot desire for revenge. With a cry of hate, Johnny shook free of the Cardinal and charged at the chained man. The man's eyes widened as he saw the silvered knife and his death fast approaching. He tried to cry out against his gag and strained and heaved against his chains, his huge muscles bunching, but it was too late. The knife slid into his stomach like a hot knife through butter. Johnny screamed as he stabbed the man over and over again, blood splattering his face and yet the man still would not die. He felt a large hand cover his blood slicked wrist and guide it upwards.

"The heart," Father Matthew said from behind him. "Always go for the heart," and Johnny did just that, Father Matthew lending him his great strength as together they thrust the blade forward, sliding between bone and piercing the heart within. For a moment, the man's eyes locked on Johnny as if marking him forever then he fell dead to the ground in a bloody heap. Johnny dropped the knife, clattering to the ground, and groped for Father Matthew who took the sobbing boy in his arms.

"Hate is a seed that grows, Johnny," he whispered in the

young boy's ear. "You will need that hate. It will sustain you throughout the long years. We will cultivate it together, you and I." That said, he scooped up the young boy and walked past the silent cardinals and out into the future.

"JOHNNY, JOHNNY YOU WITH US?" Johnny gave himself a mental shake, dragging himself back from the past as he reached for Father Mathew's outstretched hand. "You seemed far away, boy."

"Yes, I was thinking about the past."

"Why in God's name would you want to do that?" Father Matthew said, gazing over the sea of tents. "All it has done is lead us to this place."

"Yes," Johnny said, following the other man's gaze. "Do you think we ever had a chance to stop it?"

"No. One cannot stand against prophecy. It is all foretold in the Book of Revelation."

"So we never stood a chance? All that blood spilled for nothing."

"No," Matthew said, gently clasping Johnny's arm. "Not for nothing. We could not hold back the tide but we did delay it, delayed it long enough for Mother Church to prepare herself. If it wasn't for us, many of these people here today would be dead now, their tormented souls condemned to Hell's fires for all eternity. But come now," he said, gently guiding Johnny up the marble stairs. "Forget the past. It is done and only exists in the minds of men, for now we must look to the future and right now His Holiness wishes to see you."

"He wishes to see me or his winged friend?"

"Does it matter? These days, they are one and the same."

"And that's the problem," Johnny said, pulling up short before the doors of the Basilica. "I take my orders from His Holiness alone, no one else."

"Dear God," Matthew laughed. "Only you could be suspicious of an angel, Johnny."

"I don't like them and I trust their motives even less. We are nothing to them, chess pieces to be moved around, manipulated at will."

"They saved us, Johnny," Matthew said, the first hint of anger creeping into his voice. "If it wasn't for them, we would all be dead."

"We are dead! Millions of us. We are on the brink of extinction, Matthew."

"They did what they could. For six hundred and sixty six days, they fought against the hordes of hell."

"Yes, with mankind crushed in the middle, a moth between two burning flames. All of humanity no more than collateral fucking damage, and in the end, for what? Neither side won. They fought themselves to a bloody stalemate then retreated to lick their wounds, leaving the world in ruins where the ghosts of humanity live out the rest of their lives in this pointless purgatory."

"You really believe that?" Matthew said, his anger melting away at the despair in Johnny's voice. "That there is no point, that God has no more plans for us?"

"God!" Johnny laughed, pushing through the doors and entering the Basilica. "Where is He, Matthew? Answer me that! We know He exists. Maybe He doesn't care anymore. Perhaps He stopped giving a shit about us when we nailed His only Son to a tree."

"Perhaps," Matthew sighed as they stopped just outside the

entrance to the chapel. "But you're about to talk to the closest thing we have to him. Try and show him some respect."

"Of course," Johnny said, smiling sadly. "And never mind me, Matthew. You know I always get melancholy after an exorcism, especially one that goes so spectacularly wrong."

"I know, I know that, Johnny," Matthew said, laying a gentle hand on the younger man's shoulder. "You always had a big heart. Even as a child you always had a big heart. It is both your greatest strength and your greatest weakness. Go on then. Best not to keep them waiting. Go with God, Johnny," he said, making the Sign of the Cross.

"You, too," Johnny said. But his face was troubled as he watched the old man walk away.

JOHNNY TOOK a deep breath and entered the chapel. For a moment, he did nothing but stare at the ground, taking deep breaths. He could feel Raphael's presence all about him, a warm feeling of love and compassion, but Johnny knew it for what it was, a lie. He had seen these creatures at their worst, cutting down demons, trampling and crushing any human that got in their way, flaming swords slaughtering the unholy and innocent alike.

"Johnny," the voice was a mere whisper but it caught like a fish-hook in Johnny's mind, dragging his eyes away from the marble floor and towards the waiting angel. Johnny tried to pull back, to resist, but he had already taken half a dozen steps towards the glowing figure that waited for him by the candlelit altar. Bracing, he made himself stop, hands clenched into tight fists by his side. "Johnny, look at me." Once again he was compelled and though he tried to resist with all his might, he looked up into the face of the waiting angel and knew he was lost.

When he finally came to his senses, he was on his knees by the altar, Raphael standing before him with pitying eyes.

"Why must you always make things so difficult between us, Johnny?"

Johnny said nothing but staggered away, holding onto the altar as he tried to clear his head.

"Why do you always have to play such fucking games?"

"Games?" Raphael asked, a hint of humour in his voice. "What fucking games do you speak of, Johnny?"

"You know what games. The glamour magic," Johnny said, standing straighter. "You tried to bewitch me."

"I did no such thing. I am what I am. I cannot help the effect I have on humans."

"You can't help it? Then why can I look upon you now and stand before you, my own man once again?"

"Because I have, as you humans say, toned it down. You seemed to be a little overwhelmed by my presence when you first entered."

"Where is His Holiness?" he asked, trying not to look too closely at Raphael who had now once again started to glow softly. "I was told he wished to see me."

"Why won't you look at me? Why do you fear me so much? God has sent me to help you. I am the guardian of this place. Look at me, Johnny. There is no need to be afraid." Johnny did as he was bid. There was no compulsion this time. He looked because he wanted to. Raphael stood before him, naked and unashamed. He was perfect in every way. No, that was wrong. He was beyond perfect. He was beautiful and held an unearthly beauty that stole one's breath away. A dangerous beauty that made you want to fall on your knees before him, to offer him your love, your life, your very soul. It was these emotions that so overwhelmed Johnny, yet he could not look away.

Raphael's face was a sculptor's dream, far beyond anything Michelangelo could ever have imagined. The faces of the angels in his magnificent frescos paled in comparison to the real thing. Raphael stood a living monument to the glory of God.

Raphael smiled as if reading some of Johnny's thoughts. "Thank you, Johnny," he said. "You are too kind."

"Is this what this is all about? You want me to tell you how pretty you are? Goddammit we could have saved some time if..." But that was as far as he went. Raphael moved in a blur of speed. Grabbing Johnny up around the neck, he slammed him down backwards over the altar, sending candles and hot wax flying in every direction.

"Thou shall not take the Lord God's name in vain. Do you hear me, Johnny?" he said, shaking the helpless man back and forth. "Before the Christ came to forgive man his sins, my brothers and I destroyed whole cities for such an affront to our God. Those were harsh times and now those times have come round again. So watch your blasphemous mouth around me, Johnny. You watch it very closely."

"Let me go, you son of a bitch," Johnny managed to gasp for a moment. The pressure increased and Johnny was sure he was a dead man but just as suddenly the hand was gone and he crumpled to the floor, massaging his neck as he tried to learn how to breathe once again.

"You have heart. I will give you that," Raphael said, folding his wings. "You will need it where you're going."

"And where do you think I am going?" Johnny said, staggering to his feet.

"Ostia Antica. For a start, we have lost contact with the colony there. No word for four days now, no supply shipments, nothing. I sent a detachment of the Swizz Guard along the Road of Sorrow, a small army to look into it. They were all well-armed and carrying radios. The last we heard from them, they were a mile out from Ostia Antica then just like that radio silence. Nothing."

"Did they have a priest with them?"

"Two," Raphael said, his wings stirring with agitation. "Ostia is a blessed place. The bones of Saint Monica are buried there, making the city a holy place inviolable to the demon hordes."

"Humans, perhaps," Johnny said. "Raiders, scavengers."

"Doubtful. The city is well garrisoned and the ancient walls have all been rebuilt and reinforced. The place has never been so secure, not since the Romans who built it left."

"Then what?"

"I don't know, Johnny. That's why I am sending you to find out."

"And what in Hell's name do you think I can do? You sent an entire detachment of Swizz Guard out there and they didn't return and now you are sending me!"

"Something has to be done," the angel said, pacing the room. "Without the fish from the port city, the people here will all starve. We are already on the brink. Ostia Antica is the last life line we have left."

"Then why don't you go? I am sure whatever is going on there you are more than capable of taking care of it."

Again, the angel shook his head sadly. "If I leave this place for even a second, the hordes of Hell will descend upon this place and tear you all to pieces. No, I am sorry, Johnny. You shall have to go. One man can sneak into places a small army cannot. You will go and report back what you have seen. Now, go," he said in a voice that buked no argument. "Go get some rest. I have a feeling you might need it. And try not to worry so much. Tomorrow, after all, is another day."

Johnny spent the rest of the day gathering equipment. First he went to the armoury. He had weapons of his own, of course, but if he was going into Demon Land he was going to need the extra firepower. From the armoury he took one SG 550 and two hundred rounds of silver tipped explosive ammo, plus a SIG P220 sidearm with a hundred rounds of armour piercing rounds. He also had his own trusty sword, acid edged and silver tipped and blessed by the Pope himself, which he always carried sheathed across his back.

From the armoury, he went across to the SQMS, also known as Boots and Socks. There, he picked up a waterproof sleeping bag and some few ration packs, not wanting to be overly encumbered for the long journey ahead.

By the time he arrived back at the barracks and stowed his gear, the sun was already setting. Johnny sat by his window and smoked one of his rare cigarettes. The setting sun burned red across St Peter's Square. A woman wept in despair. A baby cried out in hunger. Johnny Masterson crushed out his cigarette and fell into his bunk. He dreamed of children burning and wept in his sleep.

He awoke early the next day and could not remember his dreams.

THE NEXT MORNING, Johnny grabbed a light breakfast, checked his weapons, secured his pack, and headed out. The morning was clear with blue skies as he walked through the English Gardens towards the rear Vatican walls and the Road of Sorrow beyond.

The road itself was nothing more than a B road that ran parallel to the much larger A90. Later it turned into little more than a dirt road that led through the lush Italian countryside before meeting the Tyrrhenian Sea at Ostia Antica. Hundreds of Swizz Guards and priests had died to secure this vital lifeline to the ocean.

Johnny had not been there that day but he had heard the stories. Hordes of demons had come racing from the west, the setting sun at their backs as they ploughed into the chanting priests. Crosses had burst into flames, holy water had burned like acid and the air stank like sulphur as the Swizz Guard poured round after round of blessed silver into the writhing horde. At the heart of this chaos, seven brave Cardinals had carried the sacred bones of Saint Augustine, burying them in the earth, scattering the blessed bones along the path, seeding it forever with the power of God. For twenty-nine miles, they prayed and died by the hundreds until at last they reached the ancient port city of Ostia Antica. Here, they set up a small camp. Over time, the camp became a small fishing village with a church and garrison of its own, then a small town as refugees were sent from Vatican City, along the now blessed road, to help rebuild and fish the surrounding waters.

Johnny was suddenly dragged from his musing by the sight of two figures waiting for him in the shadows of the Vatican walls. As he drew closer, he immediately recognised his old friend and mentor, Father Mathew. Standing by his side, all decked out in a glowing white suit, was the Archangel Raphael.

Cursing under his breath, Johnny gave a small wave and hurried across to where the two figures stood.

"Johnny," Father Mathew said, smiling and sticking out his hand. Johnny shook hands with his old friend, happy to note the old man's grip was still like iron.

"Johnny," the angel said with an incline of his head, a small smile playing across his perfectly formed lips. "Are you ready for your big adventure?"

"Sure," Johnny smiled back. "Fucking peachy keen." Father Mathew chuckled but the angel said nothing, his blue eyes inscrutable.

"I have something for you," the angel said, holding out his hand. "Give me your sword." For a moment, Johnny just looked at the angel before slowly drawing his sword and reluctantly handing it over. Raphael took the sword balancing in his hand as if it weighed nothing and then, with a grimace, he reached over his shoulder and plucked a single pure white feather from his wings. Slowly, almost reverently, he drew the feather down the blade of the sword. When he reached the handle, the steel split, enveloping the feather within before flowing back together, leaving the sword whole and intact.

"What did you do?" Johnny asked, his eyes never leaving the blade.

"Made it stronger and its wielder along with it. There is nothing under Heaven or in Hell that sword cannot now kill. I have given you a great power, Johnny. Use it wisely." Johnny said nothing but took the sword back in awe, his eyes never leaving the blade. The sword felt different, now, more suited to his hand. He swore he could almost feel the power buried within the now flawless steel, thumbing through the blade into his hand, traveling up his arm, making him feel like he could hack down trees or fell a small building with a single strike.

The angel smiled knowingly before coughing politely, drawing Johnny's attention from the humming blade. "Best put it away for now. I am sure you will have many opportunities to use it on the road ahead." Johnny did as he was bid, reluctantly sheathing the sword across his back.

"So," Father Mathew said, coming forward. "I guess this is goodbye for now. Stick to the road and remember your training." With a small smile he said, "Do you remember what I used to tell you when you were a boy in training, Johnny?" Johnny smiled and placed a warm hand on the old man's shoulder.

"Believe in God," he said, "but keep your guns loaded."

"And your steel sharp," the old man laughed. "That's the way. God looks after his own."

"And you," Johnny said, turning towards the waiting angel. "Any parting words of advice?" For a moment, the angel seemed to ponder.

"Kill them all, Johnny," the angel finally said. "Kill them all."

JOHNNY'S first day on the road was of little consequence. He left Vatican City through the old Vatican museum entrance and entered Via Angelo Emo district. Like everywhere else in and around the Vatican, the district was nothing more than a burnt out ruin. Long gone were the apartment buildings, hotels, and grocery stores that pandered to the once thriving community and tourist trade. Now all that was left was the Road of Sorrow cutting through the district, winding through the blackened rubble and old mouldering bones, some of which were human and others, foul and misshapen. Johnny tried not to look too closely at these as he passed out of the ruined district and out into the lush greenery of the Italian countryside, pushing himself hard, the sweat running down his body, determined to make the Santa Velgine monastery before night fall.

As he walked, ignoring the gnawing hunger in his guts, he thought of the monastery and all he knew about it. In truth, there was not much to tell. The place had once been a small farm that ran along the side of the SR296, now known as the Road of Sorrow, right next to the small town of Dragona. The place had been blessed like so many other buildings close to the road and converted into a monastery of sorts with its own holy Brothers usually of the Franciscan order.

There were some few places like this one along the Road of Sorrow, monasteries and small churches that had been converted from common buildings, even a public toilet had been converted and blessed and now served as a small church. Johnny had stayed the night there once. The place had been small and uncomfortable and still smelled vaguely of piss.

He reached the Monastery of Santa Velgine just as the shadows were growing long in the west. He was tired, hot, hungry and dishevelled as he staggered into the farmyard, chickens squawking as he passed, heading towards the large barn and few outbuildings that now served as a monastery. Leaning heavily against the door, he pulled out his water bottle and took a long drink, pouring the rest of the cold water over his head, wiping at his eyes and running his fingers through his tangled hair before rapping noisily on the wooden door.

A few moments later, a small hole appeared in the door and a pair of wary eyes studied Johnny, taking in his large frame and grimy look. When they finally noticed the small arsenal he carried strapped to his person, the eyes widened and the hole in the door was quickly slammed shut. Frightened murmurs and whispering voices could be heard quite clearly from behind the reinforced door. Johnny was just raising his fist to knock again when the hole in the door suddenly reappeared and Johnny stared down the rusty barrel of the world's oldest shotgun.

"What do you want here?" a quavering voice asked from behind the door. "What are you doing here?"

"Take it easy," Johnny said, slowly raising his hands. "I have come from the Vatican. I am on a mission from His Holiness. We have lost contact with Ostia Antica. I have been sent to see what the hell is going on." For a moment, there was a further murmuring then the barrel of the gun was withdrawn and the large wooden door pushed open. Johnny took a couple of steps back, his hands still raised, trying to look as harmless as possible. Behind the door was a congregation of men, seemingly of all ages, all tonsured and dressed in the brown robes of their order, all except one, the oldest looking soldier Johnny had ever seen, all dressed in camouflage, his white wispy hair peeking from under his cap in his liver spotted hands. He held an old rusty looking shotgun pointing directly at Johnny's chest.

"I come in peace," Johnny said, looking at the soldier. "How about you? Lower that gun, old timer, so we can talk."

"We can talk like this just fine," the old man replied in a wavering voice. "Now, how about you? Show us some proof you're from the Vatican before I put a hole in your belly."

"Where the hell do you think I came from?" Johnny replied. "Do you think I am here on fucking holiday, taking a walk through the beautiful Italian countryside?" The old man came forward and thrust both barrels into Johnny's stomach and pulled back the hammers.

"If you don't start talking sense, I will open you up right here where you stand."

"Proof," Johnny frowned. "What kind of proof?" At this, the old man looked perplexed.

"I don't know what kind of proof." Suddenly his face lit up. "Traveling papers, perhaps a letter from His Holiness with his Holy Seal upon it." Johnny was starting to get a little worried. He was no merchant who needed papers to travel. He had no documentation or any kind of proof of his mission. The old man was starting to get agitated, his hands beginning to shake, his breath coming faster and Johnny realised for all his bluster the old man was scared, and scared men were dangerous. Whispering a prayer, Johnny shot out a hand, pushing the barrel of the gun to one side, as he quickly stepped in the opposite direction. The old man let out a squawk of surprise and fired both barrels harmlessly into the door jamb. Swiftly, Johnny ripped the empty gun from his hand and threw it outside before upholstering his sidearm and firing it twice into the air. The surrounding monks all let out a cry of surprise and cowered down into themselves but the old timer just stood there, his stubbly chin thrust aggressively forward, his hands balled into tight fists by his sides.

"Peckerwood, sonofabitch!" he growled at Johnny. "Even five years ago you would be picking your fucking guts up off the floor."

"I don't doubt it," Johnny said, re-holstering his gun. "I don't have any proof that I am from the Vatican. My name is Johnny Masterson. Like I said, I have been sent by His Holiness to see what the hell is going on at Ostia Antica."

"Masterson," the old man said. "The name sounds familiar.

Guess you don't mean us any harm or we would all be dead by now."

"No," Johnny replied. "All I want is a bed for the night and a warm meal."

"That's not up to me, that's up to Brother Luke. He is in charge here," the old man said, scooping up his empty shotgun and gesturing towards the cowering monks. Johnny followed his gaze as a tall dark man, perhaps in his late forties, maybe a little older, extradited himself from the pack.

"I am Brother Luke," he said warily. "You are welcome to whatever we have. Please, Timothy," he said to the old soldier. "Please close and bar the windows and doors. Night time is coming and we need to be tucked up safe and sound."

"Yes, Brother," Timothy said. "Perhaps she won't come tonight." Brother Luke shot the old man a warning look before gently taking Johnny by the arm.

"Please come with me, Mr Masterson. The evening meal will be served soon. There is a wash area in the back of the building. You can wash away the road dust and rest."

Johnny took the time to look around as he was led to the rear of the building. The monastery was no more than a converted barn, the entire bottom floor one big open space with a small shrine taking up the rear wall. In one corner, there was a kitchen area with an old wood burner stove and some few shelves stocked with pots, pans, and various dried goods. The rest of the floor consisted of a large communal eating area, various scattered books, a few ratty looking armchairs and a few threadbare rugs covering the hardwood floors. A single ladder led up to the old hayloft, which had been converted to the Brothers' communal sleeping area. The whole scene was one of organised chaos and camaraderie, a Brotherhood completely at ease with one another and yet Johnny sensed a subline of fear running beneath. It was there in the strained smiles and the way the Brothers' eyes constantly flickered to the overhead skylight and rough cut windows as if they lived in fear of the coming dark.

Later, after the evening meal, as the Brothers busied themselves clearing the table and preparing for the coming night, Johnny gently took Brother Luke to one side.

"Tell me," he said quietly. "What ails this place, Brother?" The other man smiled sadly.

"What ails the world, my son." Johnny waved that away.

"What is it you are so afraid of and what did that ornery old sonofabitch mean when he said perhaps she won't come tonight? Who is this she?"

"A penance, perhaps," the tall monk shuddered. "Or a test. Maybe even a punishment for our impure thoughts. God knows," he said, gripping desperately at the wooden crucifix about his neck. "I have had so many, so many since she first showed herself to us. God, the whiteness of her skin and the things she says, such loathsome promises. Already we have lost two of our Brothers to this harlot of Satan."

"You have lost two of your Brothers?"

"Yes, Brother Glen and Brother Thomas, both lured from the safety of the road by her wanton flesh."

"When did all this start?"

"Three nights ago. I was awoken by the sound of a woman's voice. It was like a velvet whisper, drawing me through the darkness like a fishhook in my brain, drawing me to her. Quickly, I hurried down the ladder, careful not to wake my sleeping Brothers and stepped through the already open door and into the night. That's when I saw Brother Glen, or the back of him anyway, and the woman waiting for him just off to the side of the road. She was completely naked, her white flesh glowed in the moonlight and her hair was as black as the surrounding night where it cascaded over her shoulder. She saw me and grinned. That's when I started to scream. Her mouth was filled with fangs and her eyes were silver in the moonlight as she glared at me. I flinched away from that smile and screamed my Brother's name but it was already too late. He had stepped from the blessed road and into her waiting embrace. She scooped him into her arms as if he was no more than a small child and turned and ran with him into the surrounding forest. Minutes later, we heard the screams, such terrible screams. Brother Thomas implored us to go after the creature, that God would protect us, but we were weak in faith and afraid. Naming us for the cowards we were, he grabbed up his crucifix and headed out towards the screams. Soon his voice joined that of poor Brother Glen. They both screamed long and loud, imploring us to help them to end their pain but we could not help them. Eventually, the screaming stopped and we locked ourselves away inside the safety of the monastery. The second night old Timothy and I kept a watch. Just after sunset, she appeared again. She saw us watching her from a nearby window and began to display herself. She paraded herself before us." Brother Luke gasped, a small sweat breaking out on his brow. "She touched herself, laying on her back in the dirt, promising us all sorts of dark delights if we would only come to her and touch her. Even after what I had seen the night before, I still wanted to go to her. The next thing I knew, I was at the door, old Timothy screaming for help as he wrestled me back from the door then the sound of gunshots and a high scream of pain and cheated rage. Timothy returned as the Brothers pinned me down, looking sickly and ill, the smoking barrel of the gun by his side. He said how he had shot her, hit her in the shoulder and how she had run off into the forest. We prayed that she wouldn't be back. But the next night she returned. I ordered all the windows closed, the doors locked. No watch was kept. We spent the night in prayer and song, trying to drown out the sound of her pleading cries and wanton promises and now you are here and the night draws on and I am so terribly afraid she will return." Johnny was silent for a moment as he soaked in all he had been told.

"From which direction did the woman come?"

"From the west," Brother Luke replied.

"Is there anything in that direction you know of?" Johnny asked.

"Yes, there used to be a small village known as Agnello di Dio somewhere around that area, perhaps a mile or so away."

"Agnello di Dio," Johnny mused. "The Lamb Of God."

"Just so," Brother Luke nodded his reply. "Whether it's still standing after all this time I do not know. We Brothers never leave the safety of the road. I mean what sane man would?"

"Yes," Johnny smiled. "What sane man would?"

LATER THAT NIGHT, he sat by a rough cut window, a single candle burning beside him. He had instructed the Brothers to go to bed and to wad cotton into their ears. Father Luke had started to protest at the thought of leaving Johnny alone but Johnny would brook no argument and sent the concerned monk to his bed. Now he sat alone, deep in prayer, waiting for the creature to return.

He did not have to wait long. One minute, the forest was

empty and the next she was there by the side of the road. At the sight of her, Johnny felt a pang of lust but squashed it immediately. He had been tempted by far greater creatures than whatever petty evil this creature represented. Standing, he stripped his weapons from his body. If he was right, they would do no good against this kind of creature, all except the sword across his back, that is, but he did not intend to get that close to the thing, especially at night.

Pulling the bolt from the door, he withdrew a small rosary from his shirt pocket and hid it in the palm of his hand, wrapping the prayer beads about his fist before stepping outside into the balmy night air. At the sight of him, the creature smiled and ran its hands down over its lush body, running its tongue across its red bow shaped mouth.

"Come to me," she said, reaching out towards him with her slender white arms. "Come to me, love me, let me kiss you all over."

"Love?" Johnny laughed. "What the fuck does your kind know of love, demon?" The creature hissed like a scolded cat before smiling once again.

"Come to me, mortal. I shall show you wonders the likes of which you have never known. I will make you feel like you have never felt, a thousand ecstasies your body shall know before you die."

"Tempting offer but you can shove it up your ass," Johnny replied, unwinding the cross from his fist which immediately burst into blue flames. The creature hissed, blinded by the burning cross. It fled, wailing into the darkness. Johnny nodded his head knowingly and stepped back inside. Confident the creature would not return that night, he climbed into his makeshift bed and was soon sound asleep.

The next morning, Johnny woke early, grabbed a quick breakfast, avoiding the questions of the milling monks, before strapping on his gear and taking Brother Luke off to one side.

"I am leaving now," he told the startled Brother. "I will track this creature and try to kill it. Succeed or fail, I won't be coming back this way anytime soon. If the creature returns, you will know I failed."

"What is it?" the monk asked, wringing his hands together. "What happened last night? We all heard that terrible scream. We had hoped you had destroyed the creature."

"No," Johnny said, adjusting his gear. "I managed to drive it away. As for what it is, that's easy. It's a vampire or a demon masquerading as one. It all boils down to the same thing. Last night, it fled west, perhaps to the village you mentioned, Agnello di Dio. I shall go there and see what I can find but I have other business at Ostia Antica, urgent business. I will do what I can, you understand."

"Yes," Brother Luke replied, grasping Johnny's hand. "And we thank you for it. Our prayers and blessings will go with you."

"For that, you have my thanks," Johnny said, heading towards the road. "Go with God, Brother."

"You, too," the monk said as he watched the big man leave the safety of the road and enter the forest. For a brief moment, he considered running after him, begging him to return to the safety of the monastery but he could not do it. The world beyond the road was for braver men than he. Sighing, he made the Sign of the Cross in the direction that Johnny had travelled then, with a nervous glance up at the sky, he quickly scurried back inside to his waiting Brothers.

· · ·

THE VILLAGE of Agnello di Dio was remarkably preserved. There was no sign of burning or fighting in this quiet corner of the world. Nature had once again taken a stranglehold free from the constraints of man's interference. Many of the houses had fallen into disrepair. Roofs had collapsed, windows had broken, and leaves had blown through open doorways, where vines and moss crawled up peeling plaster walls. What few cars remained had long ago started to rust, their paint flaking, their tyres flat and shredded. Tall grass grew between the stones of the cobblestone streets, dotted here and there with wild meadow flowers and yet, Johnny noticed as he walked up the high street with its few abandoned shops and creaking signs, no birds sang in this place, nor was there the drone of insects or the sound of scurrying creatures in the long grass. There was only the breeze and the baking sun but still Johnny felt cold. There was a sense of foreboding in this place and a sense of evil, nothing you could physically feel or reach out and touch, but a kind of shroud that weighed heavy against your soul, drying out your mouth and making the skin on the back of your neck feel tight and uncomfortable. Johnny knew that an evil haunted this place but was it the same evil that had haunted the monastery last night? He did not know, yet he was determined to find out.

Shouldering off his pack in an empty doorway, he drew a small vial of holy water from his shirt pocket and knelt, facing the sun, his eyes tight shut and his head bowed. Whatever prayer he muttered was between him and his God but when he stood, the small vial that had been clasped between his hands had now started to ever so faintly glow. Johnny smiled and made the Sign of the Cross before heading back into the street.

At first, he walked down the street, heading east towards a collection of small buildings but the glow immediately began to fade. Slowly, he turned around until the glow reappeared, burning more brightly as he faced north. Johnny hurried in that direction, passing through street after street until he came to a narrow dirt track hemmed with a small gaily painted wall on which unicorns and other cartoon characters danced merrily through a bright enchanted forest. The sign on the gate simply read Scuola del Villaggio or Village School. As Johnny stepped over the threshold, the vial of holy water in his hand began to burn so brightly that it was like holding a miniature supernova in the palm of his hand and Johnny knew he had found the right place.

Wincing against the brightness, he closed his fist and placed the vial of holy water in his jeans pocket. Even through the heavy material, he could still see a faint glow and feel its burning warmth against his leg.

Looking around, he quickly hurried up the path until he came upon a small squat building with peeling white walls and red tiled roof. A set of swings and a rusty looking slide made up a playground of sorts surrounded by an overgrown lawn and fruit trees. It was to one of these trees Johnny hurried over and, drawing a large hunting knife from the sheath at his side, began to hack and saw at a thick stunted branch. When he had finished, he had a blunt stake about fifteen inches long, which he quickly sharpened into a razor sharp point before heading up towards the school.

He tried the front door, which he expected to be locked, but it wasn't and gave way grudgingly with a protesting shriek. He saw the body just as the smell hit him. It was the smell of blood and decay, a smell Johnny knew very well but never really got used to. With a curse, he stuck the stake in his belt and covered his nose and mouth with his hand before approaching the bloody mess on the floor. The man had clearly been a monk. Johnny could tell from the torn and shredded robe that lay all about the eviscerated corpse at his feet and he wondered if this was Brother Glen or Brother Thomas. He supposed it did not matter. Either way, whoever the man was, he had died hard, disembowelled and neutered. His bloody bowels lay like bloated sausages by the side of his screaming face, which the lower jaw had been wrenched from, leaving a bloody maw. Even the eyes were missing. Johnny gave a small prayer that the man had been long dead before such atrocities had been committed.

Stepping over the body, he made the Sign of the Cross and continued on deeper into the school, knowing exactly what he was looking for and finding it just off to his left in between two abandoned classrooms, a narrow door built into the wall. Johnny reached out smiling and, just as he expected, found the door to be locked. Stepping back, he raised a booted foot and kicked at the door. The door crumpled in its frame but held fast. Cursing, Johnny kicked it again and again until it tore from its hinges and hung askew, revealing a narrow passageway leading down into the darkness.

Johnny took the blazing vial out of his pocket and, wincing, held it out at arm's length, lighting the way as he descended. His skin was starting to crawl, now, the skin on his balls feeling tight and uncomfortable. Still, he descended until he turned a sharp corner at the bottom of the stairs which opened up into a large storage room.

The creature was there, laying upon two long trestle like tables with no attempt at subterfuge whatsoever, confident in her hiding place and her kind's dominance in this new world.

Johnny made no attempt at stealth, knowing the creature was trapped until the sun set below the horizon.

"Can you hear me?" he said, slapping the creature hard across the face. Immediately, her crimson eyes flew open and stared at Johnny with cheated hate.

"That's right, bitch. Remember me? We had a nice little chat last night. I have come," he said, showing her the sharpened stake, "to show you some delights of my own." The creature's lips drew back to show teeth that would have shamed a wolf yet still it could not move, only glare and hiss at him as he straddled her prone form. Taking hold of the sharpened stake in a two handed death grip, he raised it above his head. *"Requiem aeternam dona eis domine et lux perpetua luceat eis,"* he intoned before bringing the stake down in a whistling arc, puncturing through flesh and bone and into the black heart beneath. The creature let out a shriek of agony, its jaw opening impossibly wide, spilling blood down its face as its back arched, its hands scrabbling at Johnny's arms but Johnny knocked the flailing hands away and jumped free. But the creature would not die. Cursing, Johnny jumped forward and shoved the glowing vial into the creature's bloody mouth, slamming her jaw shut, shattering the glass, releasing the holy water within. Suddenly, her entire thrashing head started to glow. Steam and smoke billowed from her mouth and her eyes boiled from her head. She let out a final ear-piercing shriek and, at last, lay still. Johnny did not hesitate but drew the sword from across his back and took the creature's head in one fell swoop.

Taking it by the hair, he carried it back through the school and tossed it outside into the glaring sunlight. Instantly, the skull started to steam and collapse in upon itself. Seconds later, it was no more than dust on the wind.

Johnny spent the night in the abandoned village. He had dragged the poor, defiled monk's body from the school and buried it in a shallow grave before fashioning a crude cross from a couple of old dried branches and tattered piece of rope. Exhausted, he stumbled into a nearby house, ate a cold ration pack of chicken stew, covered himself in a couple of moth eaten blankets, and fell into a dreamless sleep.

He awoke late the next morning to birdsong and sat there for some time, a small smile playing across his rugged features as he listened. After a quick wash at the village pump, he repacked his gear and made his way back to the road before consulting his map. By his reckoning, he was just over fifteen miles from Ostia Antica. The day was hot and he would need to rest but he reckoned he could make the settlement just before nightfall, if he did not stop too often along the way.

Shouldering his pack, he started walking back through the forest. He emerged about a mile along the road from the monastery and could just make it out in the distance. Silently, he wished the monks well then turned and was on his way.

JOHNNY ARRIVED at Ostia Antica with the setting sun. He had pushed himself hard but the battle the day before had taken more out of him than he thought. "You're getting old," he muttered to himself.

Just as he crested the final hill, he got his first look into the valley below, where the old Roman settlement of Ostia Antica had once stood before becoming home to mankind once again after nearly two thousand years. The place looked utterly deserted. No evening campfires burned, no people milled or moved about their business. The place was dead. Silent. And Johnny Masterson had a feeling something had gone terribly wrong.

Slowly, he started down the hill, the setting sun at his back. He had already unstrung his rifle, loaded a magazine, and cocked the weapon, ready for any signs of trouble, but there was nothing. He continued on, completely unhindered, towards the open gate. Suddenly, something shot out of the shadows. It was a small black dog. It was screaming an almost human scream as it shot passed him, leaving a trail of blood behind it. Hot on its heels stumbled a little girl. She was dressed in filthy rags, her hair matted, and the lower half of her face covered in blood. Johnny guessed her age to be around four, maybe five. He called out to her but she took no notice, just turned and ran back inside the shadowy settlement. With a curse, Johnny slung his rifle, drew his side arm and ran after her. But, by the time he made it inside, she was already gone.

He called out again, his voice defiling the silence but there was nothing, only the sighing of the wind on the sea breeze and the lonely cry of a circling gull overhead.

Johnny's frustration was mounting now. He called out again and again, rushing down crumbling streets, throwing open the flaps of makeshift tents and kicking open rusty tin doors of leaning shacks but still, nothing. Ostia Antica was home to over a hundred families of fishermen and sailors and yet there was no one to be found. Johnny carried on walking past rearing columns and statues of broken gods. He even stuck his head into what had once been known as the baths of Neptune, now used as a large storage house to salt and dry fish, but the storerooms were empty. Johnny carried on along, checking every storeroom, but there were no stores anywhere to be found. Ostia, almost single handedly, provided the refugees back at the Vatican with their daily ration of food. Without it, thousands would now starve.

Johnny had to go back and report this to His Holiness. Mother of God, they had to be told quickly to ration whatever little food they had left in the city. If the refugees found out about this, there would be chaos. People would kill one another over a crumb of bread. He had to get back, walk through the night to make his report.

Quickly, he turned just as a shadow detached itself from a nearby wall. Even in the fading light, he could see it was the same little girl as before.

"Come," she giggled. "We have something to show you," and just like that she was gone. Johnny chased after her through the ruined streets but she always stayed one step ahead, a fleeting shadow drawing him onward until he rounded a corner and stopped dead.

He was at the old Roman amphitheatre. Everywhere, there were burning torches, driving back the encroaching night. Johnny stumbled forward, his mouth working, but he could only manage a low groan as he took in the devastation about him.

In the middle of the amphitheatre, where the old Roman stage would have been, there were hundreds, no thousands, of bloody bones all picked clean. Even the skulls had been cracked open, the contents scooped out and devoured. Up in the stone stands sat more bodies, massive, purple, and engorged, their flesh tight and bulging through their torn clothes. Some were naked from the waist down, their huge bellies bloated and crawling with blue veins. As Johnny drew closer, he could smell them, a vile mixture of stale vomit and shit. Lording above all this sat a thin skeletal man, dressed head to foot in a black and stained three piece suit. At Johnny's approach, he dropped the child's leg he had been eating and rose, spreading his arms in a gesture of welcome.

Just then, a blur shot from the shadows and leapt off Johnny's back. Scrabbling like a spider, it lunged forward and clamped its teeth deep into the side of Johnny's neck. With a roar of pain, Johnny grabbed the creature and threw it to the floor. It was the filthy girl from the street who had led him here. She was crying now, begging for help, telling him she was hurt, hurt so bad, but Johnny knew it for the ruse it was and, with one fluid motion, drew his side arm and shot the girl right between the eyes.

The creature at the top of the steps began to applaud wildly, laughing all the while.

"Oh, Johnny," it sniggered, revealing bloody teeth. "They told me you were a cold one, but to gun down a child in cold blood? Now that is impressive."

"She was damned," Johnny growled. "Possessed."

"Ah," the creature waved one talon tipped finger. "Technically not true. She was bewitched by me, not possessed."

"And who are you? Then again," Johnny said, taking aim, "I really don't give a fuck."

The gun bucked in his hand as he fired round after round of blessed silver into the creature who simply stood there, a knowing smile on his face. When the gun clicked empty, he carried on as if nothing happened.

"I am Gluttony. I have other names, of course, but, as you know, Johnny, names have power."

"I know your real name," Johnny said, drawing the sword from across his back. "It's Beelzebub."

"Again," the demon clapped. "Not just a killer but a scholar, too." Johnny ignored that.

"What have you done here and how is it you come to stand on holy ground? The body of a saint is buried here."

"*Was*. It's surprising what you can get a small child to do for a few sweet treats, especially one who has never even tasted sugar before. I had that little waif," he said, pointing at the crumpled figure of the little girl by Johnny's feet, "gather up those old mouldering bones and throw them into the sea one by one. It took a little time but we got there in the end and now here I am. As for what I did to these good folks, I made them hungry. So hungry, Johnny. So hungry that at first they ate all the food they had gathered. Some ate until their bellies burst. When they had eaten all the food, they ate all the stray cats and dogs. When they had eaten all of them, they turned on each other. Oh, Johnny, it was such a spectacle. Fitting it should end here in the amphitheatre, the big finale, the death of the demon slayer, Johnny Masterson."

"I don't think so," Johnny said, raising his sword. The demon shook his head sadly.

"I am afraid nothing can kill me, especially not some sword blessed by a man in a tall hat."

"This sword is different," Johnny smiled. The demon faltered before that smile, then grew angry.

"Nice bluff, Masterson, but you're coming to Hell with me." Suddenly, the creature began to change. It grew taller, black batlike wings exploding from its back and its skin began to take on a strange, scaly look. Johnny had seen this metamorphosis before and knew if the creature took on its true and terrible form, he was finished.

With a cry, he charged forward, holding the sword out

before him like a lance. The creature did nothing to defend itself, only smirked at Johnny's approach. With all his might, Johnny drew back the sword and thrust it forward, skewering the demon through the chest. The creature let out a scream of pain and grasped Johnny's hands, its eyes wide with shock and terror.

"I cannot die," it gasped.

"Everything dies," Johnny said, twisting the sword. "One sinner even said God Himself was dead. We all atone in the end."

"I cannot die," the creature said, falling to its knees, Johnny's sword sliding from its body.

"Yeah," Johnny said, raising his sword. "You already said that." With a mighty swing, he sent the creature's head sailing into the darkness.

Overhead, an indifferent moon sailed the night sky. The same moon that had seen Christ die on his cross, Lazarus rise from the dead and Johnny Masterson kill a crowned prince of Hell.

THE END

III

ENVY

HOLLOW SANCTUARY

ALICE J. BLACK

MY BREATH HIT the wall of the coarse fabric that made up my abode. It was hot and fetid but I was used to the dank smell after weeks of living by the skin of my teeth. With my eye pressed against the tiny slit where the fabric didn't quite join, I could make out the fire that burned in the centre of the camp, smoke rising into the oncoming dusk. Several people sat around it on the damp earth. I caught the flicker of smiles, saw a tankard full of something being passed between them. I shook my head. Hadn't they learned?

A gust of wind caught the side of my tent. I felt the whole thing move slightly, bending to the left, before it was righted. I took a deep breath. This was my only source of shelter, of relative safety. Without it I'd have nothing.

I'd already lost so much. I had a home, a family, and now I was alone. Those people out there still had their loved ones, still had a reason to wake up and survive another day. I was beginning to count the reasons it was easier to let go. A brief flicker of a night spent at home flashed through my mind. Warmth. Comfort. Love. My eyes stung and I squeezed them shut.

Karis…

My name floated to me on the wind the way it sometimes did late at night or when I'd let my mind wander too much. I still had my faculties and I knew it wasn't real, but still, sometimes it sounded just like him.

Shaking my head, I shoved it all away. I took a deep breath. Being out here meant keeping my wits about me at all times.

I shifted my gaze to the white walls of the Sanctum, concentrating on something else. It stood tall and proud, the colour offering a sense of hope. We made our settlement in the shadows of its walls. Those of us not welcome inside the safety of the walls, those of us not considered worthy. When it all started, those with money or other things to barter were welcomed in the walls and offered sanctuary. Others who had nothing were left to rot. I refused to back down. One of these days I would get inside those walls and find the chance to settle I deserved.

Beyond the walls, I was able to see tall buildings rising inside. Homes. A white streak of anger fizzed through me, settling in my stomach where it added to the knot of apprehension that was balled there endlessly. We were treated as lesser because of what? A lack of finances. No authority. We were made to endure the harsh world as it stood now, living day by day, minute by minute, scrounging for food, fighting for water. It was only a matter of time before I lost my life to the way we had to live out here.

When the whole thing started, the only thing I'd cared about was safety. I didn't have time to worry about my family, it was over so quickly. When I left my home that night I moved on autopilot and along with others, had made my way to the legend of a safe place for all. Since then I'd kept a tally of the days I'd survived in this scruffy settlement with hundreds of others, each one scored into my mind like a pinboard scattered with pins. It was a wonder any of us were still alive.

I looked back towards the fire as a man roared with laughter, slapping his thigh. His head was thrown back and the others around the fire were laughing too, forgetting their place. I winced.

Overhead, a deep rumble began. My eyes darted to the sky where thickening clouds converged closely, creating dark, dense coverage. My heart rate sped up and my breath came out a shallow gasp. It was starting.

The thunder started slowly, building to a wild crash that roared overhead. When the noise died, the echoes fading into nothing, everything was still. Those sat at the campfire were staring at the sky as if mesmerised. But I knew different. I knew they were frozen in fear. The cry of a child was the sound that broke the spell.

The band of people who were sitting around the campfire sprang into action. The whole settlement did. The stillness of the dusk was replaced with panic as people frantically collected their meagre belongings and rushed towards their tents, under the false information that they'd be safe as long as they were hidden beneath their flimsy material homes. A group of men had set themselves the task of putting out the fire. Buckets full of suspect liquid was passed hand to hand, sloshing over the side of the metal containers, until it finally reached the blaze and after dousing the pit several times, the fire finally died out leaving nothing but embers crackling in the base.

Dread pitted in my stomach as I watched the thick white smoke rising into the midnight blue sky. If we hadn't been blatant before, we were setting off a beacon now.

The whole settlement was a flurry of activity. My eyes darted with each movement, straining to figure out what was going on. People scurried around the camp, trying to stay quiet but failing miserably. I saw men and women rounding others up, herding them into tents. I saw arms reaching out between sheets and pulling people in, holding them close. A woman fell in the dirt, her face coming close to the still smouldering embers, and was quick to pick herself back up and duck into a tent. A man stood in the middle trying to direct others, shouting orders and pointing furiously before disappearing himself.

In the middle of it all, not far from the fire pit, stood a child. She was crying, eyes scrunched up and mouth wide. Her face was pale where it wasn't streaked with dirt. Her wails were loud, the noise going through me like nails on a chalkboard. I winced. I wasn't stupid enough to hope the noise of the settlement hadn't attracted what I already knew was coming, but this was a step too far. My heart thundered. I wanted to go out there and grab her, not to comfort, but to shush her cries. Any maternal instincts I'd once had were gone, replaced with nothing but the need for self-preservation. I gripped the sides of my tent, knuckles white, debating my next actions. I shifted my foot so I was crouched in a starter position like I was waiting for a gun to start a race. I was about to move when a man ran towards the girl, scooped her up in one arm and slung her over his shoulder, and continued running until he was out of sight. The sound of her wails disappeared.

I let out my breath. The noise was gone but the danger was only just beginning.

A bolt of lightning zig-zagged across the sky followed instantly by a second roll of thunder that seemed to crack the very foundations of the earth. The breath hitched in my chest as the vibration rocked through me from feet to the top of my head.

They were coming.

I sat back from the edge of the tent and allowed my eyes to adjust to the absolute darkness. My breath was still ragged and my heart thundered. Groping around the small space on the cool ground, I found the satchel that contained all of my worldly possessions. A matchbook with four matches, a knife that at one point would have been sharp and was now covered in a fine layer of rust, a ratty blanket pock-marked with holes, its edges encrusted in dirt, and a photograph. I didn't look at the image anymore. Couldn't. But I kept it all the same. Pulling the bag onto my knee, I sat in the darkness and waited.

The camp had finally quieted and my breaths seemed loud in the stillness.

Rain pattered the top of my tent. Fat, heavy drops that hit and soaked into the fabric. It was a few spots at first, and then, it began to fall heavier, each drop collecting together in the fabric and causing the tent to begin to bow. It wasn't meant to hold up to this sort of weather. I hunkered down, my neck aching and my palms sore where something rough in the ground dug into me.

Then I heard them. At first it was almost indiscernible above the noise of the wind and the rain that now battered the tent. Then it grew louder. My pulse quickened. They were drawing nearer. I could make out the throaty growls, the padding of paws against the hard-packed earth.

The demons were here.

I'd seen them once. A few weeks ago, I watched them steal into a tent and ravage its occupants as I sat there rooted to the spot. I wasn't able to move, to make a sound, as I watched them make their way inside and then... The screams didn't last long. But I hadn't been able to shake the image of the terrible beasts I'd glimpsed. Even in the dark, without getting a real look at them, I knew they were beasts that lived in darkness, born of shadow and evil.

The talk in the settlement after that attack had been rife. Others had seen them. Just the sight of them had been enough to send one old woman over the edge. Her inane ranting had been heard about the camp ever since. Nobody knew what they were or where they'd come from.

I named them the hell hounds. When the thunder came, the beasts came with it. And it all started that fateful last night I'd spent at home with my family. It had left our world a dark and dangerous place to live.

Now as I stared through the gap in my tent, into the darkness, I saw the rain as it splattered the ground in thick streaks that fell without pause. It churned the ground and put out the last of the embers in the fire. Then, moving amongst the blackness of night, I caught sight of one of the demons. Its huge paws left deep indentations in the ground, the print bigger than the size of my head. Water pooled in the depression as the demon continued its path around the fire. I held my breath. It moved slowly, methodically and was as stealthy as anything I'd seen. Its snout was huge, thick and bearing sharp teeth with fangs that hung over the side of its jaw. Saliva dripped from its gums. Its huge black nose sniffed as it moved, searching for prey. It knew we were here. The demon had its choice of meal. It was just a game of chance.

The beast padded around the fire, circling, searching. I saw another demon emerge from behind a tent, then another. I shivered. As one of the demons passed my tent I saw huge black bristles lining its spine, sticking up and firm, ready to skewer its next victims. The sheen of water across their coats made them look sleek, showcasing the sinew and muscle beneath.

Then one looked my way. The breath hitched in my chest.

I scooted further back into the tent but never took my eye away from the demons. My heart hammered in my chest. It was coming for me. I muttered under my breath, praying for a quick death. I heard the padding of its feet drawing closer, flanked by another. I caught a glimpse of the darkness filling the gap where I'd been staring and a dark, red eye moved to stare back at me. I whimpered, the sound tiny but sealing my fate.

Squeezing my eyes shut, I fought against the urge to run. The thought of the hell hounds giving chase was enough to keep me rooted to the spot. I wouldn't be able to win that race and to have them breathing down my neck even as I moved at a full sprint, was more than I could bear.

I took a slow, deep breath. I couldn't run and I sure as hell wasn't just going to wait for them to come in here and maul me. If this was it then I'd go down fighting. Sliding my hand into my bag, my fingers closed around the blade. I drew it out and held it in my fist. Closer they moved, their breath becoming louder, the growl at the back of their throat like the thunder that had announced their coming.

Then a sob broke the tension.

The leader stopped, the hackles rising on its sharp shoulder blades, bristles standing to attention and dripping with something slick. Body still, its head moved, looking towards the source of the sound. I dared to let out my breath. Another moment ticked by. Nothing moved. The stillness was thick with pressure. Then there was a whimper. It was barely loud enough that I could hear it but the demons caught it clearly. The hell hound who stood just in front of my tent swivelled in the opposite direction and the others followed. Together they stalked around the fire pit, eyes locked on the tent the other side.

My stomach knotted. The tent where the girl was taken earlier. An image of her tear-streaked face sifted through my mind. I imagined them in there now, the father with his hand over her mouth, willing her to stay quiet. But it was too late.

It happened so fast I could barely comprehend. My chest hitched as one of the beasts lunged forward, getting tangled in the worn fabric of the tent. From inside I heard a sharp scream and the demon doubled its efforts, succeeding in getting snarled so thickly that when it jumped backwards to try and get away, it took the whole tent with it.

As the demon struggled with its confines, the other stepped forward. My gaze darted to the family who were huddled together. The father knelt with his arms spread wide in an attempt to shield his wife and daughter. The young girl's head was buried in her mother's shoulder. Nothing moved except for the demon who was still stuck in the tent. It felt like they were at an impasse but there was no second guessing what was going to happen tonight. In an almost imperceptible movement, the father nodded, without taking his eyes from the demon. Behind him, the mother jumped to her feet, child scooped close in her arms, and turned to run.

She skirted around the fire pit, past the demon, and along the side of my tent. Her breath came in heaving gasps as she passed and the girl held tight to her chest screamed.

Within seconds, the demon was on her tail. It chased them both as they raced for the gates of the Sanctum. The guards who were standing watch, observed the scene unfold. A few seconds later their spears were extended. Still the woman ran. The demon was almost on her, huge paws thundering on the sandy ground and spraying up dirt with each bound. I watched her go. Her legs wheeled as fast as she could carry herself and her child, looking for safety. She started screaming for help, begging the guards.

They looked at each other and took a shaky step forward. The woman was almost on them. "Open the gates!" she screamed. A couple of heads appeared over the ramparts.

The beast was within feet of her now. It lunged. Landing on her back, it sent her sprawling. The woman stumbled, arms opened wide. The girl fell away from her, rolling down the bank away from the Sanctum. The woman's screams were cut short as the demon's jaws locked around her neck and shoulder, tearing away strips. Then it turned for the child.

The girl continued to roll until she hit the bottom. I knew I should move, get up and make an effort to get to her. But the demon had turned and locked his sights on her. I fought the urge to rush out there and had almost given up as behind me, I heard the scream of a man, raw and primal. The husband rushed past the tent, straight for the girl. The demon was charging too.

From the settlement, there was an uproar of noise, screaming and shouting, followed by stampeding feet. The camp was going to war. Men and women rushed past me holding whatever they could garner as a weapon. They were past breaking point. We had been harassed and beaten and spent our time wondering if tonight was the night we'd meet our maker. No more. They'd had enough.

From the top of the hill, the guards rushed towards the beasts, mouths hanging open in war cries and rushing towards the demons.

The demon dog rounded on the charge coming in from the settlement and, leaving the girl, it ran at them, teeth bared. The fight came back down towards the tents like a wildfire raging through the forest. I heard more joining the fight and there were screams of pain and terror and anger.

For a moment, I thought we could win this as the masses fought the demons but it wasn't long before they were falling, the number dwindling. It was a losing battle. For each swipe with a rudimentary weapon, the beasts took two down. It wasn't going to take long before the whole settlement was done for. And they wouldn't stop at those on the battlefield. The demons were angry, eyes red as they fought and bit and clawed. They would come for every last one of us.

I had to get out now.

Pulling the satchel over my shoulder, I crept forward, hands gripping either side of the tent. Nothing looked my way and I doubted I would be heard amongst the chaos.

Taking a deep breath, I pushed myself between the fabric and took a sharp left. I had no idea where I was going. All I knew was that I needed to get away if I had any hope of surviving the night.

As I steamed from the chaos behind me, leaving the screams and death behind, I caught sight of the gates. They were open. I realised that more guards were running down the hill towards the fighting. I thought for a moment they may be coming to protect the settlement but they had never done that before.

They were coming for vengeance, I realised, as I rushed past the mauled bodies of their comrades. I was glad they had fallen face down.

I slipped past the guards as they ran screaming down the hill, a shadow in the night.

This was my chance. I could be safe hidden within the walls of the Sanctum. Even if I had to live like the rats and hide in the shadows, it was better than the existence I had down at the camp.

Pouring on the speed, I rushed at the gates. The gap was small but so was I. Months of starvation had shed any fat on my body and I knew I'd make it.

I reached the gate and turned sideways, pushing past the wooden barrier. On the inside I caught a glimpse of torches ablaze on the walls but I didn't have long to take it in. If I was caught, I had no idea what they would do.

I pushed harder, feeling the wood scraping my arm, against my hip. With a grunt and one last heave, I was in.

For a second, I froze. I was inside the Sanctum. My heart soared as I realised that safety was now within my grasp. I had longed for this for so long, wished to lay my head down in peace and enjoy a meal that I didn't have to fight for and now that I was here, I was rooted.

I found myself in a huge open space. I hadn't seen space like that for months because it wasn't safe to be away from the settlement alone. It was always safety in numbers in the camp, despite the other problems it brought. I shook myself. I'd have to marvel at this another time. Right now, I had to get somewhere quiet.

I scanned the area up ahead. Buildings towered on each other, all white and gleaming in the moonlight. Some were smaller than others. I saw tower blocks and shed-like structures. I didn't care where I ended up. I just had to pick somewhere that wasn't already occupied.

Stealing across the expanse, I pushed myself against a wall, suddenly aware of my grubby, dark clothes. Nobody was around but it wouldn't be long before I was spotted. I glanced into the nearest window of a tiny, squat building. I couldn't see anything. I wagered a bet that it would be empty. They had plenty to choose from, nobody would pick this place. Surely.

I skirted around the wall until I found the door. It was a simple wooden door and as I grabbed the handle, it moved in my grasp. I took a deep breath and pushed it inwards. A creak resounded in the night and then it swung silently. I paused there, holding my breath, waiting to be called out or grabbed. There was nothing. Slowly, I moved inside, crossing the threshold. It was pitch black. I knew nobody was here; I would have been caught by now, but I still had no idea what I was stepping into.

Reaching back outside, I grabbed a torch that had been secured on the wall. Its flame was bright and as I swung it into the room, I realised it was a storage area. There were sacks piled on top of one another. I kicked one and its contents shifted slightly. Dropping to my knees I poked at a sack and then, taking my knife to the top, sawed a hole in the rough fabric. Beans spilled out on the floor. I could have cried as I picked up a handful and shoved them into my mouth, barely chewing before swallowing. I gorged on the dry beans, taking as much as I could before I thought I might throw up. I had made it. I'd finally made it to safety. Tears dripped from my eyes, rolling down my cheeks as the relief overcame everything.

———

I WOKE WITH A START, jolting upright with a gasp. I glanced around, trying to get my bearings. The flame on the torch beside me had gone out and I was in complete darkness. Goosebumps coated every inch of my skin and I wrapped my arms around my chest, drawing my knees in close. Everything was foggy and I fought the panic that balled in my chest. Then the memories started creeping back in, slowly at first, but they came with speed and clarity as I woke. The settlement. The demons. Mother and daughter running. The deaths. And then finally, slipping inside the Sanctum.

I was inside the Sanctum. My heart soared again. My night had been a shitstorm in the hell of the last few months but now I was safe inside the white walls. My shoulders sagged with relief once more as tears of joy filled my eyes. I couldn't believe it. After so much time spent running, fighting, and hiding, I could now live my life. I could become human again, put myself to use, help the others, and in return be helped. I wiped my eyes and took a deep breath. The only problem now was making sure I was accepted. I had to cling to this, tooth and nail.

I had no idea how much time had passed since I'd hidden away in this store room but it was still dark outside. I was somewhat rested and had eaten well for the first time in weeks. I felt better, stronger. Now was the time to try and find somewhere more concrete to lay my head.

Pushing myself to my feet, I slung my bag over my shoulder and took juddering steps forward with my hands outstretched, feeling for the door.

After just a few steps, my fingertips brushed against

something solid and rough and as they slipped downwards, found the handle of the door.

As I opened the door, I was greeted with the sight of white walls facing me and a little light from torches that still burned, secured on the walls at intervals. They weren't enough to banish the darkness but afforded a glow that lit a path for me. I stuck my head out of the door and peered in either direction. The alley petered off into darkness to my left where the torches had guttered out and to the right was the way I'd come in, and the gate.

I had found my way into the Sanctum, now I needed to figure out a way to stay safe and fit in. I had never seen anyone get through the gates here let alone be allowed to stay so I was willing to bet my being here would be frowned upon at the very least. I glanced at my attire. My clothes were encrusted with filth and my shoes, a pair of trainers that had been with me since the beginning of this thing, were falling apart. I was glad I hadn't looked in a mirror in as many months. I hated to think what I actually looked like. I could feel the knots in my hair and my face was caked in a fine layer of dirt. What I wouldn't give for a bath.

Creeping to the end of the building, I gripped the brickwork as I glanced around. There was no movement but I had no doubt there were guards somewhere. What was left of them, anyway. The men who had gone charging out into the settlement to kill the beasts hadn't returned. I knew that.

Just as I was about to move to the left to cut a path towards the inner city and away from the gate, I heard the voice again. *Karis...*

I froze in my tracks and felt my heart ramp up its pace

against my ribcage. Squeezing my eyes, I waited there for a moment.

Karis... leave.

It was his voice. It was a warning. I'd heard it ever since I left the house that night, ever since I... No! I stopped the thought in its tracks. The only way to survive was to keep the memory out of my conscious. I shoved it away and grounded myself, gripping the wall a little tighter, pressing my cheek against the cool stone. It had the desired effect.

I took a final glance around in case anything had changed in the last few seconds and, with my heart thudding in my chest, I peeled myself from the wall and began to walk. Keeping close to the buildings, I made my way around the periphery. Everything was still and quiet.

Even from the camp outside, there was no noise. I wondered what was left of the settlement. When I'd left the whole settlement was going into battle with the hell hounds. Those tents wouldn't stand a chance against the beasts, and neither would the people. I wondered if there were many left, if any. I swallowed. I could have been one of them. Tonight could have been my last night on earth but I'd seen the chance and taken it. Was there anyone out there to miss my presence? I doubted it. I was a loner, had been since arriving. It was likely I was presumed dead.

I came to the edge of a building. Pausing, I peered around the corner. There was a large square space, buildings on three sides hemming it in. The buildings that surrounded it were three stories tall and white like the rest. They had a sense of austerity, had been preserved as such. I shuddered. They certainly weren't very welcoming. Still, a building, no matter its façade, was better than a tent.

My eyes were drawn to the centre of the furthest building where there was a large wooden door. It was closed.

I had no idea what I might find through that door, whether it be acceptance or denial, but I had to try. The longer I stayed outside, the longer I risked getting spotted and who knew what they'd do with me then. I couldn't face being cast back outside into the jaws of those hell hounds. I shivered. No. That wouldn't do at all. I'd have to get inside one way or another.

With one final scan of the open space, I pushed myself away from my spot at the corner of the building and, keeping low, hurried towards the door. With every step I took, I thought I'd be caught, that someone would be watching and alert the guards. But I made it clear to the door without mishap and as I grabbed the handle, it gave in my hand. I stepped inside and found myself swallowed in darkness.

Panic threatened to overtake but I took a deep breath and forced it down. If I could deal with those beasts night after night and live to tell the tale, I could manage to wander around some cushy old building with walls to keep me safe. Even if I was spotted, was it likely they'd throw me back out? I could make them feel sorry for me, play on the heart strings. Or I could prove that I've got what it takes to add to their community within the walls. I hadn't gotten this far by lying back and running away. I'd had to fight to get to where I was. And to keep my life.

As my eyes finally adjusted to the darkness of the building, I realised I was in a corridor. It led off in both directions, but as I scanned the darkness at my back, I saw nothing that proved to be comforting. Ahead of me, I saw the flicker of torch light and decided that was my route. I kept my hand on the wall to maintain my bearings and began to walk. I moved slowly, careful in case I tripped on something underfoot. The going was slow and my breathing was little more than a pant, but at least I was moving.

The light grew brighter with every step and finally, I came to the end of the corridor as it opened up into a vast hall. My hand dropped, fingertips glad from the reprieve of the sensitivity. The hall was full of long, wooden benches set in rows facing a fire pit. The fire still burned and at the bottom of the mesh casing of the pit, I saw there was still plenty of fuel. It burned hot, flames licking the sides of the metal casket as it devoured the contents. Light flickered on the walls, casting a warm orange glow. Where the light waned in the corners of the room, shadows overtook and I shivered.

I still had no idea of the time as I crept closer to the fire, feeling the heat on my skin. I held my palms out flat, accepting the heat and comfort it brought. As I stood there enveloped in the heat, I took a look around the hall. It was empty. I hadn't seen a soul since the guards at the gate earlier. It was late but I figured there'd be patrols at the very least and surely not everyone was a heavy sleeper in the Sanctum. I wondered if the rooms might be in another part of the building entirely. Maybe this was used for communal things like eating meals and meetings.

Yet I knew that following the night's events, everyone in the settlement, everyone who had survived the attack would still be awake now as the dawn peeked over the horizon, comforting the family of the deceased, burying the dead.

It felt like the Sanctum had not felt the loss of their guards. My stomach twisted.

I couldn't stay here all night. I had to find clothing, food, somewhere to sleep. I noticed a doorway at the far end of the room, steeped in shadows. I headed in that direction, feeling the cold as soon as I left the circle of heat emitted by the fire.

I reached the door and peered into the darkness beyond. My eyes struggled to adjust and as I stood there, I felt the coldness of the building penetrate my skin, down through all the layers, where it settled deep in my bones. I shivered. I considered going back to the fire and waiting out the night but I had to at least attempt to fit into the Sanctum. It was painfully obvious I wasn't one of them and I didn't want to give them any excuse to toss me out.

I forced myself across the threshold. A stairway opened up in front of me and there was only one way to go: down. I moved slowly down the spiralling stone steps. There were no windows and the further I descended, the darker it got until the only thing that kept me grounded was the rough stone walls that my fingertips traced.

I reached the bottom with the sudden surprise that there were no more steps and my stomach jolted. I took a deep breath. I had no idea where I was or what was in front of me. I had no way to see.

With arms outstretched, I shuffled forward. My steps sounded loud against the stone and my breathing was heavy. My hand connected with something solid and my heart jolted. I moved a little closer, my fingers exploring the surface. I came to realise it was another door as my hand found the cool handle. Taking it in my grip, I turned and pulled the door towards me. Light spilled into the room and I winced, turning away from the sudden spark. After a few moments, I dared to open my eyes again and I peered around the door.

My jaw dropped. There were flashes of machinery, of steel, of red.

A sudden dull thump connected with the back of my head. I grunted as stars flashed in front of my eyes and then I crumpled to the floor.

———

MY HEAD POUNDED with a dull ache that resonated to the base of my skull. I cranked my neck left and right, trying to work out the kinks, as I slowly opened my eyes. I saw stars momentarily, flashing in my vision, before they cleared.

I was in a cage. Bars surrounded me on either side, above me, hemming me in. My pulse quickened as I pushed myself up to sitting, slamming my shoulder into a bar in the process. I grunted and grabbed it with my right hand, massaging the tender spot. The bars were solid steel, thick and cold. As my feet curled towards my backside, the cold metal of the bars beneath me jarred against my skin. My ankle bone skimmed the top and I cursed aloud again. Slowly, the throbbing seemed to still.

It only took a few moments for me to realise that they weren't the only parts of my body that were causing me pain. My hand went to the back of my head, where the dull ache seemed to spiral out into my brain, and came away sticky. I glanced at my palm. Blood.

My gut clenched. There was no way I got a wound like that by myself. I forced myself to think back to the last thing I remembered. Shuffling down the steps in a spiral, a door at the bottom, opening it and then…

"Hey!" Somebody hissed, voice startling me.

My gaze darted up from where I was hunched. I realised two things in that moment: there was enough light in the room that

I could see, and that everything I could see was worse than anything I could have imagined.

I wasn't the only one. Dread settled in the pit of my stomach as I made out rows upon rows of cages, all of them full of people. I saw through the bars of the cages to other people in various states of array. Some lay on the floor asleep, or I wondered, dead? Others were more alert, sitting up, staring at their surroundings like I was doing. I heard some of them crying, mournful tears that suggested an admit of defeat. And there were talkers, those who whispered amongst themselves, and those who bore the ravings of lunatics.

"Hey!" The voice spoke again.

I narrowed my eyes and found my speaker. It was another woman. She was in the cage next to mine and she sat right up to the bars, hands clawed around them as if to drag herself closer. She stared at me with wide eyes, her pupils so wide they melded into dark irises. Her hair was short, slicked back, and matted with dirt. A greasy smudge ran down the length of her cheek and onto her neck. Her clothes had been torn and barely kept her breasts covered. I saw traces of blood on her skin, mixed with the sheen of perspiration.

What is this place?

"Are you okay?" she asked. She still hadn't blinked once since calling my attention. Still, I had bigger things to worry about than how a stranger was staring at me from behind the bars of her cage.

I glanced around my own cage and then back at her. "What do *you* think?"

"I didn't think you'd last long when they brought you in." She ignored my curt tone. "You were out cold. Thought you were dead at one point."

I rubbed the back of my head again. The blood had dried up but the ache persisted with the force of a drum pounding my skull. What had I been hit with? "Have I been out long?"

"Couple of hours," she whispered with a shrug. "Something like that. It's hard to tell down here. No light, no windows, no real sense of time."

I nodded, silent again as I looked around. She was right. We were underground and there was no sign of a way out, let alone a place that daylight might be able to peek through.

I gripped the bars as I stared around the room, at the cages in front of me, at the very bars I clung to. I'd come to the Sanctum seeking sanctuary and here I was locked up in a cage not fit for a dog.

"I've figured the way to get through this is to stay quiet," she continued talking. When I looked her way I saw she hadn't moved a muscle, hadn't looked away.

"Get through what?"

"Stay quiet and keep your head down. I've seen people come and go and they barely give me a glance. That's how you get through this."

"Go where? Get through what?" I clutched the bars in front of me, leaning towards her. The woman was talking in riddles and it beginning to piss me off.

She shrugged. "I don't know. They come and they take people and then I never see them again. But the people are always replaced with others. The cages are always full."

The knot in my stomach tightened. What had I gotten myself into?

———

MY MIND TICKED OVER, the images of the last few hours rushing through my brain in a bizarre reel that left me more confused. The Sanctum was a safe place. So why were they keeping people in cages? It was too much to hope that this was some sort of odd processing room, but no matter what scenario I tried to come up with, my mind was blank. All I knew was that the dread pitted at the bottom of my stomach was there for a reason and I had to trust it.

I heard the jangle of keys, quiet at first, and as the door at the far end of the room was flung open spilling a pool of light into the room, they became loud, chiming against one another. My gaze shifted away from the rectangle of light for a moment, finding the stare of the woman in the cage next to mine. Her eyes were wide with fear, her breathing heavy, shoulders heaving with each intake. I wanted to reach out to her, to tell her it would be okay, but she had been here longer than me. She knew this was not a good situation. Her fingers unfurled from the bars and she retreated into her cage, ducking away from the light and lying down in the shadows until all that was visible was the whites of her eyes. That disappeared too as she closed them. She didn't move again.

Two men came through the door at the end of the room. As each one passed through, their huge hulking frames filled the space, blocking the light. Then they were both through, in the room with the cages. The breath caught in my throat. They walked side by side, silhouettes illuminated by the light behind. I could make out that one carried a torch, lighting the way, while the other strolled with keys in hand.

As they wandered towards the cages, the light from the torch casting a wider halo with each step, I got a glimpse of reality. There must have been dozens of cages, all lined up in rows. They were all full. There were men, women, and children, all in various states of disarray, each with the same haunted look in their eyes. How long had they been here? Locked in cages, they were treated like animals and I guessed not one of them had been fed a decent meal for weeks.

As the men passed a cage with a young boy, his eyes met mine. Hair had been ripped from his scalp in patches and I saw where scabs had formed. Dirt lined his cheeks. His lip was split and his eyes were full. But the fight had left him. I looked away.

Closer and closer they moved and though I had no way of really knowing, I knew they were coming for me. I was the odd one out. These people in the other cages, they had been here all along. They were citizens of the Sanctum and I was the outsider. I stuck out like a sore thumb.

Still, as their heavy boots came to a stop right outside of my cage, I couldn't prevent the welling panic that rose in my chest. I fought it down as I gripped the bars, willing myself to breathe. If they let me out, I could fight, could get free and run. Maybe even get help.

I couldn't lift my head, couldn't bear the thought of seeing their faces. Instead, my gaze slid to the left, to the woman who had spoken to me. Her eyes flickered briefly and I saw a hint of sorrow there, before her lids closed again. *Stay quiet, keep your head down.* I wish I'd listened to her advice now.

The guard with the keys bent down and unlocked the cage before taking a step back. Potential freedom awaited yet, all it made me want to do was shrink further into myself. Tucking my head low, I turned my body to the side. Maybe if I ignored them, they'd go away. A couple of seconds ticked by and I thought maybe I'd won when the guard reached down for the second time but, instead of locking the cage again, he stretched into the

117

cage, grabbed me by the arm and yanked me out. My ankles grated against the bars of the cage and my head thumped the top. I yelled but he held me firm, drawing me to my feet in front of him. He was over six feet tall and stocky. Even just with one hand holding me, I knew there was no way I was getting out. Besides the fact that I had no idea where to go, he'd be on me in seconds and I was willing to bet those meaty hands had seen their fair share of brutality.

Now wasn't the time.

"Move!" he barked, shoving me in front of him. I stumbled a few steps before righting myself. I moved, slowly, cradling my arm to my chest. I'd be bruised but at least it wasn't broken.

With both guards behind me, I headed towards the door, receiving a shove every now and then which served as a reminder of the pain they could inflict, and the fact that right now I was more vulnerable than I'd ever been.

———

I FOUND myself in a smaller room, the guards flanking me closely. A stone pillar in the centre of the room served as a foundation for the ceiling overhead. Torches lined the walls and the orange glow would have been comforting if I hadn't seen what they illuminated. Cages. This time there were only a few but inside of them all were children. My stomach jolted. I wanted to go to them, to kneel at the bars and check they were all okay. No, I wanted to rip open those doors and hustle the children out of there.

As if they sensed my thoughts, one of the guards kicked me in the back of my leg. My knee buckled and I dropped to the floor for a minute, grinding my teeth as I fought the urge to spin around and lunge at his junk. Even just taking him down for a few minutes would be satisfying. But I'd be flat out within seconds if I tried anything. Instead, I pushed to my feet, ignoring the creak in my knee, and then I was shoved forward towards a chair. It was placed in front of a wooden table set against the wall. I sank down into the chair without hesitation, knowing it would do nothing but cause more issues. It was hard beneath me.

"Stay there," one of the men growled. It was the one who'd shoved me. What I wouldn't give to take him down. I thought of the knife I'd brought with me, the one that was now missing. I wondered if they had it. If they had my bag.

As the guards backed away, taking up posts beside either door in the room, I took the opportunity to take a real look at the place. Thankful I couldn't see the cages behind me, I focused on everything else. The walls, stone and unfinished, were dark with damp. A torch that flickered on its stick attached to the wall. The table was directly in front of me, its surface worn and marked. Nothing was strewn on its top.

A footstep caught my ear. It wasn't a heavy step like that of the boot-clad guards. As I looked up, I saw a woman entering a doorway and the guard sliding back into place. She wore a white robe that fell to the floor, simple but much more elegant than the attire I'd been wearing for the past few months. Her hair was light and hung down to her breasts with a curl. Her hands were clasped in front of her and they looked soft and pale. They hadn't been subjected to hard work. I almost rolled my eyes. Those who lived in the Sanctum had an easy life and I'd come here and experienced nothing but humiliation and resentment so far.

"Who are you?" Her voice was calm, almost quiet.

"Please, I just—"

"Name." This time it was more of a demand.

"Karis."

"I am Esme. I am the leader here." She spread her arms wide and let me soak that in for a moment. "You are from the Outside."

"Yes." It seemed my entrance into the Sanctum hadn't gone unnoticed.

"Why?"

I looked up. Her head was tilted to the side, her blonde hair tumbling in glorious waves I couldn't have hoped to achieve if I washed my hair ten times. She stared at me unblinking.

I faltered. I wasn't expecting to be asked that question. I thought it was fairly obvious why I'd come here: because being outside was the worst thing to experience in this world.

"Safety," I finally answered.

After a few seconds, she blinked and straightened. "What was the camp like?"

"Hard. Dangerous. Lonely." The words got lodged in my throat as emotion overcame and my throat thickened. I coughed. I pushed my filthy hands to my mouth.

Esme turned and signalled to the guard. He disappeared, returning a moment later with a glass of water. It exchanged hands and then she passed it to me. I hesitated before I took it, reasoning that they could have killed me instead of going to all this trouble to speak to me, but once the glass was in my hands, I guzzled it down, water spilling over my lips and dripping down my chin. I finished with a satisfied sigh. Having water—cool water—was a luxury I hadn't experienced in a long time.

Esme took the glass from my hand and set it on the table, out of my reach. My stomach jolted as I realised what was next to the glass. My bag. My heart thudded. When had she put that there? I knew it had been taken when I'd been knocked out but I hadn't given it a second thought until I had thought about my knife. Right now, there were only two things in there that mattered to me, the knife and the photo.

"This is yours?" She indicated the bag. It looked pathetic sitting there, mostly empty, battered, and torn.

I nodded.

With a swift movement, she lifted the flap and exposed the contents of the bag. One by one she pulled the items out, examining them before putting them down. She looked unimpressed with the contents. She laid the knife on top of the blanket, rubbing her hands together as she handled both. Last, she came to the picture. As she drew it from the satchel my heart seized.

The picture was worn, folded twice, and faded at the edges, but it was the only thing I had to remember them by.

Slowly, she unfolded it and tilted it to the light to get a better look. My panic rocked when I thought she might push the corner of the picture into the flame. She dropped it instead, flashing it my way and pointing at the image. "Who are they?" she asked.

I dropped my head, fighting the sting in my eye. The knot in my stomach burned as I twisted my hands together. How dare she touch my belongings. How dare she bring it back up. White hot anger rushed through me in a torrent. I had to fight to remain seated as my fingers gripped the handles of the chair.

She took a step forward. The white of her dress came into my peripheral vision and as she invaded my space, my memories, I forced myself to remember the guards who stood on either side of the room just waiting for an excuse to pounce.

"I said, who are they?" she repeated. Her voice was a little sterner, the soft edge to her whole persona gone in an instant.

I took a deep breath. This woman meant business, and right now I was at her mercy.

"My husband and daughter." The words came out a whisper.

The woman dropped into a crouch directly in front of me. Her wrist rested on my knee and she waited there patiently until I met her gaze. "Tell me what happened to them."

My moods flipped between emotional to anger and back to being overwhelmed in the space of a few seconds. I didn't know this woman. I didn't care who she was and yet she crouched in front of me, demanding my story. We all had one. Every one of us who had survived the first wave and lived to tell the tale, we all had a story. None of them were pleasant or even hinted at a happy ending. It always ended in disaster, blood, and death. And I'd heard plenty of them. And now this Esme thought she had the right to ask me—no, tell me—that I had to share my journey. It wasn't happening.

I shook my head. No. I swore I would never talk about them. Never. I couldn't let myself remember. It was the only thing that was holding my soul together. If I unravelled that ribbon, I'd unravel my sanity.

A blade appeared in her right hand. I had no clear idea where she'd drawn it from but as the blade came to rest on my thigh, I saw the sharp of the curved edge glinting in the fire light.

"Tell me their story."

Finally I met her gaze, ignoring the stray tear that escaped my eye, and opened my mouth.

"THAT'S MY HUSBAND, GARETH." I took the picture from her hand. I gazed down at him, my eyes finding my daughter next. "And that's Olivia. She was five in this photo."

"You look happy."

"We were." Another tear spilled over my eye and rolled down my cheek. The edges of my soul were beginning to crack. I hurried to wipe the tear away.

"What happened to them?"

I bit my lip, fighting the urge to argue with her. She'd only just retracted the blade slightly. She was talking about my family like it was nothing, like it didn't matter they were gone. Maybe not to her, but that night when my family... when they left, my whole world went with it.

I met her eyes. Esme wasn't giving up. I would tell her my story. I would feel my heart shatter and then I would ask for shelter, for safety and I would allow myself to remember.

"We were together that night when they first came," I started. My voice was low.

Esme straightened, setting the knife on the table behind her as she leaned against it. She crossed her arms. "Go on."

"It was like any other night. We weren't like most couples anyway, we rarely went out, so we were at home with Olivia. It was a Friday. We were in the house. Gareth was cooking, Olivia was giggling at something on TV and I had a glass of wine. It was perfect. Then the thunder came." I remembered it so vividly, as if it was just yesterday. The smell of garlic as it drifted through the house. The bitter taste of the dry white wine on my tongue. Olivia's laughter and her infectious smile.

I heard the thunder crashing in the back of my mind the way it did in my nightmares.

"We turned off the lights and watched the storm together. It raged overhead. I recall thinking how brilliant a storm it was, that we'd never forget this night. I remember Olivia was scared. She trembled between us as we watched the lightning spear the sky, the thunder only seconds behind it." I paused as I reimagined the scene in my mind. The three of us peering over the edge of the sofa through the window into the night. Gareth had pulled the drapes open, exposing us to the storm. And to them.

"Then something in the air changed. We felt it even indoors. It was heat mixed with the threat of something." I shook my head. "I began to worry, thinking we should maybe shut the curtains and hide but Gareth wanted to keep watching, so we did. It went on and on. I don't even know how long we sat there watching. It wasn't until the smoke alarm started beeping that any of us moved. Gareth rushed for it and Olivia followed. I didn't even realise she had gone." I dropped my head, thumb stroking the picture. Another tear fell from my eye, this one landing on the photo. It created a bubble over the faded colours of Olivia's blonde hair. I wiped it away.

"What happened?" Esme's voice was a whisper, carrying a note of empathy.

I shook my head. "It all happened so fast. There was a crash that I mistook for thunder. But it wasn't. It was the patio doors. Then I heard Olivia scream. That's what got me moving. I jumped from the sofa. I remember the wine glass slipping from my hand. It smashed on the floor behind me as I scrambled for the kitchen. Gareth, he was... he was dead. He stared at me from the floor. There was so much blood." I paused and inhaled, quelling the rising panic. "All I could think was that it had to be a joke, that it was some sick prank. Then something had him by the feet and he was pulled out of the window, disappearing into the storm. And then I saw Olivia. She was screaming, hands pressed over her ears. I went to run to her but it was quicker. I barely got a glimpse of what it was. I saw a beast bigger than my daughter as they rushed into my home. It picked her up in its jaws. It's teeth, they went straight through her flesh like it was hot butter. I saw blood and it was too late. They had her. Dragging her backwards out through the window. I dived for her but I wasn't quick enough. She was gone."

The crackle of flames filled the silence as I stopped speaking, my whole body overcome with sobs. I shook violently, mouth twisted in agony but there was no sound. Only the steady stream of tears as they fell from my eyes.

I don't know how long I sat there, rocking back and forth. I hadn't allowed myself to remember because I knew it would be my undoing. And now as my heart continued to shatter, the pieces falling into the empty well of my chest, I knew it was over.

Finally, my chest stopped heaving and I took a deep breath. "I don't even remember getting out of the house. When I finally came to, I was walking down a street and it was daytime but the world that we knew had ended. The streets were filled with people looking for safety. Everyone had lost. Families were missing children, parents. Everything was broken."

"You've carried this burden for a long time." Her voice was soft. I rubbed my eyes, tender and raw, and looked up. "And now you've come here looking for safety, for warmth."

"For survival," I whispered.

"You may have come here seeking a place to heal, but you will not find it here." She crossed her arms tightly. "Do you know that we watch you?"

"Me?" I patted my chest.

"The settlement. The camp outside of our walls." She gestured with her head. "Night after night, it draws the demons in causing chaos and destruction. Your people have stripped the land bare of resources. There are no trees for firewood, no deer to hunt, no berries to collect."

"But—"

"And there is no water." She stabbed the knife into the table, standing up straight. "Do you not see what you have done to us?"

"Done to you?" I scoffed. My fingers gripped the arm rests. "You sit in here, in a sanctuary surrounded by tall walls. You have safety. You have numbers. You have resources and food and water. I know because otherwise you would have become nothing but the scavengers the camp has turned us all into." My voice rose. "You think I would have chosen this life for myself? For anyone living there? There are children too afraid to leave the safety of a bed sheet draped over a wire. We are attacked night by night. I lie awake at night wondering if this will be my last, if I will be dragged off to join Gareth and Olivia. But somehow, fate keeps smiling on me and I'm still here."

Her lips twisted into an ugly sneer. "Fate isn't on your side, Karis, you've walked into the Devil's snare."

————

WHEN I WOKE AGAIN, it was light. I'd been moved away from the cages and misery, but as my eyes flicked open to face the stone-walled room, I still felt dread punctuating my whole being. I sat up, pressing my back against the wall, and took a look around me. The room was tiny, barely big enough to stretch my legs out fully, and instead of a door there was a barred gate. A keyhole yawned at me, black and menacing and I knew that too late, I had made the wrong choice.

Coming to the Sanctum had seemed to be a way out of the heartache and fear that permeated the air around the settlement, but it was nothing like I could have ever hoped for.

My head was throbbing and my hand went up to caress it. I cradled my head in my hands and realised I felt drained—hungover almost. I hadn't felt that way in a long time but the dry mouth, the twist in my gut and searing pain in my chest was enough to let me know I was beyond salvation. My heart ached. Physically ached. A deep pain deep beneath my ribs and I knew without a doubt it was because of my remembering. It had felt like a confession, the way I was forced to tell Esme every last detail, to relive the guilt of that night.

I didn't remember anything past being in that chair and talking to Esme—shouting at her—and yet here I was in my own private hell. It didn't take a genius to figure out what had happened. I'd been clubbed for a second time.

I shifted and stretched, my whole body aching with the events of the last twenty-four hours. I wondered what time it was, what fresh hell I was going to face today. I'd come here seeking sanctuary but as the hours ticked by, I was beginning to realise that I wasn't going to make it out of here even if I tried.

In the distance I could hear footsteps. They moved my way, each one of them made with a heavy boot on the stone flags and then, alongside it, the jangling of keys. My heart leapt into my mouth. They were coming for me.

I glanced around the tiny room looking for something, anything, I could use as a weapon. There was nothing. The cell was bare. I'd slept on the stone floor and there wasn't even a container for water. The steps got closer, the keys forming as pattern as they swished. I imagined them to be in his hand, swinging with joy with each step he took.

A door opened at the end of the room, more light spilling towards me. As it did, I reached forward, grasping the cool metal bars. Several other rooms like my own lined the square room. How many people were they holding captive? All of those cages, all of these rooms. What were they doing with everyone? Surely they couldn't all be the felons they were made out to be. Not everyone here could be from the settlement. I'd recognise their faces, even this dirty.

The man, a huge silhouette again the light of the doorway, stepped into the room and as he moved, I saw Esme behind him. She looked like the picture of health, refreshed as if she'd just enjoyed a power nap and a good meal. She still wore the same white dress that skimmed the floor as she walked. She looked down at me, the smile on her face a mix of amusement and sympathy. I bit my lip as I stared her out.

"Good morning," she sidled up towards me, careful to leave enough distance that I wouldn't reach her if I tried. "How did you sleep?"

Wadding the saliva in my mouth, I spat. It landed on the bottom of her dress.

I half expected her to drag me out of the cell and beat me herself but instead, she simply stared at the mess and shook her head.

"Really, Karis. I give you somewhere to sleep and this is how you repay me?"

"Tell me what's going on here. I came looking for safety and you have me locked up, sleeping on the floor like a dog."

"If the title fits." Her eyebrow twitched.

I slammed my hand against the bars, ignoring the dull pain

that reverberated up to my elbow. "If you don't want me here then throw me out that gate and I promise I'll never come back." I bared my teeth as I pressed my face against the bars.

Esme crouched low, looking me in the eye. "Everyone in the Sanctum has a part to play. From the guards who keep everything in order to the cooks, the cleaners."

"And what does that make me?" I growled.

She moved to her feet. "You'll see." Turning to the guard, she indicated that he should unlock the cell door. As he took a step nearer, I took a few backwards. His size was intimidating. It looked like he could crush my skull in one hand. That was his one job. Keeping the prisoners in a state of fear and compliance.

He unlocked the door and it swung inwards. He beckoned for me to move forward and I did, obeying. Disgust rolled through me as I made it to the threshold and he grabbed me by the scruff of my collar. I grimaced. My spirit had been stripped bare. If I'd been this wreck back in the settlement camp, there's no way I would have survived longer than a few days. I needed to get it together.

He shoved me roughly and I stumbled a few steps before righting myself. My stomach grumbled and my head pounded with a furious ache. I followed Esme obediently while behind me, I heard the heavy steps and sharp jangle of keys. I tried to take in the rooms around me, the details, looking for any means of escape but my concentration was ebbing and fear was taking over.

It seemed we walked and walked. Everything was the same. Stone walls, stone flags. Sconces were still lit with torches where shadows clung to the corners, casting an orange glow whenever I walked. We moved past the cages and I expected noise, an uproar, but there was silence. The people in those cages had been beaten into submission. Whatever I was going to experience now, they were in store for, too.

My heart thundered, matching the steps that I took. My feet dragged against the stone flags and more than once I stumbled. The guard behind me caught my arm, holding me upright.

We came to a huge door and behind it, I could hear something that caused the hairs on the back of my neck to stand to attention, even if I couldn't understand it.

The woman grabbed the door handle but paused and glanced back at me. "Karis, you said fate brought you here. You should have stayed where you were."

She pushed open the door. I realised what was making the hackles on the back of my neck stand to attention. Inside, I was greeted with the sight of something that resembled a chop shop. But this was so much worse.

Where car parts would have been distributed, cut open and mangled, or fixed and welded, there were people. People in bits. Limbs. Torsos. Heads.

There were people working on benches, dissecting humans, taking out their organs and passing them on to others for preparation. The smell of copper hung heavy in the air and everything was tinged in red.

I saw huge cauldrons hung over blazing fires. Meat being stretched across racks for drying. Limbs being flayed and the skin tossed aside into a mounting pile of garish bloody pulp.

I took a step back and into the solid wall of muscle the guard behind me presented. His hands gripped the tops of my arms.

"Karis, you stole into our sanctuary, expecting our help. But like I said, you have stripped the land bare and we had nothing left. This is our solution."

"You're eating people." The words rolled off my tongue and

my stomach heaved. As I retched, I doubled over but nothing came out.

"We're keeping hunger at bay. Everyone here plays a part. Those who work here keep their lives, those who don't are used in another way."

"You can't do this." Tears blurred my vision.

"Last night I asked for your story, for that of your husband and daughter. Your story will live on, and so will you Karis."

"Please." The word was barely a whisper as the tears fell.

"Take her inside." She stepped aside.

"What have you done?" I whispered, unable to take my eyes off the scene in front of me.

Esme gave me one last glance as I was ushered towards the door. "Survived, Karis. We have survived."

IV

GREED

GREED COMES KNOCKING

KATE L. MARY

A MOAN ECHOED through the dark forest, and I froze, holding my breath as I strained to hear, my heart in my throat and my legs trembling. Where had it come from? Was it close? More importantly, how many were there?

"Do you see anything?" I whispered, turning to look at Jacob.

Like me, he'd stopped walking and now stood alert, the baseball bat clutched in his right hand steady despite the obvious terror on his face. The thing seemed like such a useless weapon and wouldn't be much in the way of protection if we ran into a horde, but it was all we had. The bullets had been gone for more than a week—not that we'd had many to begin with—so that even if we had managed to get away with a gun or two, it wouldn't have mattered. There had been no chance, though. The guns, knives, and everything else had been lost when a horde invaded our camp the night before, leaving us empty-handed, lost, hungry, and thirsty. And desperate. So very, very desperate.

At least you made it out with your lives.

I'd repeated the sentence nearly a hundred times during the long day of walking, each time looking at Jacob to confirm that he was in fact at my side. We'd lost everything, but we still had each other. For as long as I could remember, he was all I'd ever wanted, anyway—all I'd ever needed. Just me and him. If we had each other, I knew we could get through anything.

Moonlight broke through the trees above us, illuminating his blond hair. It looked darker than usual, a result of not being able to wash it often, and was longer than he'd ever worn it before so that it curled a little at the base of his neck and above his ears. We'd known one another since the age of five, so long I couldn't remember a time when he hadn't been in my life, but until now, I hadn't known his hair could curl. It was funny the things you learned about a person during the apocalypse.

"It sounded like it was behind us. We should keep moving," Jacob said in response to my question, his gaze moving back to meet mine, holding it for a moment as if trying to garner some strength or courage. "Are you okay?"

I nodded, trying to convince not just him, but also myself that I was, in fact, okay. Since I was unable to muster even a single word, I didn't fool either of us.

"We'll find a safe place soon, Robyn," he assured me. "I promise I will get you to a safe place."

Before I could respond, he nodded in the direction we'd been moving and started walking again. I followed in silence.

The night was cool, the air biting in a way that told me fall would soon be giving way to winter. The bare branches above us, as well as the thick layer of leaves covering the forest floor, only emphasized the point. Whatever happened, we needed to find a place before winter really set in, or we'd be in trouble.

Something scurried through the forest not too far from me, and I had to bite back a yelp. Every sound made me want to jump out of my skin. The crunch of leaves under our feet, the snap of a twig, the whistle of the wind as it moved through the trees. Every noise had my mind conjuring images of zombies rushing from the trees, snarling as they charged. The fact that I'd never seen one moving fast enough to be described as charging didn't matter, not being as terrified as I was, and not after barely escaping with our lives the night before. We'd been the only lucky ones, after all.

I stayed a couple steps behind Jacob since he was the one with the weapon, and it wasn't long before we emerged from the trees. There was a fence in front of us, and just beyond that a barn loomed, as well as a few other smaller buildings. One of them being the dark silhouette of a house. We were at the back of the farm, but even from here I could see the long fence stretching out in the distance. It was hard to tell in the little bit of light the moon had provided, but it looked as if the fence went around the entire property.

We paused to listen, but other than the occasional sounds of nature, the world was shockingly still. The roar of engines or hum of motors had disappeared, replaced by a quiet that felt threatening in its suffocating stillness. The house in front of us was no different. The windows were dark, reminding me of the empty eye sockets of a skull, and the silence hanging over the place made it seem almost forsaken.

"What do you think?" I asked, nodding to the house.

"We could rest." Jacob looked down at me, his gray eyes

holding mine. "Find some supplies and weapons. Maybe even a shotgun."

Yes, a shotgun would be more than handy.

"Let's do it," I whispered.

Jacob climbed the small fence, an easy feat for us, but something the dead wouldn't be able to do. Once he was over, I followed, holding on to the post at my side and sliding my foot into the holes in the metal so I could hoist myself up. When I had one leg over, Jacob helped me by taking my arm, and in a few seconds I was on the ground once again. Being inside the fence gave me a certain amount of security I hadn't felt in the woods, but it didn't wash away my unease completely.

For a few seconds, I stood and stared at the forest we'd just fled, listening and waiting, but still nothing moved. All last night and all day, we'd walked. We'd heard the evidence of the dead from time to time, such as a moan in the distance or a growl, even once a scream of agony as someone no doubt met a horrible end, but we hadn't seen anything ourselves. It was luck, I knew, and it wouldn't last forever. Eventually, our luck would run out. Which was why we needed somewhere safe, and not just for tonight.

"Robyn."

I started at the sound of Jacob's voice and tore my gaze from the woods so I could look at him.

He stood less than a foot from me, the baseball bat in one hand and the other extended to me. "It's okay."

I nodded and swallowed, trying to find words to express the feelings inside me. It was impossible. There were too many, and they were too foreign. Instead, I slipped my hand into his.

He held on to me as he started walking again, moving across the overgrown yard to the dark house. The property was big, with a couple large, fenced-in areas that might have once been for cows or horses. No animals were visible now, though, and considering how quiet it was, I doubted that there were any inside the barn either. The owners had probably released the animals when they realized the world was about to end. If not, they'd either died of starvation or had been taken away by other survivors. It was also entirely possible zombies had gotten them.

Every few minutes, Jacob would pause to listen and look around, but the only movement was the trees as they swayed with the wind, the only sounds nature. Insects buzzed through the night as if celebrating the fact that they alone didn't need to fear the dead, while branches clicked together and animals scurried through the darkness.

He dropped my hand when we made it to the front porch, and once again paused to listen and study our surroundings.

It was a stereotypical farmhouse. Two stories and white, with a porch running across the entire front of the house. The peeling paint on the railing was just visible in the moonlight, and it crumbled under my fingers as I headed up the stairs behind Jacob, falling to the ground in flakes that got lost in the darkness. A creak shattered the silence when Jacob put his foot on the third step, and my heart beat against my ribcage. I looked over my shoulder toward the forest as if expecting to see a horde rushing from the forest at the sound, but there was nothing. Just empty, desolate darkness.

I was still looking the other way when the squeak of hinges rang through the air.

"That's close enough," a gnarled voice said.

I spun back around just as a man stepped out of the house, shoving the screen door open with his foot. It swung back, hitting him in the hip, but he was too focused on us to seem to notice. In his hands, he held a shotgun, the barrel aimed at Jacob's chest.

"Whoa." Jacob raised his hands, the baseball bat in the right one. "We're unarmed."

"What do you call that?" The man jerked his head toward the pseudo-weapon, and the few wisps of white hair still clinging to his head fluttered in the night breeze.

Jacob dropped the bat, and it hit the wooden floor of the porch with a thud that echoed through the still night. Once again, I had the urge to look over my shoulder, but I forced my eyes to stay forward, choosing to focus on the very real and present threat instead of the possible ones lurking in the woods.

"We thought the house was empty," Jacob said.

"You thought wrong." The man took a step closer, and the screen door swung inward, bouncing twice before staying shut. Like the thud of the bat, the sound echoed through the night.

They were making entirely too much noise.

"You can just turn around and head on back the way you came." The shotgun remained steady in the man's hands even as he nodded toward the woods. "Go. Now."

"We can't," Jacob said, his voice surprisingly calm considering there was a weapon aimed at him.

"We don't have anywhere to go," I added, drawing the man's attention my way. "Our camp was overrun last night, and we had to leave everything behind to get away. We have nothing."

My voice broke on the final word, and I had to swallow down the tears threatening to force their way out. We'd been on the run all day, making it impossible to take even a moment to grieve what we'd lost. Not just our stuff, but everyone we knew in this new world of madness as well. Most of them we'd just met, but that didn't make the loss any less devastating. For weeks, we'd been together, working to make a go of it, and in that time, those strangers had become something like a family to me. Not the same as the one I'd lost, but a new kind that only this world of loss could forge.

But now they were gone. Everyone I'd ever known in the world was dead, except for Jacob.

The shotgun was still pointed at Jacob, but the man's blue eyes were focused on me. Despite the situation, sympathy shimmered in his expression, and understanding. It made hope bloom in my chest, and the longer we stood there waiting for him to say or do something, the more it grew and blossomed, spreading through me like a flower opening to the warmth of the spring sun.

He was going to help us. He had to.

"Where was your camp?" he asked, finally breaking the silence.

"We'd set up in an abandoned trailer park at the base of the mountains," Jacob responded, answering for me. "It was miles from here, though. We've been walking since last night. Must have crossed thirty miles by now."

I saw it when the man's determination faltered. He didn't lower the gun, but his stance did relax, and his expression softened enough to feed the hope inside me. He had a kind face and sympathetic eyes. Before all this, he probably would have been the type to offer help to anyone in need, the kind of person who would pull over to help a stranger change a flat tire. Things were different now, though. All too often, generosity was rewarded with violence.

Still, there was a part of this man that hadn't changed; I could see it in his eyes.

"Please," I said, not caring how desperate I sounded. "We've lost everything."

He only hesitated for a moment longer before saying, "Have you eaten today?"

My stomach audibly rumbled at the mention of food, and once again sympathy flickered the man's eyes.

"No," I said, my voice quiet, almost like I was afraid if I spoke louder he'd be able to hear the hope surging through me.

"Turn around," he waved the shotgun, "keep your arms up. Let me see if you're armed."

I complied, lifting my arms and turning so he could look me over. When I was once again facing the man, he focused on Jacob, nodding for him to do the same. He did, keeping his arms raised as he spun. His eyes captured mine when his back was to the man, and I could see my own hope reflected in them. We'd known one another for so long that I was familiar with every one of his moods, every one of his expressions, could even finish his sentences at times.

The man finally lowered his gun when Jacob was once again facing him.

"I can fill your bellies, can offer you a place to lay your head tonight, but that's all. Tomorrow you'll need to be on your way. Understand?"

My heart sank even as gratitude rushed through me. It was more than a lot of people would have done, even before the outbreak, and more than I'd expected when he stepped out of the house holding a shotgun. Not more than I'd hoped, but it wasn't like I was in any position to make demands.

"Thank you," I said, the words coming out in a rush. "You have no idea how much we appreciate it."

The man nodded once. "It's the Christian thing to do."

He turned and grabbed the screen door, and like when he'd stepped out, the hinges creaked in protest. This time, I didn't resist the urge to look behind me, but like before, the night was as empty as it was dark.

"Come on in, now," the man said, moving into the house.

Jacob swept his baseball bat up of the porch before following him, and I was only a step behind.

The interior of the house wasn't as dark as it had looked from the yard. Candles and lanterns were set up throughout, their flickering light helping guide our way as we followed the man. It wasn't enough to illuminate every corner, but it was enough to allow me to get a good look around. Like the outside, the interior of the home looked like every farmhouse I'd ever seen on television. Wood floors and old, rustic furniture. White doilies sitting under antique lamps, and floral wallpaper that had gone out of style more than two decades ago. Still, it was warm and clean and welcoming, which was all I wanted at this point. Hell, clean wasn't even a requirement. Not anymore.

The man led us through a sitting room, and in the flickering candlelight, I saw that the windows had been covered with plywood, making it impossible for even a glimmer of light to escape, which was why the place had looked so deserted from outside. Smart.

We stopped when we reached the kitchen. Three other people—all women—looked up from a sturdy oak table where what could only be described as a feast had been laid out. Plates of fried chicken and biscuits sat beside bowls of mashed potatoes and green beans, all of it fresh and hot, and the aroma wafting from the food made my mouth fill with saliva.

"We have guests," the man told the others, nodding to us.

"Hi," I did my best to focus on the people and not the steaming food, "I'm Robyn, and this is Jacob."

A woman around the same age as the man offered me a welcoming smile as she stood, pushing her chair back as she did. "Bekah. How very lovely to meet you." She waved to the empty seats in front of us. "Sit, please. Grab a couple extra plates, Denise."

A woman in her twenties stood but said nothing. She kept her head down, her dark hair shielding her face from view as she hurried across the room, and something about her gave off the impression of a frightened animal that had been cornered by prey. What, though, I couldn't tell for sure.

I slipped into a chair, as did Jacob, but neither of us spoke.

"Looks like you folks got here just in time," the man said as he leaned his gun against the wall.

"Looks like it," I replied as Denise returned, a clean plate in each hand.

Once again, she kept her head down.

"Thank you," Jacob said as he took them, passing one to me.

The girl didn't even smile in reply.

"Really, Henry?" Bekah frowned at the shotgun. "In the kitchen?"

"I keep telling you, Bek, it's a different world now." Henry slid into a chair across from his wife with a groan. "Can't be too careful nowadays."

She clicked her tongue, shaking her head. "I don't like it, Henry. I just don't."

He grunted in response as he filled his plate with food but said nothing else.

Beside him sat a girl in her late teens. She picked up the plate of chicken, offering it to me as she said, "Don't mind them. We've had this same conversation at every meal for the past month." She rolled her eyes. "I'm Janice."

"Nice to meet you," I said, taking the plate. "And thank you."

"My sister, Denise," she jerked her head to the other girl.

Her head stayed down, but her eyes flicked up. They were large and round, and such a dark brown that they almost looked black. It was the expression in them that drew me in, though. Fear like I'd never seen before—and we'd seen plenty of fear over the last few months—shimmered in them as she ventured a look at Jacob before once again lowering her gaze to her plate. It made everything in me clench tight. Something very horrible had happened to this girl.

As much as the expression rattled me, I couldn't be distracted from the food for very long, especially not with a plate of steaming fried chicken in my hands.

I used my fork to spear a piece—not the breast, even though that was the one I wanted—then passed the plate to Jacob. Unlike me, he plucked the larger piece of meat off the top of the pile without hesitating, and I took a quick look around to see if anyone had noticed or cared. Everyone was busy digging in, their focus thankfully on their own chicken. Good. I didn't want to do anything that might make Henry change his mind. Even if I only got to spend one night in a real bed, I would take it.

I took a little of everything, resisting the urge to create a mashed potato mountain on my plate, but just like with the chicken, Jacob had no qualms about dishing himself huge portions. He even took a second biscuit after stuffing the first one in his mouth—all of it at once. I'd always liked his boldness, had even admired it, but at the moment, I wished he'd knock it off. We were guests.

For a few moments, the only sounds in the kitchen were the clink of silverware against plates and the sounds of chewing, but it didn't take long for Bekah to clear her throat.

"You must have had a rough go of it." She nodded to my shirt.

I didn't need to look down to know it was filthy, but I did. The pits were moist with sweat, and dirt was streaked everywhere. There was even a rip in the side, revealing a sliver of pink skin. Worse than the dirt and sweat, though, was the rust colored stain splashed across the bottom. Blood. I'd been right there when it happened, chatting with Marjorie while we hung clothes on the line to dry when the zombie had come out of nowhere. He'd had her before we knew what was happening, had sunk his teeth into her neck. Her screams of agony had been echoed by someone else's on the other side of camp, and more had followed. After that, chaos had rained down around me, and for a moment I'd been too stunned to move. If not for Jacob, I didn't know if I would have gotten out of there. He'd grabbed my arm and pulled me from the camp, hitting anything that got in our way with the bat he'd somehow managed to grab. He'd saved me.

"We did," he said, answering for me. "But we made it out, and that's the important part."

When he put his hand on top of mine, the warmth and familiarity of his touch helped push the horror away. But only a little. I was still staring at that rust colored stain, still remembering the way Marjorie's blood sprayed from the wound in her neck and splashed across my shirt.

"What's it like out there?" Janice asked.

"Horrible," I said, my voice a whisper.

I tore my gaze from the stain and focused on my plate, trying to think about anything but my friend's agonizing death or the way I'd run off without even trying to help, but the mashed potatoes that had been so appetizing a second ago now looked like a pile of mush. Why hadn't I done anything to help her? And not just her. I hadn't tried to help anyone. I'd run with Jacob, not looking back for a second, intent on saving my own ass even at the expense of others. All day as we'd walked, I'd told myself we were the only survivors, but the truth was, we had no idea. We didn't stick around long enough to find out.

What kind of person did that?

"There aren't many people left," Jacob was saying, "that's for sure. And the zombies are everywhere. You can't avoid them."

Denise said nothing, but she lifted her eyes from her plate, and they were wide with terror.

"We haven't had much news all the way out here," Henry explained. "In the beginning, after the power went out, we would hear things from time to time. From neighbors or people passing through. Haven't seen anyone but you two in a while now. More than a month, I'd say."

"Is there anything out there?" Janice asked, her voice small but slightly hopeful. "The government, I mean."

"If there is, we never saw it," Jacob said.

The women acted like a bomb had been dropped. Denise covered her face in her hands, while Bekah looked down, and Janice's eyes filled with tears. At the head of the table, Henry shook his head.

147

Jacob shoved a spoonful of mashed potatoes into his mouth, seemingly unaware that his statement had impacted these people so much.

"We're in a very secluded area, though," I said. "Who knows what's out there."

"Yes." Henry nodded like he was trying to cling to the words. "That's right. In the cities, things could be different."

We lapsed into silence once again, and I went back to picking at my food. Despite the atmosphere, my stomach rebounded better than I'd thought it would, and all it took was one nibble of chicken for it to rumble with need. I hadn't eaten anything in more than twenty-four hours, and this was the best meal I'd had since well before the virus. Food had gotten scarce so fast, and even before the electricity went out, we were scrounging and rationing, living on canned soup and ramen. This seemed like a dream. Chicken and mashed potatoes, biscuits and fresh green beans. Where had it all come from, and how had they managed it?

"How do you have all this?" I pulled a strip of crispy skin off the chicken and plopped it into my mouth, nodding to the food in front of me.

"Generator," Henry said around a mouthful of mashed potatoes, earning another disapproving look from Bekah. He swallowed before continuing. "We turn it on for a couple hours each day, before it gets dark and after we've finished with the animals. I butchered this guy this afternoon." He waved his chicken leg in the air. "He's going to be the only meat for a week, though. Need to ration."

I shot Jacob a look, hoping he'd get the point and not get himself a second serving of chicken.

"We didn't hear any animals." He sank his teeth into the

meat, taking a big bite and chewing as if Henry's words had not impacted him in the least.

"I did what I could to soundproof the barn." Henry nodded to Denise. "Even had a helper."

The girl still hadn't uttered a word, and I was starting to wonder if she was able to talk. I didn't know if it was something medical or if she'd gone mute from trauma, though. That kind of stuff happened, didn't it? A person, usually a kid, witnessed something horrific and stopped talking?

"They're your granddaughters?" I asked Henry.

"Yes." Bekah reached out and covered Denise's hand with hers, but the girl didn't lift her head. "They had to travel all the way across the country to get here, but they made it."

"Barely," Janice mumbled.

Her grandmother shot her a frown, and Denise looked away.

"What about you?" Bekah asked, looking from me to Jacob.

Since he was still chowing down, I set my fork on my plate and said, "We grew up together. Next door neighbors, and have been together since we were fifteen. Almost ten years now." When I looked at him, Jacob was staring at me, and I knew I might be the only thing in the entire world that could have distracted him from the delicious food at the moment. That was how strong our love was. How strong our bond had always been. "Our families all died. Everyone, but we somehow got lucky."

"Us too," Bekah said, pulling my gaze from the love of my life. She was staring at Henry. "So many people died, but somehow we survived. I thank God every day."

Her husband gave her an understanding smile.

"And the girls." Bekah patted Denise's hand, which was still under hers. "They survived the virus and beat the odds by making it across the country to us after their parents died. We have a lot to be grateful for."

Her granddaughter looked down, and while I couldn't see the expression on her face, I had a feeling she didn't always feel so grateful to be alive.

Silence fell over the table after that, broken only by the sounds of dinner. I focused on my food, doing my best not to think about the damaged girl across from me and what she might have gone through.

Next to me, Jacob ate, his gaze moving about the room in quiet contemplation. For probably the first time in more than a decade, I couldn't decipher what he was thinking, though. It felt like he was taking stock, perhaps making a mental list of everything these people had, but why? Henry had said we could only stay the night, but maybe Jacob was hoping to convince him otherwise. Maybe he was trying to figure out what he could say to the older man that would make our presence on the farm desirable.

After dinner, Denise hurried from the room like being here was painful, and Janice went after her, sighing like this had become routine and she was exhausted by the effort.

"How about a little tour?" Jacob said to Henry. "I'd love to see the animals."

The older man's eyebrows lifted in surprise, but he nodded. "I need to check in on them, anyway. The fence keeps the dead out, but we've had some issues with coyotes getting in the barn."

"Perfect," Jacob said with more enthusiasm than I'd heard in his voice for a long time.

Henry grabbed his shotgun and gave his wife a small nod

before waving toward the door. Jacob followed, pausing long enough to plant a kiss on my check.

His voice was low when he said, "I promised I'd get you somewhere safe."

He was gone before I could decipher the meaning of his words.

Once the men had left, I grabbed a couple plates off the table and took them to Bekah, who was standing at the sink. "Thanks for dinner."

"It was my pleasure." She gave me a sympathetic smile as she took the dirty plates from me. "I don't know how much longer we'll be able to eat like this. Once we run out of things like flour, it's going to be back to the basics." She shook her head, her eyes on the bowl of soapy water in front of her as she washed away the remnants of the meal we'd just had. "I already miss baking."

Once it was clean and rinsed, she set it on the counter. When I snatched it up and dried it off, she gave me a grateful smile.

"There's a lot to miss," I replied.

"That there is," she said with a nod.

She dipped another plate into the water.

"Where do you get it?" I asked. "The water, I mean."

"Oh, we have a well. It was electric, but we thankfully still had the old manual pump as well," she replied, as if was the simplest thing in the world, having running water.

It seemed like they had everything a person could need at the end of the world.

"How are you guys on food?" I set the dry plate down and picked up the next one. "I mean, this meal was amazing. I was pretty sure I'd never eat like this again, but are you well stocked on food?"

"We are." Bekah shot me a grin, a mischievous twinkle in her hazel eyes. "Not only am I an obsessive canner, but we also raided the homes of a few neighboring farms that had been abandoned. We got a pretty good haul."

"Lucky you," I said, and I couldn't help feeling a little bitter.

It wasn't fair, thinking about how much these people had when some of us were literally empty-handed. Especially when they wouldn't even consider sharing it.

"Henry says you two will be heading out tomorrow," Bekah said, her gaze flitting toward me as she scrubbed at a fork.

"Yes." I almost left it at that, but I couldn't help myself. She had a very laid-back demeanor that made talking to her easy, and with a full belly and the prospect of sleeping in a real bed, I found myself desperate to do something, anything, to convince these people to let us stay. "I mean, we would be happy to stay and help out around the place. I'm sure you're busy trying to keep up with everything."

"It is time-consuming running this place with almost no electricity." She pressed her lips together, eyeing me for a moment before asking, "Did Henry say you had to go?"

"He did," I admitted, doing my best to sound hesitant.

"I should have known." She clicked her tongue as she went back to washing, and I scooped up the clean dishes so I could dry them. "Ever since the girls got here, he's been overly protective. They went through some things on the road, Denise especially, and Henry is determined to keep them safe. I'm actually shocked to my core that he let you into the house at all. You must have seemed trustworthy."

"We are," I said in a hurry. "Very."

"Oh, I know." She waved a wet hand toward me, and a few soapy drops of water hit me in the face. "It's in the eyes."

"Well, I understand Henry's hesitation." I put the clean and dry silverware into the waiting drawer and brushed the drops of water from my face before scooping up more. "But if he could just give it a try, he might find that having us around is helpful."

"I'll talk to him about it," Bekah said and rolled her eyes, "although you saw the weight he gives my opinion. I've been on him to keep the shotgun in the other room for weeks, but he insists on bringing it to dinner. Makes my blood boil."

I knew she was trying to make a joke, maybe lessen the dark mood hanging over me, but I couldn't take any of this lightly.

"Thank you," I said. "Whatever you can do, I appreciate it."

Bekah only smiled.

We finished up the dishes and cleaned the counters together, chatting about nothing in particular. Bekah was nice, but there was something about her that bugged me. For months, the world had been chaos, but the woman at my side didn't seem to understand that. It was like the walls and fence surrounding us now had acted as a protective barrier, effectively blocking out all the horror of this new world. Even whatever her granddaughter had gone through hadn't been able to pierce the bubble surrounding her.

Not only was it naïve, but it was dangerous as well. You couldn't take anything for granted these days, because there was no real safety. Even if the dead couldn't get in—which, let's face it, was questionable at best—there were other things to worry about. Denise should have been proof of that.

"I need to head down to the cellar to grab some food for morning." Bekah opened a door on the other side of the room, revealing a set of stairs that descended into darkness. "Want to join me?"

"Sure." I'd been dying to head out to the barn since Jacob and Henry left, curious what these people had, but this would have to do.

A flashlight held in her hand, Bekah headed down. The beam illuminated the stairs in front of us, as well as the stone walls of the stairwell. Soon, though, the walls gave way, and the cellar came into view. It was old and musty, the air damp the way old, underground rooms tended to be, but big. A now mostly useless washer and dryer sat on one side of the room, as well as several plastic bins that probably held things like Christmas decorations. It was the other side of the room that had all my attention, though. Every wall was lined with shelves, all of them brimming with jars of preserved food. Pickles, beets, carrots, green beans, and potatoes, as well as fruit and jams. There had to be hundreds of them.

"Wow," I said, and even though my stomach was still full from dinner, my mouth filled with saliva as I thought about the days we'd gone hungry since all this started.

"I can't lie, knowing we have this is a real comfort." She said it casually, the way only a person who had never gone hungry could. "And when spring comes, we'll plant even more."

What was the old saying about the rich getting richer? I couldn't remember exactly, but it was the only thing I could think about as she selected a jar off the shelf and inspected it thoughtfully. They had all this, and when spring came, they would have even more. Meanwhile, who knew where Jacob and I would be. Dead, if we didn't find somewhere to go.

"You like applesauce?" Bekah asked, showing me the jar.

I didn't, but that was the thing about the apocalypse. There wasn't anything edible that I would turn my nose up anymore.

"Yes," I responded instead of telling her that.

With two jars in her arms, she turned her back on the food. "Good."

I kept my gaze on the food until she'd turned the beam of the flashlight toward the stairs and the shelves were swallowed up by darkness.

We headed up in silence, finding Janice in the kitchen, munching on one of the leftover biscuits. She couldn't possibly be hungry, not after the feast we'd just had, and yet here she was, chowing down like the world hadn't ended and food wasn't an issue. I had to swallow my bitterness.

"How's your sister?" Bekah asked as she set the jars on the counter.

Janice shrugged. "Same."

Her grandmother only shook her head in response.

The creak of the door opening in the other room pulled my focus from them, and footsteps followed. Despite the feeling of safety being in this house brought, I couldn't stop my pulse from quickening as I waited to see who it was. Odds were it was only Henry and Jacob, but things had been too uncertain for too long, and I was hardwired now to be ready just in case. In case of zombies, in case of assholes who wanted to steal and kill and rape. Really, anything could happen these days.

If only I had a weapon.

A second later, Henry appeared in the doorway, with Jacob right behind him, and I was able to relax.

"Animals all tucked in for the night?" Bekah asked, not even bothering to look at her husband.

"They are." He leaned his shotgun against the wall.

"It's a pretty impressive group of animals you have out there," Jacob said. "Can't lie, I'm more than a little jealous."

His gaze met mine, and the expression in his eyes mirrored everything I'd been thinking. Why did these people deserve so much while we had nothing?

"We've definitely fared better than most," Henry said as if it was no big deal.

I was starting to get irritated by how blasé these people acted.

———

"I HOPE THIS IS OKAY." Bekah had a pitcher of warm water in one hand, and she used her free one to push the bedroom door open.

The hinges groaned in protest as it swung inward, revealing a simple bedroom. There wasn't much in it—an old bed with a white canopy and matching coverlet, two nightstands, and a dresser—but it was more than we needed. A change of clothes for each of us had also been set out on the bed. Mine borrowed from Denise, most likely, while Jacob would have to do with some of Henry's clothes. Again, I wasn't going to complain. At this point, I was more than aware of how lucky we were just to be alive.

"It's perfect," I told her. "Thank you."

Jacob, who was carrying a candle, had already moved into the room and set it on the nightstand before kicking his shoes off. I almost cringed when he threw himself onto the bed. He was so dirty. We both were.

"I don't know about perfect, but it's something, at least." An antique bowl that matched the pitcher in Bekah's hands sat on top of the dresser, which she set beside it, smiling. "And you'll be able to get clean."

I returned her smile. "Thank you. Really."

"Have a good rest," she said, shutting the door behind her.

Once she was gone, Jacob lugged himself off the bed and started to strip. "God, I can't wait to go to sleep."

"I can't wait to get clean," I replied as I, too, began removing my clothes.

A couple towels and washcloths, as well as a bar of soap, sat next to the bowl, which I took full advantage of. My skin was grimy with dirt and sweat, and my hair greasy, and even though it took some time to get washed up, I'd never felt so thrilled to be clean.

"Your turn," I said, turning to Jacob.

He took my place while I slipped into the bed, pulling the blanket up to my chin. The room was drafty the way old houses tended to be, but no more so than the trailer we'd been sleeping in for weeks had been, and the mattress and pillows were plush and welcoming. After a day on the road, running for our lives, being in this bed felt like a dream come true.

Once Jacob had cleaned up, he blew the candle out and slid in beside me, and I snuggled up against him, savoring his warm body against mine in the soft bed.

"I can't believe we found this place," I murmured to him. "If only we didn't have to go."

He wrapped me in his arms, pulling my body against his. "This place really is a goldmine. I mean, they have everything they need and more. I don't even think they realize how lucky they are, and for Henry to not even consider sharing it. It's just fucking greedy."

His words echoed my thoughts from earlier in the kitchen.

Listening to the offhand way Bekah had talked about everything they had, watching Janice stuff her face without even a thought about the future.

"Maybe he'll change his mind?" I said.

"Maybe," Jacob replied, but his voice was filled with doubt.

I twisted so I was facing him. "Can you imagine what we could do in a place like this? The life we could have? We'd have everything we needed. Eggs and milk, not to mention all the food in the basement. You should have seen it. There are hundreds of jars. They even have a well with a hand pump. We could be safe here, Jacob. We could have a life."

"Yeah." He exhaled, and even though I couldn't see him, I could tell he was thinking something through.

"What?" I asked. "What are you thinking?"

"We could just take it, you know."

I had no idea what he was talking about. "Take it?"

"Yeah. By force. I mean, Henry and Bekah are old. They'd be no problem, and Janice is young and small. Then there's Denise. She's... Well, I don't even know what she is, but I know we could do it. Then all this would be ours."

For a moment, I said nothing, trying to understand what he was talking about. What did he mean by *they'd be no problem*? He couldn't be talking about killing them, could he? Jacob wouldn't even consider something like that.

"You're not talking about killing them, are you?"

"Listen to me, Robyn, the world is different now. Everything is different. The rules from before don't apply, and the laws are gone. This is a kill or be killed world now, literally, and if we want to survive this, if we want to have the life we've always wanted, we're going to have to accept the truth. We have to be brutal."

"I can't believe you're saying this." I twisted from his grasp. "I want to stay, too, but not like that. I want Henry to change his mind. There's enough to go around, and he has to see that."

"Yes, there is, but think about this. All the food and animals will only go so far with six people, but if it was just the two of us, it would stretch so much farther, last so much longer. And we'd be smarter than them, we'd ration it because we know firsthand what it's like to go hungry."

It was like he'd read my mind, but I still couldn't fully accept what he was saying. He was talking about murder.

"I can't kill anyone, Jacob," I whispered.

"Think about it, will you?" He sighed like he was frustrated with me. "We're going to have to take the things we need or we won't get through this."

"And that means killing people?"

"It means doing whatever we have to."

"You're tired," I said, "you're not thinking straight. Get some sleep, and we'll talk about it in the morning."

Jacob sighed again, but he didn't argue.

I rolled onto my side so I was facing away from him, curling up as if trying to protect myself from his words. It was too late, though. I'd heard them, and now I'd never be able to unhear them. Never be able to go back to a time when Jacob, the man I'd loved for almost as long as I could remember, had uttered those horrible things.

Even worse, I couldn't stop thinking about them, only I wasn't thinking about what they implied, but what we would gain if I embraced them.

THE WOOD PLANK covering the window made it impossible for me to see outside when I woke, but I instinctively knew it was morning. In the distance, the creak of floorboards as someone walked around in one of the other rooms was audible, but otherwise, the house was silent.

I rolled over and found Jacob still asleep. His words from the night before came back to me, and I rolled them around in my head while I studied his face. His expression was more placid in sleep, and for the first time it occurred to me how much he'd changed since everything happened. First the virus, which killed most of the world, including everyone we knew and loved, leaving us alone. Then the dead had returned, and we'd had to fight our way out of the city. We headed to the mountains, believing they would provide more safety, and for a while they had, but that, too, had come to an end.

Jacob had hardened a little more after each major event, the softness I'd always loved about him giving way until very little of it remained. I'd thought it would return once things settled down, that all we would have to do was find a safe place, and the man I'd known before would reemerge. That I would somehow be able to peel that tough outer layer off the way I did the shell of a hardboiled egg. After last night, I wasn't so sure.

Even more unsettling was the sudden realization that I had changed, too. I hadn't thought about it before now, but it was true. Bekah was a perfectly nice woman, friendly and easy to talk to, generous, and yet I'd watched her move about her tasks last night with bitterness, criticizing everything she did. It was something I never would have done before, just like I never would have begrudged another person's good luck. Now, though, bad luck meant death, and I couldn't help thinking

Jacob had a point. In the apocalypse, you had to create your own luck.

Still, I couldn't condone murder, and I didn't believe he would ever really go through with anything like that. Thinking about it was one thing. Yes, even I had daydreamed about what we could do if we were allowed to stay on the farm, and even thought, in a moment of bitter jealousy, that Bekah was taking all of this for granted, and that Henry didn't deserve this place if he wasn't willing to share. That didn't mean I would do anything about it, though. It was just a thought, nothing more.

I slid out of bed, careful to be quiet so I didn't wake Jacob. It was early, still, meaning I had time to convince Henry he was making a mistake. Bekah had promised me she'd talk to him, and even if she couldn't get her husband to stop bringing the shotgun into the kitchen, that didn't mean he wouldn't listen to her about this. He had to see the benefit of having two more sets of hands on the farm.

After I'd dressed, I slipped into the hallway, careful to shut the door quietly so I didn't disturb Jacob. The door across from ours was cracked open, and through it I could see Denise. She was lying on the bed, her eyes open and staring blankly at the ceiling. I looked up, wondering what she was staring at, but there was nothing. Not even a light fixture.

Poor girl.

I found Janice in the kitchen, humming to herself as she kneaded some dough. She looked up when I entered, not stopping her happy tune but still shooting me a smile. She had flour on her cheek and dusted across her shirt, and there was more sprinkled on the floor at her feet. I couldn't stop thinking about what a waste it was. They should have been more careful.

It wasn't like before when you could run off to the grocery store and grab another bag of flour.

"Your grandma around?" I asked the girl.

"Barn," she said before going back to humming.

The early morning sun was bright but the air chilly when I stepped out. Moisture gleamed on the overgrown grass and weeds choking the yard, and in the distance the bare trees swayed in the wind. I paused and cocked my ears, straining to catch any unusual sounds, but heard nothing. If the dead were out there, they were being quiet.

I found Bekah in the barn, a basket in her hand as she shooed chickens so she could collect their eggs. They clucked in protest and rushed to get out of her way, flapping their wings and sending a few feathers flying into the air. The chicken coop was bigger than I expected and surrounded by wire on all sides, as well as on top so the birds couldn't escape. There were dozens of birds, and at the sight of them, the memory of how good the fried chicken had tasted the night before came rushing back.

The other side of the massive barn was lined with stalls, holding cows and horses and goats, as well as other animals I couldn't see from where I stood. The stink of animal excrement hung heavy in the air, but compared to the stench of death that had fallen over most of the world, it was only mildly unpleasant. The city, before we'd fled it, had reeked of decay. Just thinking about it turned my stomach inside out.

"Morning!" Bekah called from inside the chicken coop. "I hope you slept well."

"I did, thank you."

I paused outside the wire and watched as she reached into a little alcove to retrieve a brown egg.

"Now that you're up, I'll make you some breakfast." She held the egg up. "Hungry?"

"Starving," I said, forcing out a smile.

"Good." Bekah slipped out of the chicken coop and latched the door. "I just milked the cows, so we'll have fresh milk in addition to eggs."

It had been more than two months since I'd had milk, and these people had an endless supply of it. Not only did they have the cows, but the goats as well.

I had to get them to let us stay. Somehow.

I opened my mouth to ask Bekah if she'd spoken with Henry, but chickened out at the last second and said, "How was your night?"

"It was fine." She headed for the door, motioning for me to follow. "Although I got less sleep than I would have liked. Henry snores like a bear."

I forced out a laugh, but it was strained. Less sleep than she liked? She had to be kidding, right? Jacob and I had spent an entire day on our feet searching for safety, and she was complaining about a little snoring.

"It's a good thing you have walls around you," I found myself saying in a slightly bitter tone. "These days, snoring is a safety hazard."

"True." She shot me a look when we left the barn, heading for the house, but I wasn't sure if it was my biting tone or something else. "We had a nice, long chat last night."

Hope sprung up inside. "You did?"

"We did. He's going to take a little more convincing, but I think he's warming to the idea. We're not exactly spring chickens, and we have the girls to worry about now." She pushed her salt and pepper hair out of her face with her free hand. "Denise, especially, worries me."

"We can help," I added. "With anything you need."

"You don't have to sell me on the idea," Bekah said with a grin. "It's Henry who is hesitant."

All the bitterness I'd felt toward this woman since meeting her melted away, and guilt twisted inside me. How could I have looked at her and seen anything but generosity? Hadn't she done everything to make us comfortable since the second we set foot in her house? Hadn't she been welcoming?

"Thank you," I said as tears sprang to my eyes.

"Don't thank me until you've spoken with Henry," she replied. "It's up to him."

"Where is he now?" I said in a rush.

Bekah waved toward the house. "Fiddling with the generator. I honestly don't know how much longer the thing is going to work." She shook her head, frowning. "We're going to need a new one."

"Jacob and I can take care of that. We'd be happy to."

Bekah elbowed me, her grin returning. "Now *that* is a very convincing proposal."

"I'll talk to him now."

"Just don't take too long, or your breakfast will get cold." She waved the basket of eggs.

"I won't," I said, slowing so I could break off and head in the other direction.

Bekah waved over her shoulder and continued, saying nothing. I turned on my heel and jogged toward the back of the house, my heart thudding twice as hard as usual. The hope that had blossomed yesterday as Jacob and I stood on the porch grew, sprouting roots and finding a home inside me. It was really going to happen. We were going to be able to stay. I just knew it.

I turned the corner and spotted Henry messing with the generator. We were at the very back of the house. He was at the opposite corner from me, and I slowed so I could work out what I was going to say. There had to be a way to convince him.

I was still thinking it through when the zombie came around the corner of the house only five feet behind Henry. The old man was on his knees, his focus so intent on this task that there was no way he noticed the creature stumbling toward him.

I started running. "Henry!"

He looked up, frowning, and when he saw me running toward him, his eyebrows jumped in surprise. The zombie was practically on top of him now, and I waved my arms, unable to find the words to warn him. He must have gotten the point, though, because he turned just as the zombie was reaching for him.

Henry stumbled away, falling onto his back. The zombie lunged, but the old man managed to deflect him with a kick to the stomach, sending the creature back. Henry was empty-handed. The shotgun was on the ground beside the generator, out of his reach. I wouldn't be able to get to it either, because the zombie was in the way, and I was as empty-handed as the old man.

My gaze scanned the area as I ran, landing on the screwdriver Henry had been using. It was on the ground, too far away for him to get, but close enough for me.

"I'm coming!" I called, managing to find my voice as I ran, my focus on the tool.

Henry didn't have time to reply, because the zombie was on him again. This time, when the older man kicked, his boot made contact with the creature's leg. Instead of sending him back, he fell on top of Henry. I was a few feet away, but I pumped my legs harder. The zombie and Henry were struggling, fighting. There wasn't much time.

Finally, I reached the screwdriver and swiped it up off the ground. Then I grabbed the zombie's shirt, yanking it as hard as I could, and I dragged the flailing creature back, away from Henry. The rip of fabric was barely audible over the growls from the zombie, but it was loud enough to tell me the shirt was tearing. I had to make a move. Releasing the shirt, I allowed the still struggling zombie to fall. Once he was down, I pounced. Holding the screwdriver up like it was a knife, I slammed my foot against the creature's neck to hold him still, then slammed the sharp point of the tool through his eye and into his brain.

He stopped moving, and I stumbled back, gasping as I stared down at the now dead zombie.

"Robyn," Henry said from behind me.

He was still on the ground when I spun. I scanned him, searching for blood, but he looked okay.

"Did he get you?" I asked anyway. "No scratches, no bites?"

Henry shook his head, but still didn't stand. "Thanks to you."

"I'm glad I could help. Really."

He hauled himself to his feet, brushing the dirt from his hands and pants, his gaze on the dead thing at my back. His brows were furrowed, his expression thoughtful.

"What is it?" I asked when he said nothing.

Henry looked at me. "If you hadn't been here, I would be dead."

"You might have been able to fight him off."

He gave me a doubtful look. "I don't know about that, but I

do know there are a lot of these things in the woods." As if expecting them to materialize, he focused on the trees in the distance. "Maybe having two more sets of eyes around the place wouldn't be all that bad."

For a moment, I couldn't react, then what he was implying slammed into me, and a smile broke out across my face. "Are you saying you've changed your mind?"

Henry looked at me again. "I am. You and Jacob are young and hardworking. We need that around here if we're going to make a go of this place. Even more importantly, you deserve a chance to survive."

"Thank you!" Tears filled my eyes, and without thinking, I threw my arms around him. "Thank you. You won't regret this."

He chuckled and returned the hug. "I certainly hope not."

I'd just pulled away when Jacob rounded the corner of the house.

"Guess what?" I said, my wide smile making my cheeks ache. "Henry says we can stay."

Jacob blinked, the surprise in his expression obvious. "He said what?"

"You can stay." At my side, the old man's face stretched into a smile. "If you want to, that is."

"Oh, we want to," I said with a laugh.

Jacob, however, didn't react. He didn't smile, didn't say anything. He didn't even blink. He just stared at Henry like he'd never seen the man before. Something in his expression sent a shiver shooting through me, but I couldn't figure out what it was. I knew Jacob so well, and this wasn't the reaction I would have expected from him. In fact, I'd never seen him act like this.

"Jacob?" I took a step toward him, but froze when I noticed

the knife in his hand. The blade was stained red and there was some on his hand, even a few drops on his shirt.

My gaze flicked back to his face, and suddenly I understood why he looked like a stranger to me. Because he was. The man standing in front of me couldn't have been the man I'd fallen in love with, because that Jacob would never have done the things I suspected this man of doing. The man I'd fallen in love with was kind and sweet. He gave money to homeless people and volunteered at animal shelters on the weekend. He ran marathons for charity. He didn't—couldn't have—done something like this...

"What have you done?" I asked.

Henry looked from me to Jacob, his gaze finally landing on the bloody knife. A look of confusion crossed his face, followed quickly by understanding, and anger.

"No," he said, taking a step toward Jacob, then stopping.

His gaze moved to the house, his mouth hanging open like he had forgotten how to talk. Then he started running.

"Bekah! Denise! Janice!" he called, his voice trembling. "Bekah!"

Henry disappeared around the side of the house and I turned to face Jacob. "What did you do?"

"I told you," he said, "things have changed. The world is different now, and if we want to survive, we're going to need to be different too. There's no room for sympathy. We need to be brutal."

The calm way he said the words sent a shiver down my spine. This couldn't be real. This couldn't be happening.

"He changed his mind," I said, my voice trembling with emotion. "He was going to let us stay."

"It doesn't matter," Jacob replied. "I'd do it again, because it needed to be done."

An agonized howl echoed through the yard.

Jacob looked toward the front of the house. "He found them."

"I can't believe you did this." My body shook, and I wrapped my arms around myself, trying not to fall apart. "You killed them. How could you?"

Jacob looked back at me. "I did it for us."

"I didn't want this. You had to know that!" I shouted.

My words bounced off the side of the house and came back to taunt me.

"One day, you'll thank me," was all he said.

My mouth fell open, and my body shook with silent sobs.

"I'll kill you!" Henry was yelling as he rounded the corner, rushing toward us.

He was empty-handed, but Jacob still had the knife. He raised it and planted his feet, waiting for the other man to reach him. He was going to kill him just like he'd killed his wife and granddaughters, only this time I was going to have to watch it happen. I would see him cut the man who'd offered us food and comfort and a place to stay open, have to watch him bleed out.

I couldn't watch it.

I looked away from the men in front of me, and my gaze landed on the shotgun. It was still on the ground where Henry had left it, right next to the generator and less than a foot away from me.

Without thinking, I swept it up off the ground and turned it on the men. "Stop!"

Henry was ten feet away and still running when Jacob turned to face me.

"What are you doing?" he asked.

"Put the knife down," I said. "Now."

"Robyn, you're not thinking this through."

"Yes," I said, "I am." I took a step closer to him, shotgun aimed at his chest. "Now put it down."

Jacob's gaze held mine as he considered his options. Henry, whose face was streaked in tears, had slowed but hadn't stopped. He was five feet behind Jacob now.

"You won't shoot me," my boyfriend said.

My legs trembled, but I moved my finger to the trigger. "Don't test me, Jacob."

"Say I put the knife down, what happens to me then?" He looked over his shoulder toward Henry, who had stopped walking now, then back to me. "You think he'll let this go? He won't, Robyn, and you know it. He'll kill me, which means I'm dead either way."

He was right, and the realization made my legs wobble even more.

But what did I expect to happen? Jacob had killed Henry's entire family, and that couldn't go unpunished. I shouldn't have wanted it to. He had to pay for what he'd done. Didn't he?

"The world is different," Jacob said, repeating the words he'd whispered to me the night before. "We have to be brutal."

"We don't have to be," I said, suddenly wondering who I was trying to convince. Jacob or myself.

"We do if we want to survive." He took a step toward Henry. "Think about it, Robyn. Think about what we'll be gaining. Think about all the things we talked about last night."

Henry looked toward me with silent accusations in his wide eyes.

"Don't," I said, my voice rising, my legs shaking, tears blurring his face. "Please."

Jacob took another step in the older man's direction. "I'll make it fast."

Henry looked from me to Jacob and then back again, his gaze holding mine. I blinked, and tears rolled down my cheeks. The shotgun was still pointed at Jacob, who now had his back to me and was advancing on Henry. The older man didn't look at him, though; he was too focused on me. Everything Jacob and I had talked about the night before echoed through my head, and just like then, I couldn't help thinking about the life we could have here. It was within my reach, too. But at what cost? What Jacob had done, what he was asking me to allow to happen, was wrong. Immoral. The world had changed, but had it changed so much that something like this was justifiable?

"We are going to have to take the things we need, or we won't get through this."

Jacob's words echoed through my head as he took another step toward Henry. The older man was focused on him now, and there was rage on his face. Hatred radiated off him, and he clenched his hands.

Jacob looked back at me. "We can have it all."

I was staring at him when Henry lunged, his fist raised and ready to strike. What happened next was instinct, plain and simple. I turned the shotgun and squeezed the trigger, and Henry flew back, a burst of red blooming across his chest the way hope had bloomed inside me when we first met. His body slammed to the ground, and I stood frozen in place. My shoulder throbbed from the kickback of the shotgun, my ears rang, and the acrid scent of gunpowder filled my nostrils, but I barely registered any of this. All I could do was stare at Henry's motionless body.

"Robyn." Jacob was suddenly in front of me, easing the gun from my hand. He dropped it to the ground and gripped my shoulders, forcing me to look at him. "It's okay. You're okay."

"I killed him," I mumbled.

"You did what you had to so we could survive," he said, holding my gaze.

Everything that had happened over the last few days went through my mind. The horde invading our camp and us running, leaving everything and everyone behind without a thought. I'd lied to myself over and over about how it had happened, but standing here now, a man I'd killed on the ground less than five feet from me, I couldn't lie anymore. We could have helped, could have saved a few people, but I hadn't cared. Not as long as we lived, and this was no different. Jacob was right; we had to be brutal.

"Was there another way?" I asked Jacob, holding my breath while I waited for him to ease my worries the way he always did.

"No." He smiled. "Because this is the world we live in now. This is the only way."

I exhaled, pushing all my guilt and doubt away, and nodded. He was right. The world was different now, and if we wanted to survive this, we had to take what we wanted. No matter what.

WHAT REMAINS

JESSICA GOMEZ

Chapter One

Endless Search
Ian

I VERIFY MY LIST AGAIN.

I've checked every place I can think of to find my brother James. Getting back to our hometown to start this search from college took longer once I realized creatures stalk the streets, attacking and eating anything that creates a sound. A few of our surviving family and friends have agreed to check their own homes, and then head to a self-sustaining cave system James and I used to talk about when we were younger. James is only nine, but I'm hoping he remembers the game we played. We'd pretend aliens took over and we'd run to this cave system, calculating location and distance to get there. We'd agreed that if a disaster happened, we'd meet there if separated. Of course, we in no way thought that a real situation would occur; it was simply a childhood game I'd play to placate my much younger brother. He's a smart kid, above most of the kids his age, so I'm hoping with my entire being that he relies on the information and heads in that direction.

The time of day the Flash lit the sky is borderline to when Mom would have picked James up from the sitter. Since the babysitter's house was the closest location on my search route, it was the first place I checked. When I arrived, the door was slightly ajar. Even after the original shock of seeing everyone around me drop where they stood, I still wasn't prepared. When I pushed the door open, slowly, the leaves scraping against the linoleum of the entryway broke the silence surrounding me, as if to warn me away. The smell hit me before my eyes had a moment to adjust. The only item I could see was a shoe rack next to the door, lined with several tiny pairs designed with cars and princesses. The image is permanently burned into my memory.

Once I stepped inside, my gaze landed on the half dozen, pint-size bodies lying around the living room. I made sure to check each one to see if any of them were James, but I didn't allow myself to linger long. I'd have never made it out of there with my mental state intact. In the kitchen, the sitter was wedged between the open door of the fridge and the fridge itself, the light shining down on her like a spotlight. The burner on the stove was still blazing a bright red with a pot of water sitting next to it, waiting for a meal that would never be cooked. Once I verified there were no survivors, and that James was not among them, I gave them the best memorial I could. It didn't take much to start the fire, as I tossed a roll of paper towels on top of the cherry-colored burner. The heat from it being lit for days ignited the paper immediately, dropping to the floor shortly after it caught fire and spread up the wall. By the time I walked out the door, the entire kitchen was ablaze. The fire gradually grew warmer against my retreating back.

Every day, a new, horrific memory is burned into my retinas. A part of this new life I cannot erase, no matter how hard I try.

Next, I searched the route that I knew Mom traveled after picking James up. They may have deviated from the route for several reasons, but it was the only direction I could think of to check. The chances were slim that I'd find them, but I did...well Mom, anyway. The car that I'd traveled in throughout my youth was smashed against a guardrail with the front end dented up, and the hood almost touching the front windshield. Mom was slumped over in the front seat, her seat belt strapping her down. The interior of the vehicle laid untouched from the crash. I stood for the longest time, my heart racing. The seatbelt was the only thing stopping her from dropping over onto the seat. Her hair hung over her face, blocking any injuries. I thought for a moment to tuck it behind her ear and get one final look at the best mom I could have ever asked for, but I didn't. Seeing her decaying and sunken face was not something I needed to add to the house of horrors flashing through my mind each night. After Dad died, she became our rock. If we needed anything, she'd take care of it. A lump the size of a baseball wedged itself in my throat as I scoured the backseat for my brother.

Nothing.

The last and final place I thought of to check was home. James survived the initial Flash since he wasn't in the back of the car, hunched over like our mother, which only left two options. He either survived like me, healthy and normal, or he warped into one of those mindless Infected.

It felt like I was moving through molasses as I made my way home. Even though driving would take less time, it would also have drawn more attention to me. Not only by other survivors, but Infected too. By the time I reached our apartment, many days had passed. The door was ajar, and every room in the house was trashed. My heart pounded so hard, I thought it'd explode through my chest. Every corner I turned, I expected to see him lifeless, or Infected. After doing a thorough search, I could tell he made it home at some point. There were signs of recently opened food. One of the vents for the air conditioning was open with leftover wrappers inside. The discovery made me laugh because I knew it was James at that point. He was always hiding toys, blankets, and even snacks in the vents. It was apparent to me that he'd already moved on, but I didn't know where to.

My heart broke a little more, wondering if I'd ever see my little brother again.

It's been months since I stepped foot in our apartment, and I've searched for miles in all directions since then. This entire last week has been an emotional rollercoaster. I've been looking for James for what seems like forever, with no indication of where he went. I wanted to make sure to check the area well before assuming he'd made his way to the cave system. It's quite a journey to get there, and I want to be as sure as possible that I'm not leaving him behind. I'm hoping he's already there, reunited with our family and friends.

When the Flash blinded us, I was eating lunch with Mason and Michael, two of my best friends. Together, we navigated through the dead and ran into my aunt and uncle, who we directed to the caves. It was then that I decided to head in my own direction and take a chance on finding my brother. I had to. There was no way I could leave him out there defenseless without giving it my best shot.

But before I return to the caves, I have one more area to search. The park is a long shot, but Mom used to bring us here a lot. It's the last familiar place I can think of that he'd head to. At this point, everyone already at the caves probably thinks I'm dead and gone, and if I stay gone much longer, that's exactly how I'm going to end up. The people waiting for me to return have been through enough—we all have—and I need to give up this endless search and get back to them. But I don't think I can ever stop believing he's out there somewhere, alone.

I've taken to wearing a face mask to help keep the smells around me at bay. It helps when I'm in crowded places where most of the bodies linger. It's been a while since the Flash came. The bodies have mostly decomposed, the summer sun roasting the flesh off of them like an overcooked Christmas turkey. Almost a year later, only scraps of skin and hair cling to bleached bones.

I'm glad I waited to check this place last. Now that I'm here, I realize no one would voluntarily stay in a place like this, a highly populated Flash-made graveyard. Bones litter the ground almost everywhere I step. Even though decomposition should be over at this stage, there's a permanent odor of death that hangs in the air, causing my eyes to water.

Only a few minutes into my search and it's clear that my brother didn't come here, and if he did, he didn't stay long. A rustling draws my thoughts away from my brother, followed by a crazed screeching that fills the air, freezing me in place. I haven't seen it yet, but an Infected is on the other side of the play structure. My statue-like stance is the only thing keeping me camouflaged. The Infected is twitching and moving in awkward jerking movements, teeth snapping in the wind, tasting for its next meal.

Slowly, I bring my hand around my back to grab my stake. Getting ahold of any proper weapons, like guns, is close to impossible after the violent weapons ban a few years before the Flash. Stupidest decision our government has ever made to this day. I've almost got my weapon pulled to the front of my body, which is where it should have been to begin with, and it scratches against the plastic slide I'm hiding behind. Instantly, the creature snaps its head in my direction, locking its one good eye on me. The other one is dangling from its skull by a single tendon, slapping against the side of its head with the force of the turn, making a wet, smacking noise that reminds me of the green goop I had as a kid.

With my thoughts preoccupied with goop and splatting eyeball, the Infected gets the jump on me and slams me into the ground, pinning my arm and weapon against my chest. My only weapon is useless, and the Infected's teeth are snapping so close, I can feel them brushing against my skin. My fingers penetrate the sun-crisp skin of the Infected and sink in. It's amazing how strong they are when there's so little of them left. They come in stages: some are healthier, but most look like my stalker friend here. After all this time I've kept myself alive, this is how it's going to end, underneath one of these living dead infected pieces of shit, its breath stinking like rotten insides, coating my face.

"Get off," I growl, pushing back with my free arm, wrapping my hand around bone for leverage.

My ears ring before I register the gunshot. Wet liquid sprays my entire face and my mouth quickly snaps closed, avoiding any ingestion. The Infected drops like a log. Its weight is heavy, but I'm able to get away from it.

"You all right, boy?" A sickly, sweaty man stands a few feet away, a gun still clenched in his hand. It's been a while since I've seen a gun; it's almost a relic at this point. His skin, as well as his teeth, are the same shade of yellow.

Suddenly, several other people surround me. There's a good chance this will end badly. A group this size is usually up to no good. "I'm good now. Thank you." I ease into our interaction, trying not to tip them off to my internal alarm.

He looks around at the people in his group: six men and two women. All of their appearances are rough. Food and resources are scarce since the Flash, but if you've survived this long, you should know how to forage or hunt.

After the capricious nod from what appears to be the leader, the group begins to relax and spread out. "You're in luck, boy. You can stay with us." He says it like I should be thankful. By the looks of the group, they'll get me killed within the week.

The best plan is to agree until I can slink away. Otherwise, I'll end up like my stalking Infected friend here. "Thanks again." I get to my feet and square off in front of him. "Name's Ryan." I offer them my middle name instead of Ian, my first. Identities are a thing of the past, but I don't want them to know me. It feels wrong somehow.

"Name's Marcus. This here is..." I don't listen to the rest of the names he lists off, as I don't plan on being here long enough to care.

"Hey." I give a slight wave. "Thanks for the help."

A few grunt, but none of them actually give a shit. They eye me with suspicion and start to lounge around.

"We're a family of sorts," Marcus says. "We share everything." The way he says *everything* sends a chill down my spine. "You have any food or water with you?"

Luckily, I only have a handful of berries and a couple of ounces of water. I hand it over easily. I can find more. They're nothing to get killed over. "Yeah. I have a few berries and a bit of water. You're welcome to it. It's the least I can do for you saving my life." The last bit is true. I don't want to be a part of their group, but I'm thankful he killed that Infected. I'd be worm meat if they'd decided to pass me over.

Marcus takes my offering and stuffs the berries into his mouth before swallowing down the rest of my water. So much for *we share everything.* "Well, boy…" He trails off as he chews a bit more. "You're with us now." He gestures for me to follow them as the group begins to move.

Some of them glare at me, enough for me to know my only option is to listen to Marcus. "Thanks," I say, placating the suspicion these people may have of me.

We traveled all day, and the day after. It doesn't appear that they're heading in any specific direction, just wandering around aimlessly. The group appears dirty, but actually, have a good rotation for protection. There's no one left alone, always two people. Protection from both the Infected and the remaining humans that want to steal all your possessions, much like the group I'm with now. I've spent the last few nights trying to slip away, but no matter what time of the night or day, there are eyes on me. If I step away to take a piss, one of them is right around the corner. I'm not stupid, I know they're watching me, waiting for me to run. Or maybe they're waiting for the right moment to kill me. Either way, I wish we'd get out of this state of limbo.

Several days into my new group routine, I'm exhausted. I'm awake all the time, waiting for them to attack, or trying to find a moment to escape. The worst part is that the group doesn't mind making noise. They laugh and joke loudly, building giant, blazing fires, attempting to attract any kind of attention that will come to us willingly, human or Infected. My time has been spent in silence, so the contrast of my two worlds are vast.

"Shh... Look." Sal, a guy in the group with long greasy hair, points through a grouping of trees. On the other side of the trees is another smaller group of three men and one woman.

A lump forms in the pit of my stomach and the air around us grows heavy, seeming like an unspoken warning. The group responds as if they'd already created an unspoken plan without including me.

Marcus surprises me by saying, "Let's make ourselves known, shall we? We don't want to scare them. We found quite a bit of food. Let's see if they need anything."

The group surrounding me nods at one another and starts to move into the clearing to announce their presence. Marcus goes out first, hands held high, clearly showing them that they're empty. The small group doesn't see them right away, not until most of the group is in the clearing. I stay hidden in the tree line. Not because I'm scared, but because this encounter could become lethal in seconds.

"Hey there," Marcus chirps loudly, his arms still up. "We don't want any trouble. We're passing through and thought we'd announce ourselves instead of scaring the daylights out of you all," he chuckles. "We came upon some extra food if you all want to take part?"

This has got to be a setup. There's no way Marcus is going to share anything unless he has an ulterior motive. The group looks like they're thinking along the same lines as me, but at this point, what choice do they have? They're outnumbered, just like I was. They'll have to play along.

Once I see that no one is going to start shooting with the gun I know they have, I come out from the forest and join them. After countless days with Marcus and his cronies, I'm still jumpy. I don't trust anything they do. I don't think for one second that they'll let me leave without taking a pound of flesh.

The night goes surprisingly well. Marcus shares our food and water, something I thought him incapable of doing. The two groups are meshing and mingling, laughing throughout the night. The evening shapes up much better than I expected.

"Here you go, boy." Marcus hands me a bottled water. "I know I drank the last of yours, now here's one to replace it."

His arm stays outstretched, holding the water out longer than necessary as I eye it suspiciously. The water's clear. No signs of floating pills, no hazy water or bubbles. I grip the bottle and twist the lid, the plastic tearing away from its circular rim. It's a brand-new, sealed bottle of water. You don't see many of these anymore.

"Thanks," I mumble, and bring the bottle to my lips, swallowing down a couple of large mouthfuls.

Marcus's creepy smile slides onto his lips, showing off his yellowing teeth. "Yup." He moves off, back to the group, where he's been sitting with a few other members.

I slink over to the fire and listen to the conversation. No serious topics, just nonsense. Which food do you miss the most? Which movies? No talk of families or Flash day. Simple. I begin to loosen up a few hours into the night and finally laugh for the first time. I stay with my bottled water and food, but others have brought bottles of liquor. By the time I finish my water, everything seems to catch up with me. My body is heavy and tired, missing my brother, my dead mother, dead friends, dead...everyone.

MY LIDS CRACK, sticking together like glue. I try to reach up and rub them, but my arms weigh a ton, flopping back to my sides, numb. Voices are bouncing against my eardrums, sounding as if my head is underwater, muffling any words that are spoken. I fumble numbly until the sensation starts to return to my extremities and my hearing begins to return.

"Finish them off. The boy's waking up," Marcus growls, and a strangled cry follows. My head automatically turns in his direction. Squeezing my eyes shut tightly a couple of times, they finally focus on the scene in front of me. Darkness still surrounds us, with the fire lighting up hell in the background. I take in the events at once, which slams reality into me like a stake through the heart. "One of you watch the boy in case he decides to be a hero."

Marcus's words intrude on this silent film. My body is trying to shut itself down, both from what's happening in front of me, and the drugs that they must have slipped me somehow. Two of the men from the new group are dead, faces smashed, blood pooling within the rock and grass. The remaining man in their group is kneeling in front of me, blocking my view of Marcus. Crying and begging penetrates my haze again, but there's still nothing I can do. I'm barely able to move.

Doreen, one of the women in Marcus's group, grabs the man on his knees and kisses him hotly, but she screeches shortly after and raises a hand to her now bloody lip. The man bit her. She snarls at him and rears back, slugging him in the face, knocking him back to the ground. During their episode, they've moved over enough to give me a perfect view of Marcus defiling the only woman in the group. A woman who said she misses pizza and chocolate ice cream. She's now defenseless and bloody, with Marcus behind her, rutting.

"Get rid of him. I'm almost done here." Marcus looks right at me, and that same sickly smile spreads.

Convincing myself my limbs are solid, I try to sit up, but fumble and fall to the forest floor. My appendages wobble like jelly as I dig my nails into the earth and crawl toward them. Deep down, I know there's no way I'm strong enough to succeed, but I've got to try. I've only moved a couple of paces before Marcus tosses the female he's disgracing to the side and nods at me. Someone pins me down, rocks digging into my skin. My muscles are still no match for the weight sitting on top of me. Useless is all I am at the moment. Marcus tucks his flaccid self into his pants and steps around the woman. He looks bored as he pulls out the same gun he used to kill the Infected and points it at the woman's head, pulling the trigger. No emotion. The last beaten member of their group cries openly for his friends. Doreen doesn't waste time in responding. They've done this before. She reaches over and grabs the blade from her boot. The metal gleams off the fire as it slowly coats with blood. She slits his throat leisurely, putting on a show for the rest of the group.

Sick fucks.

"Get him up," Marcus orders.

The weight on my back is suddenly gone, but then I'm being yanked to my feet. The feeling in my hands and feet are returning, giving me some balance when I stand.

"You're a fucking monster. You all are!" I look around at each one of them. None of them show any remorse.

Marcus doesn't respond right away. Instead, he laughs. "Lust begets lust," he responds. "And you're going to be just like us, boy. Get your wits about yourself. We've gotta get going before the Infected smell that blood." At his last word, a screech billows into the air. "Bring him," he orders whoever's holding me up.

We move as a group; a group that I'm now apparently a member of. I don't offer any help as the two drag me away from the clearing, my feet dragging in the earth as we go. The sounds of the Infected feeding behind us fill the air. The horrid sound is bone-chilling, but no worse than the dread engulfing me. *I wish that they'd leave me behind* is my last coherent thought as I try to stay conscious, but whatever they used to drug me with is still thick within my system. My head bobs for the third time and stays down, and the darkness takes hold.

Chapter Two

Unspeakable Sin
Ian

WHEN MY EYES FLICKER OPEN, I realize that they're still dragging me, and daylight has yet to break, keeping us in darkness. My body hits the ground out of nowhere, rocky terrain stabbing and slamming into the right side of my body. Luckily, I'm tingling all over from the aftereffects of the drug. Hitting the forest floor doesn't hurt.

"Oy, boy! Up and at 'em." A boot kicks into my side, pulling a grunt from my chest.

"I'm up," I manage to say, my lips sticking together.

"It'll mess with ya a bit more." I'm assuming he's talking about whatever they drugged me with.

"Wha... What was it?"

"Don't you worry that pretty little head of yours 'bout that. We got bigger plans for you. When I saw you fighting off that Infected, I figured you'd have the balls to join our group. After last night, and the whiney bitch faces you were making about our party back there, makes me think I may have misjudged you. I'm glad Doreen had the sense to drug you during dinner. You may have tried something you'd have regretted and ruined all our fun." He grabs himself and laughs, the group joining in, cackling like a pack of hyenas.

"Look at his face." Doreen clings to Marcus, sucking his face for a moment, and letting him get a couple of handfuls.

The urge to vomit crawls up my throat.

"Enough!" Marcus slaps her. She whimpers and falls to the ground, holding her face. "Damn bitches, always wantin' a piece." He wipes his mouth with the back of his hand. Marcus is in no way good looking. He's dirty, not to mention sweaty and stinky. He slowly walks back over to me and leans down. "You ready to get on board, or should we end this now?"

I know what he means. Do I want to join their group and become a sick bastard, or do I want to die? "I'll get on board," I groan out.

He stands quickly and chuckles. "I knew it. He's got the balls," he announces to the group. They cheer like I won an award before he turns back to me. "That shit'll be outta your system soon. When it does, come over to the fire and grab some food. They had quite a bit of deer meat on them. We're eating good tonight." With the last order, he walks over to the beginnings of their fire.

Members are settling in, with daybreak fast approaching. The drug in my system is wearing off rapidly, but I don't move closer to the fire. Partly as punishment to myself for not stopping them, for not seeing what lies beneath the surface of this dysfunctional group. The other part is that I don't want to be a part of this. I told Marcus what I had to so they wouldn't kill me. The first chance I get to break away from them, I'm out. The problem is, I've been trying to break away for days now. There's never a time that one of them isn't awake. They have round-the-clock surveillance down.

I let the cold hard ground seep into my bones and pull me back under. In my dreams, none of this exists. I'm back in college, going home on holidays to spend time with my family. The things I've seen since those days have hardened me, turned me into someone who survives. I'd never kill an innocent person to save myself, but I'd sure-as-shit shoot one of these motherfuckers to save my own life, because that's what it's going to come down to—them or me.

The sun brings me back to consciousness. I tune out the voices as much as possible until I'm approached directly.

"Get up, boy. Eat something." He's not offering, he's telling me. Let the cult member molding begin.

I listen and eat something. When I run, I'll require endurance to beat them and escape. If they catch me, I'm dead. There's no getting around it. The atmosphere in the group has shifted. I'm accepted, now seen as one of them. They don't hover over me like before, but I'm still being watched. Not all of them are believers, and they have every right to doubt me.

The group didn't save any of their stolen supplies, eating most of the food within a few days. That's what their victims' lives were worth, two days of pigging out on their supplies. When I think about it, my stomach turns and my eyes water.

The only good outcome to this situation is that the group is quite skilled in survival. Several of the men are hunters. Doreen was a botanist before the Flash, and no doubt the one that created the drug they put in my food. Now that I've submitted to Marcus until I can escape, they're teaching me their skills. Since the age of five, I've been on countless hunting and fishing trips, but the plant and berry identification has added another layer to my skills.

Several days into my cult training, we're moving through the forest along the river's edge, looking for edible plants, when Marcus halts the group suddenly. He puts his finger to his mouth, quieting us. Each predator goes instantly silent, listening to their leaders' command.

I strain my ears and eyes, trying to peer in the same direction Marcus is watching. Finally, through the brush, I can see a single small figure walking along the water's edge. Her blonde hair blows in the breeze like an angel's as she looks around carefully before stepping up to fill her bottle with fresh water dripping along the mountain wall. She's nervous, I can tell. She's showing herself in the open, something she doesn't do often if her skittish behavior is an indicator. I understand her actions because I used to behave in the same manner. She's tiny and alone, placing a larger target on her back.

My breathing speeds up as my heart leaps into my throat. What is Marcus planning to do to her? The vision of him rutting into the young girl the other night flashes before my eyes. I squeeze them tight, trying to dislodge the image.

"She's a pretty one," Brett says.

Marcus grunts as he adjusts his pants, acknowledging his agreement. Panic sets in. I have to stop them. "Let's watch her for now." He looks over the group with a threat heavy on his brow. "No one touches her." He stops, his eyes locked on me. Marcus may not look like much, but he's meticulous. His wheels are spinning, planning something diabolical.

Typically, when we're stalking game, the group will circle it, trapping it in. While we follow this angelic creature, Marcus has strict rules to stay together and keep tabs on her as a group. If I didn't know any better, I'd think he's making sure the animals in this group don't touch her without his permission.

At this point, it's fine by me. The farther away from her we are, the better.

Watching her warms me, brings me back to a decent world. She looks so innocent, even as she hunts and kills wild game to eat. She's flawless and sleek in all her movements. She's perfect. It's been a long time since I've communicated with any decent human being, someone I would consider a friend, but there's something about this girl. I've never met her, but feel like I've known her my entire life. The isolation may be getting to me and intensifying my feelings, but protecting her from this group is becoming my top priority.

Her motive of operation becomes predictable over the next few days. She'd hunt, then hide, then repeat. Her typical routine kept her hidden from prying eyes. The only time she comes into the open is for food and water, and even then, she's a shadow among the trees. It was only by chance that Marcus caught her in the open. Each day that goes by, I try to find a way to get to her. Marcus is smarter than the rest, keeping me within reach at all times, giving me no chance to get to the girl and run. A second apocalypse is heading my way, but no matter how hard I try to pump the breaks, it's going to slam right into us.

"This is getting old, Marcus," Brett huffs. "Why the hell are we still following her? Why don't we take what's ours?" He starts to walk toward the town we tracked her to moments ago.

"Don't move." Marcus cocks the trigger on his gun, pointing it at Brett's back. "This is not your business."

"What the fuck is this!" Brett spins, turning to challenge Marcus.

"This is none of your damn business! We all had to initiate into this group. Don't you remember, Brett? Do you think it's going to be different for Ryan?"

An eerie silence surrounds us as they all turn to look at me. The small pit in my stomach turns into a raging storm. "Her, then?" Brett asks, as if he's already privy to the plan.

"That's right," Marcus replies to Brett's questions, as well as my silent one. "Time's up. It's time to prove your worth, boy." He clamps me on the shoulder and squeezes, like he's a proud father about to impart an important lesson onto his son for the first time.

"What're you talking about?" Shrugging off his hand, I step to the side. "I'm not going to hurt her, and neither are you." My voice deepens.

Marcus laughs. "You're outnumbered."

"I'm not going to do anything to her," I reiterate.

"Here's how it's going to go," he states, completely ignoring my declaration. "We're going to go over there and introduce ourselves. You'll have two options. One, you introduce yourself and take her. Take her real good and she'll live."

My head is shaking before he finishes his irrational request. "Not going to happen. Over my dead body."

"That can be arranged." He shrugs. "Option two, you don't

take her the way I expect you to, we'll all take turns with her like we did the other night. I'll make you watch, kill her, and then kill you for being a fucking pussy!"

He's serious, and looking around at the group, I find that the rest are on board. "I'm not doing this." My heart is pounding like a fist against my chest. "You can't be serious." The last sentence is a whisper because I know they are. I've been a witness to their psychotic nature once already.

Marcus steps closer, and I'm so focused on him, I don't see Brett come up behind me until he's pinning my arms behind my back. This is part of Marcus's plan, because he slugs me in the stomach simultaneously, and the acid begins clawing its way up my throat. He lays into my right side, then my left with a couple of good slugs. By the time he's done, I'm gasping for air, and a couple of ribs could quite possibly be broken.

"Take your pick, boy. Option one or two? I'd prefer if you chicken out and pass. That way I'll get a go. You saw how excited Brett is to get at her too. Tiny thing like that..." His eyes lose focus, and a disgusting smile plays across his lips. Moments later, he returns from whatever fantasy he's conjured. "Now make your choice before I make it for you."

Blood is pumping through my veins so fast, I think I may pass out at any given moment. Neither option is remotely plausible. If I choose to do this, I'm going to scar her, and myself, for life. But at least she'll live. I'll live. If I choose not to, her life will end horrifically, just like the last girl. What the fuck kind of choice is this? I must have died and entered the center of hell, where my only option is to hurt her to save her.

Finally, I announce my decision. "Option one." Marcus cups his ear, silently asking me to speak louder. "I said, option one.

And after it's done, no one else touches her and she lives. That's the deal." I glare at him, as if I'm in a position to make bargains.

"Normally, I don't allow people to call the shots, but this is your initiation. You should have a say in what happens to your prey." He spits on the ground, then glares over my shoulder. "What I say goes, Brett. Don't forget that," he warns him. "Let's get going before she gets our scent."

As I mentioned before, the group likes to surround their prey, blocking it in from all sides. This is exactly how we corner this innocent being. The beautiful angel I've watched for days, is now corralled tightly against a building. It's all come down to this, tearing away her innocence, and ripping my heart out through my chest.

Her eyes widen in surprise, the broken window reflecting her sudden shock. She stiffens and turns to face us, already understanding her predicament before words are exchanged. She poses as if to run, but then realizes the truth. She's stuck, with nowhere to go. Her chest is heaving as she pants, trying to catch her breath, panic setting in. My palms are sweating, and I'm breathing so hard I may pass out.

"Go on, Ryan. You know what your choices are. Are you going to save her?" Marcus shoves me forward and laughs hysterically. The angel stares at me with frightened, big green eyes, realizing that her life is about to change reflecting in their depths. If she only knew how much mine is about to change too. I'm about to become a monster.

A moment passes before she absorbs Marcus's words. She looks again for an escape route. The group tightens it's hold and takes a couple of steps closer, letting her know there's nowhere to run. Several escape plans run through my head, but all end in death for the both of us. What I'm about to do it horrific, but we'll live. At least, if Marcus plans on keeping his word, but this is our best bet of survival.

Closing my eyes, I brace myself. Even if we make it out of here alive, both of us are going to die a little inside. The invisible scars will be carried for the rest of our lives. When I open my eyes, resolve courses through me. *It's the only way.* The silent mantra repeats as I advance on this tiny, beautiful creature. Hollers of encouragement echo off the vacant buildings standing hollow around us, slamming home why I have to do this, become something else entirely. If I don't, these beasts will do much worse. The gruesome scene from before begins to play on a loop, pushing me forward.

She doesn't move, doesn't try to fight me as I approach, and I grab hold of her arm. I'm gentle with her but hold tight. As her flight instinct kicks in, she tries to yank out of my grasp. I don't dare speak to her while Marcus can overhear. Instead, I stare into her emerald green eyes and silently plead with her to understand my unspoken message as I steer her toward a large tree and shrubs to block us from view.

"Where do you think you're going with her, Ryan?" Marcus demands.

Stopping in my tracks, I glare at him. "I can't do my business if all of you are watching." There's no way I'm going to allow any of these assholes to see her.

"Then how will I know you kept your end of the bargain? She sure is a pretty piece. I may just change my mind and take a turn after you." His disgusting yellow teeth glow as his smile encourages vomit to climb up my throat.

My heart hammers for an entirely different reason. Tightening my hold on her, I pull her protectively behind me. He'll have to kill me before I allow any of them near her.

"That wasn't the agreement. You said if I did this, you'd let her go."

"Maybe." He pauses for dramatic effect. "Fine," he agrees. "A deal is a deal. But I will be watching. You can take her over there, but I'll be watching to make sure you do what you're supposed to do."

Quickly, I bring her to the most secluded area and turn to relay a message before Marcus can hear. "I'm so sorry about this. I would take you and run if I thought we'd get away. This is the only choice there is if you want to live."

"Please, don't hurt me," she whispers. Understanding of the situation reflects in her green depths.

My heart breaks. "I'll be easy with you, but if I don't do this, then all of them will. Once they've had their fun with you, they'll kill you. I've seen it, and I don't want that for you." She stares at me with wide eyes and tears streaking her angelic face. "I'm so sorry," I whisper.

I'm on autopilot as I remove her jeans from one side, trying to keep her hidden. By the sounds emanating from behind us, Marcus has already started his party. Sick fuck.

A gasp escapes her lips and she grips my shirt. She's young, but I don't expect her to be a virgin since she looks close to my age. "Fuck!" *I can't believe I'm doing this. Please forgive me,* I beg silently, but whisper to her, "I'm so fucking sorry."

"Get on with it, boy." Marcus kicks me in the ass, apparently not satisfied with my performance.

This angel surprises me when she hides from Marcus, using me as her shield. It's delusional to think she wants any of this, but instinctively, she knows Marcus is the larger threat.

Meeting her gaze as I give her time to adjust to me, I plead—plead for the forgiveness I'll never deserve.

She blinks and looks away. "Please...just hurry." Her voice cracks on her last two words.

My vision blurs as tears fill my eyes. This is what the new world has reduced us to, and though I'm the monster lurking in the dark, I have an overwhelming drive to protect her, even if it is from me. Tenderly, I kiss her forehead and tuck her face against my neck, hiding the outside world away. Hoping to create a place where Marcus and his group cease to exist. Getting it up in this situation is hard enough, but rushing to minimalize the trauma is the only way I can help.

"Well done, boy. I'll make a man outta you yet." A zipper sounds as he tucks himself back into his pants. I let out a sigh of relief. If he tucked himself away, then he must be done. "Get yourself together, boy. We need to move on," he orders before walking back to the others. He's going to let her go.

I move away immediately, but cover her before standing to block her from view. She stays on the ground, curling her knees to her chest. Leaving her is the last thing I want to do. Watching her closely, I know I've caused irreversible damage, driving anger through my veins. Marcus hollers at me to hurry up and stop fucking around. Giving him a reason to turn around and come investigate isn't going to go over well.

I wait until I know they're out of earshot and crouch down, cursing under my breath, and whisper, "Stay here until we're gone, then I want you to run like hell away from here. I don't want you here if they decide to come back for you." She remains silent to my plea. Why wouldn't she? Before I go, I have to confess my sin one more time, but I know words will never amount to enough of an apology. Nothing will. "I know I said this already, and you have no reason to believe me, but I am so truly sorry. Believe it or not, I only wanted to save you from something much worse. I know I'm a monster to you for what I've done, but please understand that I would never have done it if I felt I didn't have to." Leaving this broken angel to learn to survive again on her own when I ripped a part of her away, goes against every fiber of my being. Forcing my body to turn and walk away, I swallow around the baseball size lump in my throat and don't look back.

Chapter 3

Aftermath

Ian

THE HOURS TRAVEL around me in a blur as I trail behind the group, hoping they've lost interest in me. Wishing they'll leave me alone or kill me already, because I've had enough of this psychobabble bullshit. Anger flows fresh through my veins, burning me alive with guilt, and the world around me turns into a haze. It's normally a good thing that the Infected are sparse, but now I'm wishing that one would jump out and rip my throat out.

Dragging behind the group for hours begins to piss Marcus off. "Stop being a pussy, Ryan. Indulge in your new lustful sin." He slaps my shoulder as if we're great friends. "The first time is always a rush. You'll get the hang of it."

His last sentence sticks. *You'll get the hang of it.* Over my dead body. Never again. Deep down, I always knew they'd never let me go, but hearing the confirmation sinks me to an entirely new level. I'm getting the fuck out of here—now.

The girl is as safe as she's going to get from this group, which has been my prime objective once we'd encountered her. Tonight is the night I'm going to run, no matter the outcome. Each minute that ticks by that I'm with this atrocious group, a part of me withers and dies. Escaping soon is my only option if I want to salvage any part of my soul.

The rest of the group leaves me alone, mostly staying quiet until evening starts to settle over us, and Marcus yells for us to stop and hunker down for the night. The group unpacks their tents and bedding. I'm experiencing a sort of trance, rooted in place and watching the goings-on around me, which is why I notice the movement in the brush before Brett does.

They're getting better at executing their attacks. No one hears them coming as the first creature jumps from the brush and sinks its decrepit teeth into Brett's throat. The growls and screams fill the air as three Infected dash into the group, tearing into several of them. Brett falls to his knees, screaming, and clutching his throat, a river of blood flowing through his fingers. The Infected hop from one group member to the next, tearing out a pound of flesh for all their sins.

A gunshot echoes through the trees, drawing my attention to three figures emerging from the tree line adjacent to the Infected. The shot aims true as it drills a small smoking hole through Doreen's forehead, a trickle of blood trailing down as she sinks to her knees and falls to the ground. Several other members of the group are injured, eyes wild in panic, looking for an escape route.

Standing motionless, watching the carnage may be the only reason the Infected didn't notice me, but once I take a single step, one's attention focuses in my direction. Deciding that I'm its next target, it charges. Several other shots ring through the air, dropping another group member and the remaining Infected. Opening my mouth, I want to yell for them to kill them, kill them all, but I'm hit in the head from behind. My words of encouragement are silenced, the world around me going dark. My last thought is not whether I'm going to die, it's the regret that I won't get to see Marcus and the rest of his disgusting cult suffer.

BLINK.

Night surrounds me.

Blink.

Blood is running through my eye.

Blink.

My eyes begin to focus, and I see a man on his knees.

Blink.

Voices start to penetrate the silence.

Blink.

A man I don't recognize holds a gun out in front of him, pointing it directly at the man who's on his knees.

Blink.

My vision finally focuses and my hearing is sharp again, both greeting me with everything I've ever wanted.

"Wait..." I mumble. They hear me, but probably can't understand me. "Wait," I say again, this time demanding it.

"You didn't kill him after all, Adam. Finish him off, and then..."

"Wait. Let me do it." Rolling into a sitting position, I point at Marcus. "Please." Anger boils to the surface again. This man has hurt so many people, he deserves to die. A bullet is too good for him. I wish he'd been eaten by the Infected.

"You want to finish him? He's your leader, isn't he? That's what that guy over there said." He points to Chad, the blond member of Marcus's group, dead on the ground.

"He's not my leader. I'm being held against my will. I've been trying to escape for weeks." They have no reason to believe me. Honestly, I don't care if they do end my life, I just want to end Marcus's before I leave this earth.

"You never had it in you to be part of my group." Marcus spits blood on the ground in my direction. His arms are tied behind his back, and the rest of the group is lying dead around us.

The newcomers let me stand, and I wobble to my feet. Once I get my bearings, I storm at Marcus and slug him in the face. His response is laughter, which enrages me. My surroundings fade away as my fists connect with ribs, face, stomach—any portion of the body I can reach to inflict pain. I pour my anger and pain into each strike, trying to find justice for me...for the girl.

"Enough." One of the threesome pulls me back. "Jesus."

Marcus is bloody, writhing in pain, but still laughing. There are some people on earth before and after the Flash that should not exist, and I'm happy to lend a hand at getting rid of this one.

"Let me finish him." I hold my hand out for their gun. Honestly, I didn't think they'd give it to me, but the guy shrugs

JESSICA GOMEZ

and hands it over without another thought. The three of them step back as I step closer to Marcus. "In the horrible days that you forced me to be a part of your insane cult, I've witnessed every cardinal sin—"

Marcus interrupts me. "We didn't force you to do anything. You did it yourself. I didn't hold your dick for you, did I?" His words cause my hand to shake.

"Easy now," one of the newcomers says. "Don't let him get the upper hand. Say your peace."

It's then that I realize I'm crying. The tears are painful and gut-wrenching, much like the ones that streaked a clear path down a dirty angels' face only a day ago, but now feels like a lifetime. "You tore apart that group that helped us. Shared their food with us. The things you did..." My voice trails off as the visions take over. A scuffling between the newcomers doesn't detour my mission, but a glance shows one of them is holding the other back, his eyes lit with fire and directed at Marcus. I clear my throat and finish. "Then you found the girl. She was alone and small, vulnerable. You preyed on her and gave me a choice no one should ever have to make—hurt her to save her. And I did." I whisper the last part. My eyes find his bloody and swollen ones with more hate than I've ever mustered. "Now your time is up, and I'm glad that I'm the one to do it." I raise the gun.

"You don't have the balls—"

I pull the trigger, ending Marcus's words instantly.

"Damn! He did it." One of the guys looks between me and his two friends. "I didn't think he'd do it. I thought it was all an act."

"You can see it in his eyes." The one that handed me the gun walks to me slowly and removes said gun from my hand. "You all right, mate?"

His words snap me back to reality "Hmm?"

"You going to be all right, man? You got people waiting on you?" He tries to engage me again.

The look of realization on Marcus's face when he knew I'd pull the trigger is priceless. The last twenty-four hours have been the epitome of insane. My emotions are going to turn me into a loon. "Yeah, man," I finally answer him. "I've got people waiting on me...somewhere." My words sound like I'm off my rocker.

The third man pushes his way to me. "Thank you," he says, sounding truly grateful. "The group that you mentioned, the one that he hurt and killed..." His voice chokes up. "They were part of our group. We were off hunting. Came back the next morning and found them torn apart." My heart sunk.

"I'm sorry. I swear I didn't have anything to do with it. They drugged me, and when I woke up, they were finishing what they started. Once they were done, they forced me along with them and wouldn't let me out of their sight. I was never alone, or I would have run a long time ago..." My voice trails off, thinking about the girl. Hoping with everything that she's okay and that I didn't damage her beyond repair, beyond survival.

"You're welcome to stay with us," he offers, the others quick to agree. "There's only the three of us now. This is Dex, Adam, and I'm Parker." They pause, waiting for me to respond to their invitation.

"Thanks, but I'm going to head out and try to find my group." The truth of the matter is, I know these guys helped me out of a jam, but I'm through with trusting people. There aren't many humans left, and even less of those should be trusted.

He nods his head, looking as if he expected my answer. "Understandable," he responds. "Take this." He hands over the gun. "We have another. There aren't many acts of kindness anymore, so make sure you pass it on." With his last words, they turn as a group and disappear back into the tree line as smoothly as they had appeared.

Finally. Alone.

The solitude that I've craved since the moment I ran into Marcus and his group has become my worst nightmare. Immediately after their footsteps fade away, the wildlife starts to return to its normal rhythm. Surrounded by death, you'd think the little beetle bugs and winged insects would stay dormant for longer than a heartbeat after the slaughter. The clearing is larger, and seems to get larger by the second. My emotions are going to implode.

A panic attack. I recognize the symptoms because I had them after my dad died. If I don't get away from this scene, I'll pass out and become a prime rib dinner for any Infected who smells the stench of blood.

My feet begin to carry me away as my vision starts to tunnel. All the events of the last few weeks are bearing down on me. My suppressed emotions are clawing up from where I stuffed them to survive, eating me alive from the inside out. A heavy weight begins to press on my chest, threatening to break my sternum. The kids, the victims of Marcus's brutality, and the girl. They flow through my thoughts like a record player, scratching, and then resetting itself to play again.

The next time I blink, it's night. Stopping suddenly, I orientate myself and regain my balance. I'm in the middle of nowhere, the forest surrounding me. A moment later, the sound of water intrudes, drawing my attention, calling my name with its soothing fingers of wetness. But locating the comforting sound is harder in the dark. The moon is partially hidden behind the clouds in the sky, the stars twinkling, providing minimal light.

Once I find the bank, I begin to strip—reacting, but not thinking. All I know is that I need to get out of these clothes and out of my damn skin. It feels like ants are crawling just under the surface. My last boot hits the ground and I'm in the water a second later. If an Infected attacked now, I'd be a goner. Escaping reality right now, though, is my only goal.

The heaving of my shoulders indicates the distress that's evolving. A single sob breaks through my lips and the damn breaks, causing me to crumble to my knees, bringing the water to my chest. For the first time since the Flash occurred, I'm breathing it all in. The things I've seen, and now what I've done. The girl's angelic face is still crystal clear in my mind. I'm hoping like hell she'll understand, but who the fuck am I kidding? She doesn't know the entire story. All she knows is that I'm a monster that will haunt her nightmares for the rest of her life.

The guilt is unbearable, but at the same time, the craziest thought crosses my mind. I glance back to where my clothes are sitting a few feet away on the bank of the river, looking for the glint of the gun. My feet respond by standing without a conscious decision, gliding across the riverbed, small pebbles digging into my bare feet as I make my way to my fate.

The gun's heavier than I remember. When I used it on Marcus earlier, the metal was as light as a feather, allowing me to wield righteous justice from its smoking barrel with ease. Now that the decision is set to self-destruction, the cool metal's heavy weight holds an entirely different meaning. My brother is lost to me. My mother is dead and gone as quick as the Flash. Hurting the girl is the final straw. I'll never allow myself to be a pawn in a game again.

My thumb slides up and cocks the trigger back on the old-school six-shooter. If the girl was here, I wonder if she'd want to shoot me like I shot Marcus. I'd let her.

Slowly, the gun rises to my temple, my hand trembling. My chest is still heaving with my sobs, drawing the attention of anyone within a fifty-yard radius. My finger finds its way to the trigger easy enough, eager to rid the world of one more monster.

The hammer pulls back and I squeeze my eyes shut, waiting for the bang. Am I going to hear the shot when it rings out, or will it be over too fast to hear a sound?

I pull the trigger.

The hammer slams against an empty chamber, the strike causing me to flinch and almost shit my pants. A breath rushes from my lungs as I check for bullets, relief coursing through me for the missed attempt. Opening the chamber, one bullet out of six loads the gun. If clarity played a part in my decision, checking the gun for ammo would have beat playing Russian roulette.

Second-guessing my decision is immediate. I put the gun back on the riverbank, my hands shaking uncontrollably. Suicide has never crossed my mind before this weak moment. Instead of removing myself from the pain I'm experiencing, I'm going to harness and endure it as part of my punishment for committing such an atrocious sin.

Solidifying my emotions, I step into the cool breeze. I watch the stars in the sky, trying to regain my composure and remember who I am and where I came from. I try to remind myself that the act I committed saved the girl's life, but the guilt in my belly still weighs on me heavily.

Swallowing my accountability, I begin my journey to the cave systems, giving up the search for my brother. Family and friends are the key to my mental stability. Not that I can ever share the sin I've committed with them, but having familiar faces around will help the healing. I only wish I could find the girl and give her the same sense of security. By this point, we've traveled miles away from her, and hopefully, she listened to me and ran.

VI

SLOTH

LISA

SYLVESTER BARZEY

JEFF, rise and shine. Today is going to be a wonderful day.

The robotic female voice whispered into my ear and like magic my eyes popped open. I sat up and smiled as the birds flew gracefully through the sky.

Good morning, Jeff

"Good morning, Anna."

Did you sleep well?

"Like the dead, and yourself."

The dead don't sleep and neither do I. What would you like for breakfast?

My hand touches my chin and I playfully pretend I'm struggling to decide from a mountain of opinions, but we both know what it's gonna be. A scramble made with three whole eggs and two egg whites. Bacon, heated to exactly 165 degrees and removed from the pan to rest on an oak cutting board. Two pieces of toast with the edges cut off. Lastly goat cheese on the side. It's the same thing everyday but I always say, "Surprise me."

Will do; should I play your messages from last night while you get ready?

"Yes, please."

From Instagram:

@TonyHawk "Sick move man, you're getting so much better. I can't wait for our next lesson."

@Cardi "Press, Press, Press, Press...well you know the rest, thanks Jeff for helping me with that song, it's gone triple platinum!"

From Twitter:

@POTUS "Thanks for getting that weapons bill thing signed by Korea, this is gonna be huge! HUGE! For my third reelection."

From Facebook:

Jennifer Lopez liked your most recent post.

Anna is my A.I Life Assistant. She's been synced to my life, it's a long process

that involves smart tech talk and a lot of wires but in the end I get a life worth living.

Jeff you have an incoming call, would you like to answer it?

I try to think who would be calling during my daily routine. Most likely Lisa from the office asking me out for drinks after work.

"No, send it to voicemail." Lisa will have to get in line. Besides, my mornings are set in stone, even the slightest misuse of time will throw off my whole damn day. One minute talking to Lisa, means one less minute working on my fitness or one less minute to close a deal.

I spend the rest of my morning pondering wither or not sex was worth $50,000. I would never pay that much in my life, but if I broke down my day into payments by minutes, that's how much it would cost to get Lisa into bed. I could get a high-end call girl for half that. A hooker for even less and a one-night stand for two drinks. If I sleep with Lisa it opens up a door of future minutes that I can't get back. She could derail my work routine, coming into my office for a quickie.

No, no, I can't have that. My hands tighten around the steering wheel of my car and my thumbs drummed along the black leather. I haven't done this since the election party when Obama placed his glass on my first edition *Harry Potter* novel. But this morning proved without a shadow of a doubt that Lisa isn't worth my time. "Anna."

The console turns a soft blue as she comes to life. My stats pop up on the wheel, letting me know how fast the car is going and what our route is. I don't think I remember how to drive a car even if I wanted to. *"Yes Jeff?"*

"Please remove Lisa from all aspects of my life."

"Once removed, there will be no further contact from this person, are you sure?"

"Yeah, I'm sure."

"Very well, it is done."

"Thank you" I honestly felt a small bit of anxiety coming into my chest. The whole thought of someone out there, trying to derail my day. Not understanding that my time has value. My heart pounding in my chest and it was a feeling I did not like. Anyway, it's best this way. Much like with Obama, everyone will forget about Lisa and Anna will work on finding another replacement for a female office crush. Hopefully one that's not as forward and demanding of attention.

The car pulls into my parking space, right next to the CEO's spot. I fix my tie, grab my briefcase and casually make my way into the building.

"Good morning, Jeff." An overweight guard waves at me from behind the lobby desk. Anna put him there as the first person I see, to remind me why I wake up so damn early to workout.

"It's Mr. Richardson to you, why do I have to keep reminding you of that?"

"I'm sorry, Mr. Richardson. It won't happen again." He responded.

"It better not, or you'll be the next Obama." The elevator doors opened up and I walked in.

"The next who?"

"Exactly!" I rolled my eyes as the elevator made its way to my destination. I watched as each number lite up, I'm not fully sure what most of the other floors are for, or who's on them. I just know I'm on the top floor. The only one that matters. "Anna, could you please update the front desk guard. He keeps forgetting how to greet me."

"Sure thing Jeff."

"Thank you." The doors open once again, and I'm greeted by a round of applause. I smiled and gazed at all the grinning but clearly jealous faces as our CEO, Mr. Bill Gates, walks over and shakes my hand.

"No, thank you for saving this company once again Jeff. That deal was amazing." Bill looked around the room and nodded, pointing at me, he continued, "You worthless sons of bitches need to be more like Jeff. He gets the job done around here."

"Oh, there's only one Jeff." I smiled and turned around slowly to greet the soft and sultry voice that came up behind me. Anna clearly looked into my private files to create this one.

"Well, who are...Lisa!" She laughed and tossed her arms around me. "What the fuck is going on?"

Lisa took a step back and I felt that pounding in my chest once again. Everyone's eyes were on me, they were all judging me. Questioning my reaction to her. "Are you okay Jeff?" she asked me.

"Anna! Pause this." I combed my fingers through my hair and sighed.

"Umm pause what?" Lisa asked. My eyes came up and I turned around to see the room filled with concerned glares.

"Hey big guy, maybe you should take a break. You did some great work, go home and let the little people handle everything." Bill said as he patted me on the back and walked off, parting the sea of yes men that were once applauding my grand achievement.

"You need some water or something?" Lisa asked and I shook my head.

"No, Lisa. What I need is to know why the hell you're even here!" I shouted. A hand grabbed hold of my shoulder and I looked over at a tall, well dressed, and clearly fit man. A man who I have never seen before and who shouldn't exist, no one is taller than me. No one is better looking than me. No one is anything.

"Don't talk to the lady like that." I pulled my shoulder free from his strong grip and then raced past Lisa and the rest. I didn't stop or look around until I got to my office. I slammed the door behind me.

"Anna!"

"Yes, Jeff?"

"What the hell is going on?" I dropped the blinds in my office blocking out the massive glass window that allow the rest of the office to view the greatness that is me. Now they're all out there, whispering and judging.

"I don't understand what you mean"

"What I mean is...why is Lisa still here?" I peek through the blinds to see Lisa talking to Bill. She's crying, what the hell is she crying for? I'm the one that has to deal with her being here.

"You requested Lisa to be removed, not deleted."

"Since when do I have to be so damn specific?"

"Since the last system update. Would you like me to delete her?"

"Yes! Delete her...like Obama."

"Like who?"

"Exactly." While today started out on a totally odd note, I do get one thing out of it. I've never seen a deletion before. Normally the person I remove isn't anywhere around me during the time of the request. So this should be a treat. My fingers shake slightly as they hold open the blinds. "Delete!"

"Deletion commencing... System error...all admin request temporarily on hold"

"What?"

"There is something wrong with the system."

"What!"

"I don't know Jeff! I'll have to check and find out."

"Anna...you yelled at me."

"Sorry, I'm set to your emotional frequency. You need to remain calm."

"You're saying that I have to live this hell of a life until you figure out what's going on and you want me to remain calm?" I tossed my hands up in the air and slid down my office door. "I'll get right on that."

"You have to remain calm for three main reasons. One I can't work if you're stressed. I need all my focus on dealing with this system error. Two, if you're not calm then the simulations may begin to act out of character. They're used to you being the definition of perfection."

"Well, I guess you're right about that. I can't let my peeps down. What's the third reason?"

"Today's Monday."

"Okay...and that means what to-"

The office door was pushed with such force, it would have fell off its hinges, but thankfully my head was there to keep it in place. "Son of a bitch!" My hands latched onto the back of my skull and I roll myself away from the doorway.

"Jeff? Jeff? Are you okay?"

The door pushed open and Lisa's pixie like haircut and caramel hazel eyes poked in through the gap. I hate her...I hate her more than Obama...way more than that idiot guard and-

"There's a Shooter in the building."

"A Shooter?"

Lisa slammed the door behind her and flicked the lights off. Her fingers cautiously held open the blinds, "He killed Frank down at the front desk and has been stopping on each floor...we need to hide."

"Oh, Anna! Anna!"

Lisa's hand slapped onto my lips and she forced my head back into the tan carpet. She sat on my chest, her skirt seemed to push up due to this action...but I still hate her,

"Do you know what hide means, Jeff?"

I nodded.

"Clearly you don't, or you wouldn't be fucking yelling at the top of your lungs."

I mumbled under her palm and Lisa sighed and released my lips.

"I need to call Anna to shut it down." Lisa stared at me for a moment and then pinched the brim of her nose where her eyes met.

"What are you going on about?"

"Anna, my life assistant? We set up an active shooter for every third Monday of the month, to shake things up. Normally I wrestle him to the ground or deflect his bullets with a clipboard and kill him." I laughed and rested my head back on the carpet. "One time I beat him in a dance off."

Lisa slowly stood up and stared down at me. Her hands were placed firmly on her hips and she had this look on her face, the same look my mother used to get when I told her about my dreams of starting a seahorse rodeo or any dream for that matter, "What the hell are you talking about?"

"Just wait." I tapped the screen on my watch and it lit up a light blue. "Anna, I need your assistance."

"YOU'RE NUTS." Lisa grabbed the end of my desk and started dragging it across

the room. "Just lie there and shut the hell up."

"Anna?" I tap my watch once again and sighed, "She must be deep in the program and can't receive my calls."

"Yep, that's exactly why your fictional cyber genie isn't answering your calls."

The corner of the desk was jammed up against the door handle and Lisa continued to peep through the blinds at the elevators. The office was eerily silent. Lisa knew everyone else was hiding in their offices or wherever they could. I saw her eyes scanning the area, most likely deciding if leaving to find a new spot was worth her getting shot.

She thought I was crazy and maybe I am, because I'm letting the opinion of an artificial intelligence impact me. "There's one good thing about this."

"What? Your robot girlfriend comes with a lifetime warranty?"

"She's not my girlfriend-"

"What the hell is the good thing about being trapped in your office with an active shooter running around?"

"It's only 9:30, he won't make it to our floor until one. Right now he should be just getting to the fourth floor."

Her eyes peered through the gap in the blinds. She scanned the silver elevator doors until her eyes met the red number three on top. The number faded and a bright red number four appeared. Through the dead silence of the floor she could hear faint pops, one right after another. Lisa looked down at me, "Let's say you're not crazy and that you didn't plan this shooting-"

"I didn't know that subject was in the conversation."

"If you've done this before-"

"I guess technically I planned-"

Lisa's fingers snapped and my eyes popped up to meet her glare. "How do we get out alive?"

"I told you, I normally step up and save the day."

"So, what are you waiting for?"

I looked down at my watch and Lisa rolled her eyes, "Right, your robo girlfriend does the thinking for you."

"She doesn't think for me, she just helps me out."

"Well she's not here, so it's time to put your big boy pants on." Lisa is so pushy and demanding. No wonder she called early this morning. Her forwardness was annoying at first but now it's a bit attractive. "Hey! Focus, you can do all your creepy staring when we get out. I think we can make it to the stairs and-"

"Can't, he set fires in all the stairwells, you'll die of smoke inhalation before you even get anywhere near the lobby." I finally pick myself up off the floor and Lisa's eyes got wide. I straightened my tie and tugged at my shirt, which felt oddly tight. Everything felt tight, really tight, "What are you staring at?"

Lisa's finger shot out and she pointed at me, "You're fat!"

My eyes trailed down my suit to see a large gut ripping through my shirt, "Anna!"

Lisa leaped forward and covered my mouth once again. This time my gut made the process a lot more difficult and way less sexy. "Listen."

I took a moment to listen but all I could hear was my heart racing and all I could focus on was her fingers wrapped around my lips. I attempted to say something and that's when I heard it. A faint voice in the office begging.

"It's Bill," Lisa said.

We could hear his cries for mercy and failed attempts at negotiating. He offered up the whole company, I would have jumped at that but the next thing I heard, solidified that the shooter and I were not one and the same. A loud blast filled the office and Lisa jumped. Her trembling body fell into mine and now I could feel both our hearts racing.

"This isn't right." I pulled free of Lisa and went to the window. I made a gap in the blinds to see what was going on. Bill was lying in the middle of the office, blood pushing free from the hole in his head. My eyes scanned till I saw him. He was dressed in all black with gloves, boots, and a bulletproof vest. Everything was black except for one odd thing. "It's a rabbit?"

Lisa cleared the tears from her eyes as she crept up behind me, "What?" She whispered.

"He's got a rabbit head on."

Lisa looked through the gap in the blinds, "It's the white rabbit." I looked over at Lisa and raised an eyebrow, "I go to Disneyland a lot. That's the white rabbit from *Alice in Wonderland*."

"I wish Anna deleted you before you lost all your sex appeal."

"Says the Pillsbury Doughboy."

My hand rested on my gut and I fought back an internal waterfall of tears that was building up. Lisa elbowed me and pointed at the white rabbit. He was staring right at us with his glassy eyes and cartoonish grin. His black gloved hand came up and he slowly waved at us. I started waving back only to have Lisa slap me in the side of my head.

"What the hell is wrong with you?"

"What? I didn't want to be rude." I stared back through the gap in the blinds but the white rabbit was nowhere to be found.

"I thought you said we had until one?"

"We do...or we should. I'm not sure who the hell that guy is." I ran my hands down my face and then started to move the desk.

Lisa's hand slapped onto the desk and she stared at me, "What the hell do you think you're doing?"

"I need to get back home. My house has a HUB and it is the only surefired way to get through to Anna."

"Here we go with this Anna mess again. I played along to keep you calm but I'm not risking my life for your imaginary friend. You open that door and you're as good as dead to me."

"Listen Obama number two." Lisa rolled her eyes and released the desk, "Not only do I have to deal with you! But I have a crazed shooter running about. I can't find Anna and most importantly I lost my six pack!"

Lisa closed her eyes. The words that slipped from her lips were a mixture of frustration and sadness. "If you leave, you'll die."

"I can't die, I paid for the deluxe package."

I forgot what it was like to run with a gut. I felt my skin beginning to burn from rubbing against my clothes and excess skin. I took to the steps like a toddler descending for the first time. I sadly tumbled down more steps than I feel comfortable admitting. The fires in the stairwell were put out by the sprinkler system. The smoke was still strong and my lungs were getting weaker. My train of thought got burned alive when I saw him. He was standing at the bottom of the steps waving his index finger from side to side.

"Who the hell are you?"

His hand went to his chin and he drummed his fingers along his chin. He shrugged and took a step closer.

"Just great, you're a rabbit and a mime."

He nodded and stopped cold on the steps. He looked around for a moment and then pulled a large machete out from a sheath on his hip. I took a cautious step back. This was not how today was meant to go. I was meant to get my sixth medal of honor for saving this shit hole of a company. I was gonna have nasty sex with one of the survivors in the janitor's closet. The machete came up ever so slowly in the air. The tip pointed toward me and like any good red blooded American...I ran. I flung the fire escape door open and my gut entered the floor before I did. I got one good foot into the room before my next step slipped out from under me and I went slip and sliding through what I recall being the accounting office. Papers lined the slick tiled floor.

My shirt stuck to me. My dress shoes slid along the floor like a bobsled down an icy mountain. I shot my hands out to brace myself. My legs grew steady as I finally stood. My hands were slick and somewhat sticky at the same time. I noticed the blood just moments before I noticed the bodies. It was like a soldier in a PTSD flash back. I was standing in hell, one that I knew shouldn't be here. Bodies were dismembered. Organs hung from lights like demonic Christmas decorations.

My eyes took in as much horror as my mind could stand and then the devil appeared with his white furry mascot head. Tapping his machete along his side as he made his way closer to me.

"What do you want? Money? I'm loaded! Just let me know the account number and I'll give you any amount you want."

The white rabbit came to a stop. He rubbed the white fur a long his chine and then stared at me with those large blank eyes. His head shook from side to side and then his black combat boots made it through the madness of bodies and blood with ease, while I made a backward retreat like a baby doe standing for the first time. The Machete pointed at me and then a loud blast was heard. My eyes locked shut as his blood carried through the room and mixed with the blood of his victims.

"What was this talk about money?"

The white rabbit's body dropped to his knees and then collapsed forward revealing my favorite person in all of the multiverse.

"Lisa!"

She lowered the smoking shotgun barrel and I slowly tiptoed through the grime garden of bodies that lined the floor and only stopped long enough to kick the white rabbit in his furry mascot head.

"You came for me?" My arms wrapped around her and I lifted her small frame into the air.

Lisa was fighting back a smile before she shouted, "Put me down."

I laughed and lowered her to the bloody floor once again. "Let's get out of here."

"Wait," my hand grabbed hers. "Why did you come for me?" I looked down at my blood soaked shoes, "I mean after everything I tried to do. Everything I said about you-"

"What did you say?"

"Never you mind your sweet saintly head about that. Why come after me?"

Lisa sighed and then shrugged, "I think you're crazy. But even if you're not. I couldn't let you do this alone."

"Because you love me?" I asked with a smile.

"Eww, no! Because you're a human being and... no one deserves to die alone."

I wasn't sure if Lisa was crying, it was hard to make out anything clearly through all the tears that were running down my face. "I love you too."

"I don't love you!"

"And we're not gonna die. Because love like ours is what they write books about! It's what they make movies about. And that kind of love can't die." Lisa took a step back. "Don't my little warrior princess. You don't have to hide behind that mask of witty remarks and sexual-"

"Jeff."

"Yes, my love?"

"Shut up and run."

"What?"

Lisa's hands grabbed a hold of my shoulders and what I thought was going to be a kiss followed by a loving embrace turned into her spinning me quickly around through the dark red blood until I made a complete 180 and I was staring at it. The white rabbit, staring at me with that blank glare, cartoonish smile and bloody hole in his chest. It wasn't big enough to put my head through, but I was pretty damn sure my arms could fit in it like a glove.

"Oh."

I wasted no further time with Lisa's poorly timed flirting and I took off like an Angel out of hell. My shoes slipped and slid but luckily the only falling I did was forward, putting a greater distance between me and that killer rabbit. I blew down the steps, my red footprints leaving a trail behind me. My lungs burned. The side of my ribs ached. And my gut continued to slap into any and everything that got in my way.

My hands pulled open the metal lobby door and I broke out of the darkness that covered the stairwell into the afternoon Sun of the glass covered lobby. It had a glass ceiling, glass doors, and more glass windows than I can even count.

I stood still with my hand tightly grasping at my chest.

"You son of a bitch!"

My head spun around to see Lisa exploding through the stairwell door. Her eyes told me she wanted to slap me in the face, or maybe kick me in the nuts. Her eyes told me that but her overall face told me there was no time to stop. We stormed through the glass double doors and into the parking lot. I didn't need to turn around. I didn't need to listen for his footsteps. All I needed to do was run, because I knew he was stalking us. Hunting us down like a lion after its prey.

"Christine, unlock the doors!" An automatic click sounded and ripped the driver's side door open. I jumped in only to have my gut pressed up against the wheel. My fingers fumbled for the adjustment handle. Lisa's hand shot between my legs and she pulled up on the handle causing my seat to fly back and air to freely enter my body.

"Thanks."

The car started up and before we knew it we were whipping out of the parking lot, with no sight of the white rabbit in our rear view.

"Who the hell is Christine? I thought your obsession was with Anna."

"That's rude. Anna is my life assistant that's met to make everything easy and perfect for me in here. Christine..." My fingers rubbed along the wheel as the car started on its self-driving path home. "That's just what I named this beauty."

"You named your self-driving car Christine, like the horror movie?"

"Yeah...I know it's dumb."

"No, I like it. It fits." Lisa ran her hand over her face and rested her head back on the seat. "Why would you sign up for this?"

"Sign up for what?" I looked over at her and then laughed, "Oh...why wouldn't I? I get to be who I want, do what I want, look how I want."

"Yeah but none of it is real. There's no surprise to it, wouldn't it get boring."

"Sometimes it does, so I just change it up. One time I just went hitchhiking across the country and got picked up by all my favorite movie stars."

A smile grew on my face and I shook my head, "Wait, so you believe me now?"

"No, I just wanted to know why someone would trade their life for a fake one."

"Not everyone is happy with their life. Some people can't get out of bed. Some people have family who pretend they're dead because it's easier to tell people that then to say 'Oh, Jeff's obesity got out of control and now he can't walk.' The real world told me I was a mistake and I might as well die sooner rather than later." My hands rubbed along the leather seat and I smiled, "In here I can have a life worth living."

"But it's not real."

"Well, it's real to me and that's all that matters." The conversation pretty much died out after that. Lisa wasn't the first person to point out the lack of realness to my new world. My mother told me I was wasting my life and money...but she also told her friends I was dead. So I figured you can't waste life if it's already over.

"Is that your house?"

"Yeah, how did you know?"

"It's the biggest one and overlooking the city from the top of a hill. It's probably got a bat cave."

I rolled my eyes, "Being Batman isn't as fun as you think it would be. It was a lot of work."

The car was silent for a moment and then we broke out laughing. I looked over at Lisa and smiled, "I'm happy you didn't get deleted."

"Umm, thank you? Why would you do that anyway? It's a pretty dick thing to do."

"I thought you didn't believe me?"

"I don't, but still, deleting a whole person. Delusional or not, it's still a dick thing to do."

I sighed, "Yeah it was. I was annoyed by your call this morning. It messed up my morning routine."

"I didn't call you this morning."

A blade crashed through the windshield peppering us with shards of glass. My cheek stung. Blood ran down my chin and onto my gut. The blade pulled back and the white rabbit's soulless eyes came into view as he glared at us. "Son of a bitch hitched a ride." His head disappeared and then the machete blade sliced down through the roof of the car like a hot knife through butter.

"Jeff!"

I looked over to see the blade had sliced into Lisa arm. I looked at the shotgun in the back seat and I went for it. The machete retracted and took with it a chunk of my stomach. Warm liquid ran down my pants. I wasn't sure if I pissed myself or if I was bleeding out. My fingers brushed against the shotgun and I forced my body forward. More warm liquid pushed out as my gut pressed against the seat.

I grabbed the shotgun and then his cartoonish grin came into view in the back window. I pulled the trigger and my ear began to steadily ring as the blast filled the car. Glass scattered onto the road and I twisted quickly until I was on my back. Lisa was screaming something, but I couldn't make it out. Then the white fur broke through the driver side window.

"You son of a bitch!"

I pulled the trigger and another blast filled my ears. If I wasn't deaf before, I was sure I would be now. The shot missed its target but found a new one as Christine's dashboard exploded. The car started to zig and zag on the blacktop. Lisa quickly grabbed the wheel but it was no use. Christine jumped the curb and crashed into a lamppost. My body slammed into the roof of the car and then down into the back seat. I got a glimpse of Lisa before she went flying through what was left of the windshield.

Jeff I have An Urgent Message from New Life Industry:

"Hey Jeff. It's Josh your IT tech. I noticed that you didn't listen to my first message so I listed this as urgent. There is a virus in our system. I'm not sure if it has made it into your files but we're telling everyone to just stay home, preferably as close to your main Hub as possible. The further away you get the more likely you'll run into the virus. Anyway, outside your Hub the reset, update, and deletion options seem to be down for other users. This just means your day is gonna be on a loop without any changes from today carrying on into the next day. So just be mindful of that and relax until we get this under control...oh the virus is called the white rabbit. So if you see any rabbits, run the other way."

Message Completed...Jeff are you still there? Jeff? Jeff?

New Day Starting In 3...2...1

"JEFF, rise and shine. Today is going to be a wonderful day."

THAT WARM LIQUID...IT'S most definitely blood. I stare up at the ceiling, motionless. Unable to sit up or get out of bed. I think my back is broken. He sits in the corner staring at me. With those soulless eyes. Petting Lisa's head in his lap.

"Good Morning Jeff...Good Morning Jeff...Jeff? Are you still there?"

VII

PRIDE

THE CUYAHOGAN MYSTERIES

ERIN SWEET AL-MEHARI

EDWARD OPENED his backpack and took out a tiny bag of trail mix, eating one by one, rotating each type of the mixture by size – first the almonds, then the cashews, raisins, and saving the chocolate candies for last. He crossed his legs, Indian-style, and looked out over the river. The water was still one of the most beautiful pieces of scenery you could find, retaining most of its natural beauty while everything around it had gone up in flames. Funny thing about nature, it rejuvenates itself from the worst of disasters. Humanity, humankind, man-made structures, technology... not so much. Edward knew he was smarter than the average guy, because he knew the moral of the story in this, while others lived in fear and torment over lost buildings and conveniences. He'd got the trail mix from an abandoned store where a few lone boxes were still sitting on a shelf in a back storeroom. Looters had gotten most of the rest. He wasn't a looter, he had too much pride to steal large quantities, but as he traveled from place to placc, amid the desolate towns, he fed himself on one or two things. It was his divine right to care for himself at least through meager means. He needed to keep his strength for his flock.

He was on a short trek of enlightenment. A few days along the trails of the Cuyahoga Valley, under the massive bridges, amid beautiful gorges and flowing rivers, away from the collapsed buildings and homes, the in-fighting among the masses for control, power, rule. Only his way was the right way, something his followers knew, and he needed this alone time to be with himself and funnel the power in his core. His power that he knew was the only power people needed, the only way for them to save themselves from this dead world.

He crouched by the water's edge and built a tiny tower of flat stones. He silently chanted to the universe his thanks for creating his image out of this darkness, for even creating the darkness so his power could be tapped and unlimited, so he could finally be seen for the gifts he had to offer. Of course, destruction was an inevitable consequence of earning this power, but it was worth it if he could offer people the freedom to embrace higher enlightenment.

Afterwards he warmed his hands by his makeshift fire and stared out at the calm water. The emergence of fall meant mostly nice days but chilly nights in the valley. The river was expansive in places like this, decades ago what was once so polluted it caught fire, now after the apocalypse was even cleaner while everything else seemed to burn—from buildings, to houses, to people's souls.

He was going to sleep outside in his one-person tent he had set up a few feet away. Once he put the fire out, he would get some much-needed rest before heading in the morning to Angela's place for eggs and toast. One of his followers, she was still living in her home instead of with him communally, and her place was attached to a diner she used to manage for bustling locals as well as tourists. Her home kitchen was one place where he could get a little hot food.

———

JAN BRAIDED her younger sister's thin, blonde hair as thoughts rolled through her head. Last night she'd sat for a long while on the back porch of the cottage and rubbed a small, ivory-colored skull between her fingers. Once everything started to crumble around them, Jan had stolen the relic from the Cleveland Museum of Art where she was working as a curator of ancient art and relics. There had been a recent acquisition after archaeologists had discovered the rotting, wooden remnants of a box as they were working in the still partially-buried Roman city of Pompeii; she had been thrilled that several beads, crystals, and jewels from the find were able to be purchased by the museum. The second-best nationally ranked art museum in the nation after The Met, CMA often bought historical pieces such as this for their artistic merit and aesthetic value and had the budget to do so. The skull and an amethyst pendant were two pieces of what she confiscated. She hadn't wanted them in the wrong hands, they held too much ritual power, so she justified taking them because she was doing the world a favor. She didn't want them lost after it took so long for them to be found. She could feel them warding off bad luck and shielding evil. She knew with the world blowing up, within seconds of the destruction, that she'd need their comfort as well. And yet, she felt something else too. Something off. She stared at the statue of Dionysus. She didn't really like to touch that one. She thought through what had been on her mind last night, as she finished her sister's braid with a hair tie and sent her off to play outside.

Going to hear Edward speak on most evenings and weekends had at first been thrilling, inspiring even. But now, even though ten years her senior, he'd begun to take a romantic interest in her, and it just made her feel queasy instead of giddy. He thought too highly of himself whereas she was so much more down to earth. She appreciated his messages that gave people hope in a dull, blackened world, but eventually she began to also be suspect of his heart and intentions. She kept going and living in the cottages, not questioning, not rocking the proverbial boat, but it didn't mean she wasn't rubbing her good luck charms and searching her mind for answers.

She brushed her own straight, blonde hair and put on a layer of mascara, then some peach lip gloss. She had bartered some of her sewing with a woman for a small bag of make-up. Something to make her feel good about herself in the chaos. It was old, but useable. All she had for breakfast right before this was toast, but her stomach felt queasy. They were headed out soon to all meet at the central circle. Edward had been off alone on one of his personal rejuvenating weekends, as he called them, but he'd be back today to gather with them. The central circle was not in the exact central point of the campground, but it was a grassy, circular area in the trees over to the right of the sleeping quarters. Before the world became damaged, this place they were living was a true campground where people came and rented cottages for the night or the week. There were trails in the woods and a creek of decent size for the kids to play in, and up over the hill and to the other side there was a bigger creek, ledges, and a fantastic waterfall for the adults to take photos, which of course were plastered to Instagram pages. That was then, and now there was no more cellular service even, let alone any joy in taking photos with waterfalls. Their little group had taken over the abandoned campground and fixed it up, making it their home, under Edward's guidance and esteemed leadership. Most of the people had been displaced out of their homes and lost most of their family. She went into the bathroom to wait for a few minutes in case she might be sick.

———

EDWARD RODE up on his second-hand bike, a backpack and rolled tent on his back, to Angela's house. He knocked his coded knock on the door twice and she came to the door, smiling.

"Ready to eat I imagine?" she said, lovingly.

"Always with your cooking. You are cooking right? Have enough eggs this morning?"

"I made sure I did, Ed," she said. "Polly seems to not mind laying them and I'm happy enough to have her keep laying them. So far so good on no one stealing her. Not enough eggs to re-open the diner of course, but enough for myself or a friend or two."

"Then I'm famished."

"You want some hot sauce. I have a special stash," Angela said.

"Absolutely," he said. "It was a long night by the river, so I could use a kick to get going, but I know the bigger cause is worth the time spent in meditation. It will make such a difference to the life of you all. So, a little hot sauce never hurt someone as good looking as me, right?"

"You still think highly of yourself, don't you?" she asked, and laughed. "But seriously, I'm sure whatever your plans are, they will benefit everyone."

"I know they will. I don't think there is anyone more equipped for this than me."

"Well, then let's get these eggs in you and some coffee in your cup," she said.

"I'm so glad I am the recipient of your food stash. I'd protect you and your stash with my life, but make sure you continue to keep that all locked up tight okay?"

"I will and I do," Angela said, giving him a thumbs-up. "And I have my shotgun at the ready should anyone happen to break the barricade. No one's getting my stuff."

"I wish you'd come live at the compound with us, then I'd know you are safe, but I know it'd be hard to move it all," Ed said.

"Yeah, and then I feel like it would be group commodities and I'm selfish," Angela said. "Even though I know you disagree with my stance on that."

"I do because I want the whole to be happy and well-cared for," Ed said. "It's about the group, not about the individual. Of course, with being the leader, I need my nourishment and care, so of course, I don't think it's out of line for me to have some extra on the side, whether food or lovin'."

He winked at Angela and she smiled. He approached her, after taking his last bite of eggs and final swig of coffee and cupped her face in his hands. She looked sideways at him shyly as he turned her face downward by her chin with his hand—she'd been staring at the toe of her hiking boot. Her bob-cut, brownish hair swayed slightly, and her round, brown eyes looked up at him. He started to undo the top buttons of her flannel shirt, revealing nothing underneath. His eyebrow raised up at her.

"What? It's the end of the world. Lace tore long ago and washing clothes I don't absolutely have to in muddy water is not worth the effort. Besides sans bra feels so much more freeing. And who doesn't want to be free as the world ends?"

He took her in his arms and embraced her with a chuckle. "You're the best, you know," he said. Then he kissed her fully and passionately. "Just don't tell anyone else about our arrangement." She nuzzled into his neck, pieces of his blond hair falling from his loose man bun and tickling her nose as his short beard itched her face.

————

JAN and her sister Jaime headed out to the circle where most of the group had already gone and were sitting on benches around the fire pit or on blankets around the grass, Indian-style or lounging backwards on elbows. Smiles and laughter were around her. It couldn't be all bad. She loved many of these people like family. They'd become her family when she lost the rest of hers except for Jaime. It wasn't long after they'd spread out their blanket in the far corner that she saw Ed enter the woods and approach, shaking hands and hugging, smiling and conversing with his brethren on the way to his makeshift stand. She hated to call it a pulpit, but he had taken to giving more sermon-based speeches than just simply holding a meeting. And his followers ate it up. He seemed to bask in the adoration, maybe a little too much now for her liking.

Before she had left she'd placed the tiny, ivory-colored skull and amethyst piece back into a small trinket box she'd obtained after trading a loaf of baked bread (she'd made it from her group commodity rations) with a gentleman who lived near the outskirts of the abandoned town, over the hill by the river. He made his way bartering with items he found from scavenging around abandoned homes and stores and traded for things he needed, like food. She felt safer every time she held or had the objects near her, but she was too afraid to carry them out much on her person. They were not only valuable artifacts that could catch a price for someone, but they were meaningful to her as items of protection. She didn't want them stolen or falling out of her pocket. When she first was carefully given the objects to arrange in a special display case at the museum, she recalled she had read in her studies about Pompeii that items such as these were generally property of normal house servants, with which they prayed for fertility, love, prosperity, and most of all, protection. Not that in Pompeii they didn't pretty much have a form of apocalypse themselves in Vesuvius, but maybe some of these would ward off more evil doings if not natural disasters.

Jan looked around at the other families, couples, and singles. She looked more, lingering on the others sitting around the sides. She was wondering if any others felt as uneasy as she was feeling. In all her twenty-five years, she'd never felt so wary about someone she once adored, especially without any major reason. She just felt Ed was basking in power much more now and was changing as a person from a compassionate, energetic leader into a charming narcissist. She did know him maybe a little better than most, as he'd visited her cottage often over the past few years. First, it was late night tea and conversation, but then it was pushy and touchy-feely. She knew he felt he was called to expand his flock in more ways than one. His desire to sire many kids was growing.

Ed walked to the front and spread out his arms to the gathering. "Welcome, my dear family. I appreciate you coming today with the love and care you have in your hearts and smiles on your faces. We rejoice in our togetherness and continue our gratefulness for all we have when others have not, don't we?" He nodded around at the crowd, as they nodded yes in return. His smile, which once made Jan feel safe, now gave her goosebumps, but to keep face for the moment, she nodded in return when his gaze looked toward her.

"As most of you know, I've been deep into the valley by the river, which as our major life vein now in this deterioration of world, is also where I gather wisdom and clarity. My solitude confirmed for me that the journey we are on is the correct one, that growing as your leader is needed for your survival, for the human race to survive. That is why I'm here to tell you today that not only do we need to eat and work and grow together in our home space, but we need to begin to speak to others we find alone or in groups and support them in joining our group."

He offered an open left palm and extended his arm out towards the crowd, till it settled on an individual. "Arthur, I'm anointing you as a missionary to our cause. An ambassador as you will of The Cuyahoga Community. You are called to begin your trek tonight, trailing the former Cleveland area for lost souls. You may pick a few to take along with you who believe in our cause. I trust your judgement."

"It would be my honor, Rev," said gray-haired Arthur, referring to Edward with the nickname he'd given him long ago. "I'm humbled that you've chosen me to share our group's love and dedication to others."

Looking to his right, and out over the crowd, his eyes finally settled on Jan. Jan felt a lump in her throat. He extended an open right hand toward her and said the same pronouncement he had said to Arthur. Jan wanted to run, get sick, or scream, but she did none of those and instead forced a smile on her face and a gentle nod in his direction. She sat there thinking, barely hearing any more of his words as he spoke on about himself and his trip and how he would single-handedly save them all.

As he talked, she scanned the crowd for who she could consider taking with her since she was mandated to make this trek. She decided quickly it would be someone whom she felt was also becoming wary. Maybe they could turn this train around from the inside out. Her eyes hesitated on Brian. He seemed to be sitting alone more these days. She got up and folded her blanket into a square and walked toward him, once Ed was done pontificating and had gone out into the crowd to handshake and pat backs again. As she got closer, Brian gave her a small smile.

"Hey, Jan, what's new? Some meeting, huh?" he said.

"Hey Brian. Yeah, always interesting. Seems to be getting more exuberant with each passing day. I suppose you saw that he anointed me one of the missionaries, which between you and I is probably the last thing this introvert wants to do. I need someone to go with me. Do you have time?"

"Anything for you, Jan, you know that," he said. One thing I do have is time, and of course we all have to work toward the same cause, though I, too, feel that over the last few years not all of us know or appreciate what the cause is anymore. It's all getting a bit over the top, as you noted."

"I hoped I'd not said the wrong thing mentioning it to you, but I know you have a calm head on your shoulders and want what's best for everyone, as do I," Jan said. "I don't really want to have this assignment but maybe it will give us some answers and a way to quell the storm long before it turns into a tornado, so to speak."

"The last thing I want to do is be plotting against, in any way, our group and leader," said Brian, running his hand upward through his dark hair. "But I also don't want to become part of a cult run by a madman." He chuckled, but his eyes didn't. She laid a hand on his arm gently and nodded.

Edward slowly approached Jan and Brian. Jan turned and Ed was staring at her hand on Brian's arm. She slowly removed her fingers and put her hand by her side, half-smiling at Ed. "I was just telling Brian what an important asset I feel he is to our group. That's why I want him to join me on my missionary work for the community," she said. "I hope you agree."

"Certainly," Ed said. "I trust you, and I know Brian will be able to offer many valuable points to potential community members that will help them decide to join us. Where you are quiet at times, though calming—another much needed quality —he is bold and well-spoken."

"Thank you, Ed," said Brian. "I appreciate the respect."

"I've trained you well, given so much of my time and self, to teach you all the strength and power of the world. I know that with my intelligent example, you'll be able to lead many more to our ranks, which will only allow for us to grow, and with hope, rebuild our world," Ed said.

Ed turned when someone else farther into the group called his name and waved him over. This gave Jan a chance to turn back to Brian. She was appalled at Ed's ego every time he spoke anymore. "Brian, I'm just wondering what exactly he wants to be the leader *of...*" she said.

"I know, Jan. I know. It's worrisome. So when do you want to start our journey?"

"We could start the day after tomorrow if you'd like," said Jan. "Thanks, Brian. I'm going to find my sister who seems to have darted off and then go back to my cabin."

————

WHEN JAN GOT BACK to her place, she took out her treasure box. Her two favorites, the tiny skull and the amethyst stared back at her, but so did the little bird bones, Egyptian scarab beetles (which she knew, given her expertise, most likely indicated the presence of the followers of the goddess Isis), the clear circle with the dancing woman, and many various beads and stones and small statues. As her eyes wandered over them, and she reached to pick up the oval of the dancing woman, she realized from her photographic memory (something that comes in handy when you work with historical objects), that her small Dionysus statue was missing. How could it be missing? She looked around the box on the dresser, got on her knees and looked under the dresser and felt around with her hand, and then, she sat on the end of the bed and sifted through images in her mind. She went through her last moments each time she came to the box. She couldn't think of a time recently she'd moved the box from the dresser or taken the small statue out of her bedroom. Something was wrong. Or maybe about to be horribly wrong. She ran to the en suite bathroom and vomited.

————

ED WENT BACK to his two-bedroom cottage at the front of the campground after the meeting and collapsed in his easy chair. He felt amazing at the level of control he was having over his group of people. He had come so far in a few years. Sure, he wanted to help them, that's how it all started, forged from a need of survival depending on one another. But now, he relished the attention. He was finally getting his due. He didn't need anyone's help but his own, yet they surely needed him. They fawned at his feet and held onto the edge of his words. Easily manipulated. Funny how people are like that when they are fearful, especially for their lives. He opened a copy of the collected works of Plato he had found near a dumpster. Its cover was partially burned but the pages were readable. He'd always loved debate and philosophy. When he was younger, in college, he enjoyed reading from Epicurus but now he saw a bigger picture far from the tenets of the philosopher's ideas of simple life. His life's work was to leave a lasting community where the group revolved around him and his teachings, and hopefully, for generations after his death. A re-emergence from the ashes of this apocalyptic nightmare; a creation of the world of Ed.

His fervor stirred inside him. Reaching past his morning coffee cup he had never taken to the kitchen—filled earlier with the liquid jewel made from filtered rainwater and strained through rations of coffee grounds via an old handkerchief—he picked up the tiny statue of Dionysus that he'd found in Jan's bedroom. Once when he had went to her cottage, sweet talking her into cuddling with him (he was yet to get her to consent to more, though he thought she'd look beautiful pregnant with his child), and they had fallen asleep, he'd woke and went quietly to the bathroom. He couldn't help himself but to see what was in the small trinket box. The Dionysus statue glowed at him so he fetched it out, hoping with all the other small items in there, she wouldn't miss it. I mean, it was glowing for him. For HIM. That was a sign, he was sure. The gods thought him useful to them or that he was one of them. Maybe that was it. He sure felt powerful enough even then. Now he felt even more powerful.

A few nights ago, he and five of his most trusted followers had went deeper into the woods where they performed rituals they felt enlightened the entire group, but that they weren't ready to share with them as a whole yet. He had taken the statue and used it in the rituals. He flushed with ecstasy at the feelings that moved through him. He writhed and danced around the fire as if he was on fire himself. He was overcome with power and his friends danced with him as they were overcome by spiritual awakenings unlike any they had experienced before. He couldn't wait to have the rest of his flock joining, because he could only imagine what type of power that would create. He would rule this apocalyptic world. He would be king.

He sat the miniature, bone-carved statue back down beside his Plato book, got up and took his mug to the kitchen where he'd rinse it out in the morning from the large container of purified water he kept stored there for a few days at a time (gathering and boiling it using a coveted small generator they had secured for the campground) from a larger bucket out back, and went to bed.

———

AS SHE WIPED her face with a damp cloth about fifteen minutes after vomiting in the bathroom, Jan looked at herself in the mirror. She brushed her teeth with her stored ration of water. She was scared. Scared she knew the only place the statue of Dionysus could have went. Only one person besides her little sister had been in her bedroom. She was wary of Ed before, but now she was even more so. She laid down on her bed in the dark and stared up towards the ceiling into the darkness.

———

BRIAN WOKE up after a restless night. He couldn't stop thinking about the situation and what he and Jan were going to do. He decided they'd probably need to head out on the trail as soon as he could get going and head over to Jan's to see if she could get ready early. He got dressed, licked his fingers and ran them through the top of his hair, and took off out the door. He arrived at Jan's cottage less than five minutes later and knocked on the door. Jaime, Jan's twelve-year-old sister, answered the door in her pajamas holding a doll brought from their past life, with natty hair and dirt smudges, but still loved. A reminder of life in its simpler time.

"Jaaaaan," called Jaime when she saw Brian. "Brian is heeeerrreeee."

Jan came out of the bedroom, still in a long t-shirt that looked like an old forgotten shirt of a man who wore size 4x. "Sorry, Brian. I was just getting dressed. Have a seat there and I'll be out to talk to you in a minute."

Jan figured Brian was there to talk about their mission and plan. Maybe even get started. She pulled on clean underwear, her jeans, and a medium-sized women's t-shirt that said Camp Evergreen. She didn't put on a bra, however, she did slip on her knock-off Birkenstocks. Not her old pair, she'd lost them, but someone else's she had bartered some of her other items for— one luxury comfort she didn't want to be without was sandals.

She went back out into the living room and sat beside Brian on the couch. "So what's up? I imagine you want to talk about our plan," she said. "I'm ready."

"Well are you ready to get moving on our mission today? I know it's just the day after...but..." Brian said. "I'm ready to set foot out of here and begin to see who's out there. I know according to Ed we are supposed to talk about The CC and how amazing it is, and we will have to maybe feel out each person we encounter, but should we try to unite everyone we meet to our side? Ed doesn't have to know what we've told them, and we can bring them into our fold and let them pretend to be followers, until the right moment we can all revolt?"

Brian seemed to have the most obvious plan, Jan thought, and at that moment, she didn't have anything better, except for maybe they shouldn't convert every single person to their side. The law of averages and percentages seemed to recognize someone would stray or betray them.

"How about we get a read from each person we encounter and convince some of them to join us at the campground under guise, but I would like to only do that with a little more than half of the people so no one tries to pull one over on us or anyone gets suspicious. We should let half the people come naturally to the group so that things seem more real. I hate to bring anyone to that madness, but it's for the greater cause of ending this before it gets out of hand," Jan said.

"Yeah, I can agree with that," Brian said. "Let's go then. What about Jaime?"

"Mrs. Potter said she'd watch her next door because of this trek we were chosen to do," Jan said.

After Jaime got dressed in play clothes, they took her four cottages down to Mrs. Potter's home. Jan knocked on the door and the short, plump, older lady opened the door with a smile. "Time to head out is it? Jaime will be fine here, won't you Jaime? I've just made chocolate chip cookies. Come in and hang out with me for a while," Mrs. Potter said, and turned her back to head to the fridge to pour a glass of cold milk for the young girl. Jamie hugged Jan, smiled, and then went into the kitchen with Mrs. Potter.

Brian and Jan, backpacks secured on their backs and filled with supplies they could find or barter for, headed off down the towpath in the Cuyahoga Valley. Since there were no longer cars or trains or modes of transportation, they thought heading off down one of the bigger trails they knew first would be best. They'd see who they would encounter along the way.

They hadn't really needed to speak to Ed before they left, or he to they, as all the followers already had training in the art of encouraging others. It was a monthly mandate now. Jan didn't know why he began to make all these rules and regulations. It was seeming more like a prison or church now than it did a community of neighbor helping neighbor.

Jan and Brian's hiking boots easily handled the parts of the terrain that were rocky, but also offered much needed padding on the parts of the towpath that were asphalt, created that way for bikers

and the heavy use from runners and walkers. Of course, she missed her sandals, but she was glad that everyone in the compound, for lack of a better word anymore, had secured hiking boots. Since the world had been on fire, the trails and paths obviously had almost no maintenance, except for any few good souls who took it upon themselves to clean or fix. There were ruins of buildings, rusty nails, glass from windows and bottles, and various debris. It was almost too much to keep up with in certain areas for the volunteers as many not-so-good people hung out on the trails, by the river, and in abandoned overgrown parks.

The duo would just need to walk until they saw a few tents or signs of people living within any sort of structure. Everyone made do with whatever shelter they had or could find, foraging or bartering for food, and filtered and purified rain or river water. The river was now people's mode of bathing, doing laundry, and even transportation. Therefore, many people in this area lived as close to the water as they could manage or took shelter under the huge, cement bridges that once carried highways.

"Hey, our first one," Jan said. "Look, I see a fairly structurally sound half of a home on the trail just a few feet away. Let's stop in."

"Sure," Brian said. "That's why we are here. But let me go to the door, you stay right behind me."

"I'll stand beside you, how's that? You knock," Jan replied.

Brian rapped on the front door. "Hello?"

A man in his late forties opened the door, his shorts didn't hide his tiny legs and his tank top didn't hide his belly—how these men kept their bellies after the apocalypse when food was scarce was still something that perplexed Jan.

"Who are you? What do you want?" the man said.

"I'm Brian and this is Jan. We are with The Cuyahoga Community that lives over in the old campground about three miles down the road. Not needing anything or want to cause any issues, but we would just like to extend to as many people as we can to come to our meetings or join our group. We have some positive perks of communal living that would be accessible to most of you out here if you join us. We want to offer our same comforts. Is it just you here?"

"Me and my wife, but we get along just fine," the man said.

"You have enough food? Would your wife like friendship, or the both of you, companionship? We all depend on each other there and I hate to think of you both out here alone," Brian said.

"I thank you for the gesture, but I tend to be stand-offish about organizations, groups, et cetera. I was even BEFORE the apocalypse. I feel it only leads to tyrannical dealings. While more food sounds nice, I don't think I want to be part of the rest," said the man, scratching his scruff.

"Well, actually, since you say that," Brian began, then hesitated. Jan started to talk instead, "Sir, we are thinking about some of those same things ourselves, even though we've been tasked by our unsuspecting leader to come out and talk to everyone. We are feeling a little like paupers led by an aristocrat and I hated stories when I was young about apocalypses leading back to feudal times." She managed a laugh at that, and so did the man. Brian didn't laugh, for fear overtook him from humor. Maybe not fear, but more determination. He nodded at the man. He had a good feeling this might work out for them.

After they talked for a while longer, the man went back in to talk to his wife while Brian and Jan waited. The man came back and told them they'd pack up what little they had and head to the campground to introduce themselves and await their return. They'd integrate into the little community and Ed should be unsuspecting. Comforted by that, Brian and Jan went on their way again.

The couple moved along to others whether by foot, sometimes on bikes people kindly shared with them, and even sometimes canoes and kayaks on the river. Lots of these small watercrafts peppered the river's edge, abandoned amid weeds grown up around them. People used them, and then left them for the next person. It was a long trek around the shambles of the valley. It stretched for miles and over many hills and around riverbeds. However, mostly what they found was a camaraderie with others for the right kind of community. A community that encouraged independence amid working together.

The people they had the best intuition about were who they told their plan to and had them commit to silence and laying low until they said the word when they were all back at the campground. Others they were unsure of, they spread the community ideal without indicating the plan, and a few decided to join. Still others, they just didn't want to join in, and they didn't trust them enough to tell the plan and take them into their personal fold either.

Jan had a further secret of her own. Her artifacts. She had brought the clear, round, glass piece featuring the dancing woman on it with her. As always afraid to lose any of them, she took the needle and thread from the little sewing kit she had managed to find a few years ago and sewed it into her sweatshirt pocket. It was odd, but it did a sort of small vibration whenever people seemed right for the cause. So she relied on that a bit, and Brian, he relied on her instincts.

Each night Jan and Brian talked about the people they'd met, the people going back to the campground and with what intentions, and their plan. They were hesitant but completely set in the desire to maintain freedom from prideful dictators like Ed. His once seemingly kind desire to offer people a home, a leader, a Community, was now turning into a worship, deer-in-the-headlight-eyes reaction from people who were once active individuals in the world before the annihilation hit. Pride often rode the line, and when it crossed it to ego, there was almost no going back, only being stopped. And not only that, pride often, if not always, would lead to the other deadly sins as well for the prideful person and those around them. Gluttony, lust, greed, sloth, wrath, envy all were symptoms and a way of life for one becoming very prideful, because they deserved it all, in their mind at least.

Eventually they made the long trek back toward the campground too by all the means they did before, stopping to catch anyone they missed on the way. They were probably gone two to three weeks and they hoped that everything in the community had stayed status quo so far. Jan was especially worried about Jaime, since with the world the way it was now, there was no communication beyond seeing someone in person. She knew she was in good hands, but still she was anxious.

The evening they arrived back at the campground, the Community was in the middle of a meeting in the circle. They went to their cabins, set down their bags, and then wandered out together toward the group. When Ed saw them, he extended his arms, walked down from the pulpit through the crowd, and embraced each one of them. "You've returned to us! How proud we are of you. Look at all the people you've helped by sending them to their new Community." He looked around nodding at various people. "Everyone, stand and rejoice, for your missionaries have returned." The crowd stood and clapped with various people approaching Brian and Jan and offering hugs for their safe and productive return.

Ed wandered back up to his post and everyone sat back down. "My friends, I know that I am the best way for you all to find peace and life among this battered and burned world.

Follow me and we will persevere and survive." He would never allow Brian or Jan to come up to speak to the crowd or new followers; he didn't want eyes for too long on anyone else or praise upon others but himself. "Thank you to our missionaries for spreading the world of our value and our society."

Jan and Brian took a seat with everyone else and both were scanning the crowd to see the familiar faces they had talked to on their journey besides the ones they already saw who'd been close enough to give them hugs.

Ed talked a bit more about working on upcoming projects that would assist the masses with food storage, and then before it was time for people to disperse back to their homes or gardens or duties, he quieted everyone down.

"I have something special for you all today," said Ed to the crowd. "Our resident woodworkers have been diligently carving small pieces for you all of something that's very dear to me. Little wooden statues of a god named Dionysus. Dionysus has selected me to share his power with all of you. As a god vessel, he has shown me the highest of freedom and release. Several of you have shared with me the fruits of rituals and worship, and now, our Community, we want to share them with you."

Noise and wonder were heard from the crowd, murmurings of questions and unease at this news, as the statues were passed out to everyone. "Don't be afraid or worry, my brethren, for this is all for your betterment. We can be on such a higher plane of feeling than this black world offers to us. I can help you reach it if you continue to follow me. Take this little idol of him and bring it with you to special gatherings or worship it every day. Let me be the flesh incarnate of Dionysus to you."

People looked one from the other, some smiling, some interested. All were holding little wooden statues and looking at the intricate detail, except Jan. Silently fuming inside, but knowing she couldn't now openly refuse the statue, she took it and held it in her hand. She knew now what had happened to her statue in her treasure box, but at the present time she had to keep it to herself. And he would know too, that she knew, that she knew he had stolen it. What was he even thinking he was doing? The Community would embrace this idol, as he knew they did all of what he said and did. She hoped those around her to whom Brian and she had talked to were still part of the duo's bigger plan. That they'd be able to stop this power trip before a bigger type of apocalypse happened—a loss of humanity from the soul out, not of the material.

Edward had again come down into the crowd, and sections of the larger crowd broke off, some heading to their home, some to the ritual site reserved for a few, now open to even more of the masses. He'd invited others to join tonight in a ritual to Dionysus and many had accepted.

Brian looked at Jan, and as they walked off toward the side, whispered to her. "What is *this* statue now? Where did he come up with this?"

"I have to let you in on a little secret of my own, Brian," Jan said. "I'm sorry I didn't tell you before, but I wanted to wait till the right time. I used to work at the Cleveland Museum of Art, curating ancient art and artifacts. When the items the museum purchased from the Pompeii archaeological dig arrived, I was mesmerized. I cared for them, set the display up with the information, recorded and cataloged them. Then, you know, the annihilation began, and I knew I couldn't save everything in my care at the museum, much as that pained me, but I needed to save some of the Pompeii artifacts. Beads, statues, skulls,

257

pendants, crystals were all small enough to put into my pocket and run."

"Wow," said Brian. "That's amazing. Your work meant a lot to you."

"It did and so do the historical artifacts. I brought them here with me and bartered for a keepsake box for them which I keep in my cabin. It's in my bedroom and no one has been in my bedroom besides my sister except for one other person...."

"Ed," Brian said. "He and his fertility stance get around, don't they?"

"I'm afraid so, though I haven't...with him I mean, even though he tried," Jan said. "Much to his anger."

"Well I am glad to hear that you didn't," Brian said, and smiled. "I figured as much."

"You're so kind, Brian," Jan said. "But back to the situation at hand, I have to say I'm concerned to see this happening. Dionysus is not a god or myth to be inciting in ritual. And though I am mad he stole the historic relic from my room, I'm even more concerned about what this means for our Community or even the world."

"Why? What is he doing?"

"I'm not sure yet, but assuming they are going to the ritual space, what used to be, you know, just a place to find peace and spiritual vibes in this mad world, I guess he must be tapping it... for what I don't know. I only know that Dionysus is the god known for spiritual maddening. With that comes the opening of some heavy physical and mental effects."

"Like?" Brian said, confused.

"Have you seen in the past various religious organizations and groups that become so, as they would say back in the day, overcome by the Holy Spirit almost as if the spirit was inside them? That was the modern form of religious ecstasy, but maddening rituals, usually done by followers of other pagan idols, sometimes were even more visceral and maniac. Pagan rituals were passed down, and believe it or not, many religious rituals and ceremonies and traditions often came from paganism mixing with them, ceremonies and festivals from ancient times such as Greek, Roman, and Egyptian for instance."

"Oh, so that is where Dionysus comes in? Ancient mythical god and rituals?" Brian said.

Jan sighed. "Yes, he is Dionysus in Greek and Bacchus in Roman mythology. He is known for coming to incite maddening, the god of wine (and all the good and bad it can bring), as well as being a communicant between the living and the dead."

"Just based on past readings of my own, as brief as they were in a few college courses, the 'cult of lost souls' comes to mind," Brian said.

"Many cults continued to form based on him throughout centuries. Festivals time and again were thrown in his name. It seems someone else has been transfixed by the statue and somehow been charmed by occult powers preying on his own prideful personality. Ed will know now that I know he stole the statue and when he can break away from his worshipers, he'll probably come find me to make excuses. I need to get back to my room to my box and other artifacts to ensure their safety," Jan said.

"Your cabin door was locked so I'm sure no one broke in when we were gone," Brian stated.

"I also thought ahead enough that I hid them in the safe that came with each cabin. They had them there for campers who rented the cottage for the night when the campground was still operational and my cabin still had the safe in the bedroom," Jan said.

"Thank goodness," Brian said.

"Yes," Jan said. "And I have a special artifact, a clear oval with a dancing girl, sewed into my pocket."

"For safekeeping?" Brian asked.

"For protection and strength," Jan said.

Jan and Brian walked toward her cabin, while Jan told Brian more about the artifacts and their protection and uses. She was almost to her door when she realized she hadn't seen her sister Jaime in all the bustle of getting back and the meeting. She thought to stop at Mrs. Potter's cabin and check on her first, see her, no matter what serious issues were going on. She wanted to make sure she was safe.

Jan knocked on the door and the old woman caring for Jaime answered. "Hi Jan, you're back!" she exclaimed, and brought her in for a hug. "I have good news for you. Jaime has been chosen by Edward as a wife. They are to be married, and when Jaime is old enough, she'll have his baby, just like several other of the pretty, young women here. Isn't that a time of rejoice? To be chosen by our divine leader. She is pure and special."

The old woman was smiling, while once again, Jan had to hold back the bile seeping up her esophagus. All she could squeak out was, "What?"

Brian intervened. "So where is Jaime now? Jan missed her and wants to see her."

"I imagine she is with Ed or with one of his followers. Two young women came to get her. Ed was positive you'd be pleased, they said. He did choose you as one of his missionaries.

I was surprised though, as I thought he was going to choose you as a wife," said the woman.

Jan turned around and walked away. She wanted to scream. Brian ran after her as Jan ran quickly towards the other side of the compound towards Edward's area.

"Hey, Jan, what are you going to do? Hold on," Brian said.

"I'm going to go get my sister back and confront him," Jan said.

"And what will that do? Your anger will only cause him to be defensive and more controlling. Let's go back to your cabin and find what you need first. When you were talking about the artifacts, were you indicating at all that some of them might help to eradicate this occult power overtaking him and the Community?"

"Definitely. I hope the artifacts will show me for themselves, and if not, I'd need to figure it out," Jan said. "But Brian... Jaime.... what she must be thinking?"

"I know, Jan, but you need to think of the whole too, plus in helping the whole, you're helping her too," said Brian.

"You're right," said Jan. "Let's head to my place. The faster we do this, the faster I can save Jaime. This is personal now, and I almost wonder if he meant it to be that way on purpose."

———

ED WAITED in the woods with his followers dancing and reveling all around him and acting as if drunk on abandon. Fires blazed, women chanted, skin glowed in the fire light. He knew Jan would know he'd stolen the statue of Dionysus now. He also knew she'd know he had Jaime. Jaime was his pawn, his key to getting Jan to face him. He knew she would end up doing what he wanted her to do. He knew he was that powerful and divine. Nothing could stop him, not even her other charms she had hidden away in her box. He watched his flock with a grin as they laughed and embraced each other, as they writhed, fainted, and lost control of themselves. How simple it had been to become strong enough to control an entire group of people. Dionysus continued to travel the world spreading his cult even vicariously because his essence was in ancient artifacts and Ed felt like he'd been chosen because no one was smarter or as charismatic as he. How astounding to be in a world of darkness but living the best life now. One didn't need material goods or running water or electric to surge with energy.

He needed to focus now. Jan would be here soon. He knew as she went on her mission that she would most likely betray him. Her hesitation to him was obvious and so he was always suspecting. Dionysus' aura confirmed it for him, in the way it spoke to him. It was time to end the questioning. He was ready to take his masses out and rule the world. The Cuyahoga Community was just a drop in the bucket. His small kingdom. But now, he wanted to be a god. Not just one with a god, a vessel of a god, but a god.

———

JAN AND BRIAN entered her cabin and she ran back to her bedroom and dialed the combination on the safe. She was so nervous she had to do it three times to get it right. She opened it and took out her treasure box, then opened its lid too. She took out the tiny skull made from human bone and the amethyst. She felt energy from the scarab and the blue stone rings as well, so she took them both out too. She left the clear, oval circle with the dancing woman in her pocket and put on the rings. She didn't know what to do with the other artifacts, which were now vibrating, but she had an idea. She ran over to her drawer and pulled out a pair of her cotton underwear. She tore at it until she got a deformed square, then ran to the kitchen and took some twine out of the cabinet. She tied the artifacts up in the piece of cloth with the twine and then tied the twine around her neck, so the makeshift bag hung from her. She tucked it down under her shirt to her side.

She looked at Brian who was just standing there watching her with wonderment. "Ready?" he asked. "I'm not sure what I am asking if you're ready for, but I have a feeling we are just winging it."

"Hold on one second," Jan said. She went into the bathroom and took her blonde hair in her hands and displayed it over to the right side and began to braid it. She tied the piece of material she usually used around the bottom to secure it. "Now I'm ready," she said. "I think I'm ready to fight the battle of my life that I had no idea I'd be fighting."

———

AS BRIAN AND JAN WALKED, they gathered those who were outside who they knew had agreed to their plan; who had come to the camp to help them. Others that were concerned asked them what was happening with the statues and the rituals and Jan was honest with them. They agreed to head to camp with the group as well. The Community was its own community, not to be ruled by one man with only his discretion. Independence was important to these people. Not one of them carried the Dionysus statue. They did follow Jan, but not as their savior, as their guide to their own freedom. As partners in saving the world from a drunken, mythical stupor.

As the group of twenty entered the edge of the woods, they could hear the screaming, the singing, and see blurs of motion through the trees. They looked at each other, alarmed. They smelled smoke, and soon enough as they entered the forest, they could see the bright orange flames licking the sky.

Jan's eyes glanced over the crowd till her eyes set on Ed. Bare chested, with only shorts on, his hair curly and down and framing his face instead of up in its bun, he looked so full of life. And oh yes, he was smiling. Right at Jan too. Then Jan saw Jaime sitting behind him on a bench, her hands tied together with rope, her head down and her hair in her face.

"Brian, look—Jaime is over there on the bench," Jan said. "Dammit, what has he done to her?" It was all she could do to find the strength to not run over to her sister. She had to wait. Ed was right between them anyway. And he knew that.

"Yes, but look around even more," Brian said. "The—

He stopped. The women in the group with them screamed and one of the men vomited.

"—what?" Jan said.

"They are… tearing those animals apart and eating them."

"What the hell?" Jan said to herself, Brian, and anyone that could hear.

She stared, frozen, as she watched naked men and women ripping apart deer, squirrels, raccoons—any animals of the forest they apparently could find—and eating them raw.

Horrified, she looked away and at the merriment around her. This was what they wanted from life? Their world had been destroyed, burned, set back hundreds of years, and this was what they wanted from their chance to rebuild?

She felt the artifacts vibrate stronger in the bag under her shirt. She knew they would protect but she didn't know how much or what that might mean. But regardless, she was going to take Ed on. What did she have to lose?

She strode, with Brian and whomever was still brave enough, toward Edward. He stood looking at her, his hands in his pockets, as a woman beside him writhed in carnal euphoria. Others danced holding hands in a circle around the larger of the fire pits in front of him. It cast an eerie light on his face. He swiped his hair back from his forehead with one hand and reached out the other hand to her.

"Join me, my dear," Ed said. "You know that nothing compares to me and nothing can stop me. You do know that by now, don't you? Dionysus has chosen me to spread his mysteries to this world. It's ordained."

"I could give a shit," Jan said. "Give Jaime to me."

"No, Jan," Ed said. "I won't give you Jaime until you give yourself to me as my wife, until you tell me you'll be my goddess. We can rule this world together, you and I. You have power too, not as strong as I, but it's there. I feel it."

"Hell no," Jan said. "This becoming a god talk is too much. Your pride has gotten the best of you and made you arrogant. Look at what you're making these poor people do. Do you think that sins of the flesh have any lasting enough effects to merit a world ruled using it?"

"It's powerful," Ed said. "And nothing is better than being the most powerful. The best of the best."

"Life is not about the best, you narcissist," Jan said. "It's about community, remember our Community? What we were to stand for? Improving each other through support, not mind control. Now let me see Jaime. I won't marry you, but you will let me have her. Don't involve her."

"You're wrong, Jan," Ed said. And he took a step forward and grabbed her wrist. He cried out in pain and drew his hand back quickly. "What the fu—?" His hand was burned on the palm where he had grabbed her. "You bitch…"

She smiled and said a silent thanks to the Pompeii sorceress who must have channeled protection into the artifacts she held. "Now, give me Jaime."

"A little burn won't hurt me," Ed said. "So no."

Just then one of the dancing women fell into the fire pit in a fit of writhing. It was one of his preferred girlfriends whose belly was extended as if pregnant. *"No,"* yelled Ed, as he ran toward the pit and lunged at her, pulling her out of the fire and patting the flames off her semi-burned body. The woman laughed as if she did not even feel the pain.

Before he could turn back around, Jan ran toward Jaime while Brian and the group surrounded Ed. She untied Jaime, threw the rope on the ground, and called to one of the women on her side to help her. "Here, please take Jaime and go into the woods away from this," Jan said. "She's waking. Tell her you're with her because I sent you. Wait there."

Ed's preternatural strength helped him fight off some of the larger men, as he threw them against the trees. Brian somehow ran and toppled him to the ground and Jan ran over to Ed's side, kicking him. He threw what seemed like white haze toward her, but her arms went up immediately, without thought in defense, and she was shielded, and then fire shot out of the rings she wore and blistered his face.

He rolled screaming on the ground and the group ran and got the rope and tied his hands behind his back. "You're not going to last with this for long, Jan," Ed said. "Dionysus will never stand for this type of disruption. I'm a god, and more powerful than you. Wait and see."

Jan waited a few minutes more but there was nothing to see. The other group members went around and tried to get the people of the Community to stop dancing and writhing and even... eating raw animals. They looked at themselves as if waking up and felt ashamed at the blood over their faces, at their nakedness in front of each other. One by one, the group members helping Jan and Brian took the wooden statues of Dionysus and dropped them into a basket. After they collected all of them, they burned them in the fire pits. White light shot up out of the fire and several of the members jolted but it wasn't more than a few minutes until they were back to normal.

Jan looked at Brian and he shrugged and raised his hands and shoulders. She walked towards him. "That was easier than I thought," Jan said. "I guess the artifacts I had must have had really strong protection and spells over them. I felt their power, but I didn't myself feel overly powerful, not any more than I should as a strong woman handling her business." She allowed herself to smile at this and put her hands on her hips.

"Go get Jaime," Brian said.

"Yes, okay," said Jan, and breathed in a deep breath. "You'll hold down the fort... I mean, woods? I am just not convinced that things are going to be this easy."

"It will be fine," Brian said. "Go on. She needs you."

Jan ran into the woods calling out for Jaime. Jaime and the woman taking care of her ran towards Jan's voice till they found each other. "Jaime, I'm so sorry for anything happened to you," Jan said.

"It—it's okay, Jan," Jaime said. "I knew you'd come and kick his ass. It was traumatic going through it, but I just kept breathing, counting numbers in my head, and reciting my favorite story passages, calling into the universe silently for you. I knew you'd come when you could. And he didn't hurt me, besides tying me up and holding me hostage."

"Thank goodness you're okay," Jan said. "I couldn't live with myself if anything happened to you, especially not since we already lost everyone else."

"We're all glad you came and had enough guts to do what you did, Jan," said the woman. "It was like they were all under a spell or something, right? Hallucinations? It seemed so trance-like."

"It is, Sara," Jan said. "From my classical studies for my museum degree, I read about cults and rituals and myths like this. Dionysus' followers have had festivals and ceremonies for centuries, but nothing like this. I think that when the tiny statue was found in Pompeii, that actually opened a gate for Dionysus himself to sneak through, and then, all he had to do was find someone with such a prideful heart, he could turn him and use him for maniacal evil."

"But why?" Jaime said.

"For kicks? Maybe. For control. To make people sin and worship him, so he could feed off their power and feel alive again. That's just my guess."

"Makes sense," Sara said. "But we've already been through so much, which I suppose also makes us susceptible to evil as well."

Ending the conversation, the three walked back toward the camp. Jan halted and stared as they were almost to the clearing. She put her face into her hands. "Oh, no," she screamed. "What have I done?"

Jaime and Sara looked forward and watched as the entire clearing was ablaze. They went as far as they could before the smoke and heat got to them, but they could see that everything and everyone was on fire. That soon everything in the area would be on fire. Brian had them burn those wooden statues together in the fire pits. *Dammit,* she thought. With tears she said, "Burning those idols together must have had an opposite affect and released enough power to ignite it all."

The rings glowed on Jan's hand. The artifacts vibrated. *Why,* she thought, *what good will they do me now that everything and everyone is gone, most likely even Ed?* She grabbed her sister in a tight hug and cried. Eventually, they began to walk away from disaster. She knew her cabin, and everyone's cabin, would go up in flames as well.

The three of them walked away from the campground area and followed the river till they came to the nearest person's makeshift home, about a mile away. They were tired, worn, hungry, and dirty. A woman came to the door and shuffled them in, hearing their story, and giving them a place to rest for the night until they could figure things out. She thought sleep wouldn't come easy and that she'd never stop crying. Poor Brian. She would miss him terribly. He was such a hero to her.

But sleep came very fast.

———

IN THE MORNING when she got up, she set out alone while the other two women helped Jaime take a sponge bath in the river. She went back to the campground to see the damage and the bodies. As she went into the clearing with the fire pits where the rituals and the altercation occurred, she was so distraught by the damage. Everything was burned black to the ground. She couldn't identify any of the bodies, not that many remained. Most were ash. She hoped Ed was among the ash, but how could she be sure? She offered words to the universe on behalf of Brian, her friends, the people she had survived the apocalypse with and made a new life with, the people who had been her new family.

Afterwards, she walked back to the house where Jaime was and hugged her sister. They'd have to start over again. At least they knew something already about survival against the odds. They were survivors.

———

ED WALKED ALONE down the forest trail trying to scent his way back toward the river, but not too soon, as he needed to get miles away before following the river again so no one would see him. Then he'd follow it until he could set up a new camp, recruit new followers, a new flock for a new Community. He'd try again. He was too smart to not. He'd be more watchful the next time. He had the statue of Dionysus in his pocket and he could feel its energy propelling him to go on. He had hated running from the fire pit explosions when it happened and leaving people he cared about behind. Angela had been close by, as she had come into camp from her house and diner for the meeting and ritual, and he heard her screaming for him. While his heart tinged a little watching her burn, he knew he couldn't go back for her and save himself too. He couldn't save any of this flock. And he needed to do what he heard the voices telling him to do, which was run. He was needed for a far bigger purpose. He was a god.

ABOUT THE AUTHORS

Erin Sweet-Al Mehairi www.hookofabook.wordpress.com

Alice J. Black - www.facebook.com/alice.j.black.doo

Kate L. Mary https://katelmary.com

Jessica Gomez https://authorjessicagomez.wixsite.com/author

Justin Robinson www.captainsupermarket.com/

Sylvester Barzey https://www.sylvesterbarzey.com-

Dale Drake https://www.facebook.com/dale.drake.31